For Patty

Norma Bork

TEN MILES
FROM THE NEAREST SIN

D1706493

NORMA KOESTER BORK

WINEPRESS WP PUBLISHING

© 2006 by Norma Bork. All rights reserved

WinePress Publishing (PO Box 428, Enumclaw, WA 98022) functions only as book publisher. As such, the ultimate design, content, editorial accuracy, and views expressed or implied in this work are those of the author.

No part of this publication may be reproduced, stored in a retrieval system or transmitted in any way by any means—electronic, mechanical, photocopy, recording or otherwise—without the prior permission of the copyright holder, except as provided by USA copyright law.

Unless otherwise noted, all Scriptures are taken from the King James Version of the Bible.

ISBN 1-57921-842-3
Library of Congress Catalog Card Number: 2006921388

MVFOL

DEDICATION

To Paul, the love of my life, and to Paul Kevin, Susan, Terry, Jane, Kate, and Max

AUTHOR'S NOTE

Dear Reader . . . in case you're wondering . . . this book is completely fiction. The people portrayed in the story, along with their struggles, their fears, their joys and their Christian experiences do not now and never have existed. Each of the characters is completely a product of my imagination. My family and close friends will recognize that I have used their names almost exclusively, but don't be tempted to think I have borrowed their appearances, their life choices or their sins as well. I have not.

My favorite character, Karis, was named after Karis Lynn Koester because I remember the day my brother chose what he considered a very special name for my first niece and his first daughter, and also because she *is* special, and I like the name.

The events described did not happen, but they could have. Christian homes and colleges have never been immune to the intrusion of evil but, happily, faculty and staff background checks readily available today give school administrators a way to increase protection for their students. My hope is that they are routinely used.

The End-Time colleges in my story are like, in their conservative culture and isolated locations, what hundreds of other small, Christian colleges were like in the '50s and '60s. Most of us who were students in one of those schools during those turbulent years remember them as nurturing and safe; good places in which to make life-determinate decisions of career, spouse and a relationship with Christ. It was only after we moved beyond our college years that we realized how oblivious we had been to what was happening in the world outside our restricted space.

I hope you will find the book interesting and thought-provoking. The ugly reality of childhood sexual abuse and its far-reaching consequences in the lives of its victims, their families, and often even their acquaintances, has been an unmentionable subject among Christians for much too long. Surely, we thought, we were protected. Surely, we thought, these evil things don't happen in Christian circles. My hope is that this book will help to promote a discussion of ways to eliminate this terrible sin and its terrible cost.

ACKNOWLEDGEMENTS

An affectionate and sincere thank you to my friends and family who, though doubtless sick and tired of hearing about "my book" were able—most of the time—to resist the temptation to suggest other topics of conversation, and were still willing to let me use their good names for my characters.

My special thanks, appreciation, and love to Paul Franz Bork who, though unaccustomed to reading novels, persevered and loved me anyway.

An enormous thank you to my sons. Terry, who read drafts, took notes at a critique meeting, advised on police matters and, most importantly, gave me his honest opinion about needed changes, and to Paul who constantly encouraged and cheered me on even when I wouldn't let him read it.

Two of my favorite nieces gave me invaluable help. Amanda Umek Granados walked much of the geography of the story while I timed the action, and Crystal Hardy read, found inaccuracies and made good suggestions.

Thank you to Gary Golden, Col. USAF, retired, who coached me on service rank and regulations.

Previous faculty colleagues Jane Igler, Barbara Youngblood and Herb Ford, each of whom attended and taught in colleges similar to the ones in my story, were invaluable in their comments and contributions.

Dr. James Walters, Professor of Religion at Loma Linda University, gave me important encouragement at a critical time and introduced my manuscript to his book club for critique and comment. I am grateful to the members of his book club, Fiction Addiction, who each read and made ever-so-gentle suggestions on ways to enhance the book.

Herb and Anita Ford and Charles and Peggy Bell gave me needed shelter, sustenance, and encouragement while I walked the walks and drove the streets of the book's setting.

A thank you to Dr. George Summers who painstakingly proofread an early draft. His comments about the suitability of some of my word choices gave me pause and led to substantive changes.

Lyle McCoy, teacher of my sons and volunteer fireman of many years, taught me how a small isolated community protects itself from fire.

Gary Simpson, Sheriff of Napa County, California, and former student during my teaching years, provided important insights into the complex relationship between law enforcement and college policies.

Finally I want to thank, posthumously, my avid-reader sister, Eileen. who thought an early manuscript was "just wonderful" and was sure that Oprah would immediately "snatch it up". I miss you and your extravagant encouragement!

PROLOGUE

September, 1934

Silver Spring, Maryland

Ten-year-old Jack Stevenson brushed his tears away with a dirty sleeve, hunched his thin shoulders, and fixed his eyes on his father who stood ten feet in front of him gripping the bat. He shuffled his legs farther apart, pushed his glasses up on his nose, took a deep breath, raised his arm over his head, waited . . . and threw the ball. It curved to the left and landed in the neighbor's yard.

"Didn't I tell you NOT to throw that way?" As Reverend David Stevenson, Vice President of the End-Time Christian Church, walked toward his only son the vein in his neck pulsed and his always-florid face flamed. "You throw like a girl. A pantywaist. Have you been practicing? Like I showed you? Well, have you?"

His six-foot beefy frame threw a shadow on his small son who stood with his chin touching his chest to hide the tears that had started to flow.

"Aw, quit bawlin'. If you're gonna act like a baby you can just go on in. Go on, get outta here."

Shaking his head Rev. Stevenson watched as Jack stumbled toward the back door of their home. As he turned to follow Jack into the house their next-door neighbor, General Anthony J. Williams, picked up the ball and walked across the lawn that separated their properties.

"Kinda hard on him, weren't you?" the general smiled as they shook hands.

Stevenson chuckled. "Hi, General. Naw, I'm just tryin' to toughen him up. His mother's makin' a regular sissy out of him."

General Williams glanced toward the boy and then back at the father. "Handsome boy you've got there," he said. "That black-hair-blue-eye combination's my favorite. 'Black Irish' they call it."

"Yeah, he looks just like my mother, and he's about as athletic as she is, too. He's smart enough, just no coordination."

The general's eyes went again to Jack. "I've been watching him struggle with that ball . . . you know, my new orders won't come through for a couple of weeks. I'd be glad to coach him for awhile each afternoon—that is, if you'd like me to."

"Hey, I'd really appreciate that, General. I'm gone so much I don't have much time with him."

At the back door Jack hesitated, his hand on the door knob, watching the two tall, well-built men as they talked and laughed together. Then he rubbed his sleeve across his face again, opened the door quietly and slipped inside.

Located in Silver Spring, Maryland, one of Washington, D.C.'s upper-middle class bedroom communities, the large, brick Stevenson home looked sturdy, even impressive, from the outside. Inside the walls were thin and Rev. Stevenson had a booming voice that matched his large, solid body. Jack's bedroom, next to his parents' room, gave him nightly opportunity to hear all but their most intimate conversations.

He doesn't like me; he's ashamed of me, maybe he wishes I was dead. Maybe I'll get dead and he'll be glad. Mom likes me—I think. Jack wrapped his arms around himself and pretended that his mom was hugging him. It felt good, having her arms around him, peaceful and warm. He always felt safe with her arms around him.

Every day after school his mom would ask him how his day had gone. Usually Jack didn't tell her the truth, because often it hadn't gone well. Also, he was afraid she'd tell his dad; like the time he told her about that big kid in the sixth grade who had grabbed his lunch money. Sure enough, she'd told him.

"David, please," his mom pled when his dad tried to show him how to fight back.

"OK, Son, first, you stand like this and then—"

"—Oh, David, don't." But, as usual, his dad had his way—he always had his way.

That night he had heard them arguing in bed.

"Ruth, I want you to quit hugging and kissing him all the time. He's too old for that now."

After that Jack tried to fight back, but the big kid just grabbed his money anyway and then laughed at him. He sure wished he was big and strong like his dad. Still, even though he was too old for it, his mom's hugging did feel real good.

The Reverend David Stevenson was widely respected by his colleagues as a loyal, dedicated servant of The Lord and several of them were known to have hinted to their wives that the matronly and subservient Ruth was a model End-Timer wife. The Reverend's discipline of Jack was thought harsh by some observers, but if anyone had so much as hinted that he didn't love his son, he would have been incredulous and insulted.

Rev. Stevenson's plan for Jack's future had long been settled. When Jack was eight days old he was dedicated to The Lord in front of the congregation and, later that same day, in a private family ceremony in their home, Rev. Stevenson promised The Lord that he would raise his son to be a faithful laborer in His Work. He meant to keep that promise. For Jack to succeed, his father was convinced, he would need a strong masculine image and so far Jack was just too soft and "pretty." And, there were even times, in moments of rare introspection, when he admitted to himself that he was sorely disappointed that Jack was not a tall, strong, strapping image of himself.

The next week

The general was patient with Jack's awkward throwing efforts on Monday, Tuesday, and Wednesday afternoons and Jack was beginning to respond to his kindness and careful coaching. On Thursday it rained. Jack didn't know if he was supposed to go to the general's house when it rained or not. Standing hesitantly on the general's doorstep, catcher's mitt in hand, he was wondering what to do when the door opened.

"Come in, Son, come in," the general said, putting his arm around Jack's shoulder and leading him into the kitchen.

"Mrs. Williams isn't home today, but she left us some milk and cookies. After you're finished we can go down to the 'rec' room. I've been wanting to talk to you. You know, man to man."

That night Jack told his mother that he didn't want to go to the general's house ever again; but although he cried and begged, his mother reminded him of his father's firm order. "Just try to be patient with the general, Son. Think how proud your father is going to be when you show him how you've improved."

The night after his second trip to the general's "rec" room Jack listened to his mother's pleading murmur followed by his father's booming voice coming through the thin wall. "No, he can't quit. What would the general say?" . . . "Don't be silly, Ruth. He's a general. He's sure not going to hurt some little kid. We're just lucky he's willing to take the time." . . . "You're making a mama's boy out of him" . . . "Anyway, the general'll be leaving soon; so make sure Jack is there every day 'til he leaves."

Jack hid his head in his pillow to keep his father from hearing him cry. His father had always told him that "The Lord's real men" don't cry, and more than anything he wanted to be a "real man"—like his father.

It rained a lot that autumn. The general was always waiting as Jack's reluctant steps led him to the door. After the requisite milk and cookies, Mrs. Williams would stay upstairs while the general led an unwilling Jack down the stairs to the recreation room in the dimly lit basement. "To show you how real men, strong men, act. This is how your father acts with other men," he assured Jack.

It was shortly after Jack's eleventh birthday that his mother found him with the cat. She was getting dinner when she heard the fearful howling. Running to the door she saw the mother cat lying still on Jack's lap, its head at a strange angle, its eyes staring. There were fresh claw marks on Jack's face and arms but he seemed unaware of the blood dripping down on the cat's white fur. Transfixed she watched as Jack pinched the cat's swollen belly over and over, an eerie smile on his face. Finally he stood up and threw the cat under a bush.

"I didn't want to hurt you," he shouted at the dead cat, "you should have let me do it."

In a box nearby six newborn kittens mewed and squirmed.

BOOK ONE

Chapter 1

November 15, 1939, 10 P.M.

Silver Spring, Maryland

Fifteen-year-old Mary Lou Schuster kept her head down as she quietly opened the front door to her home. She hung her coat in the closet and, crossing her arms over her chest and moaning softly, she tiptoed up the stairs toward her room.

"Is that you, Mary Lou?" her mother, Donna, called from the living room. When she got no answer she walked into the entry hall. Looking up the staircase she saw Mary Lou doubled over in pain.

"Oh, Honey, what's wrong?" she cried as she bolted up the stairs and took her in her arms.

"Oh, Mama, it was so terrible, I tried to get away, but he was too strong." Her body shook as she clung to her mother and her soft crying became a wail. "I couldn't help it, honest, Mama, I couldn't make him stop. I tried, I really did, but he wouldn't stop."

"Hush, Honey, it's alright. You're home now and it's late. Let me help you get ready for bed and then you can tell me about it." Donna's heart was pounding as she gently led her trembling daughter into the bedroom and sat down beside her on the bed. As Mary Lou's sobs began to subside Donna helped her pull her dress over her head. It was then she first saw the bruising evidence of the assault.

Thirty minutes later, after aspirin, taken to dull the pain and one of her mother's sedatives to help her sleep, Mary Lou was beginning to doze intermittently. Donna Schuster's carefree outlook on life changed in those thirty minutes.

As soon as he entered the house and saw his wife's hardened face, Art Schuster knew that something terrible had happened. Donna was dry-eyed; but her voice, usually so soft and full of laughter, was hard and raspy as she described their daughter's ordeal.

Pacing before the fireplace, his face reddened with fury, his fists clenched, he asked Donna again, "You're sure she wasn't raped? You're absolutely sure?"

"Yes, I'm sure of it, although that was clearly his intent." She began to cry then, "Oh, Art, you should see her breasts—all bruised and scratched."

"That little monster, I'll break his neck," he said, starting for the door. "I'm going over there right now."

Donna caught his arm, "No, not yet; it's after midnight." She wiped her eyes and pulled him down beside her on the couch. "Let's think this through first; we need to have a plan, we mustn't forget who his father is . . ."

By first light the plan was ready.

The next morning, The Stevenson home

"*When we walk with the Lord, in the light of His way . . .*" Ruth Stevenson was singing one of her mother's favorite hymns as she gathered her fifteen-year-old son's dirty clothes from the floor of his bathroom. "*When we do His good will, He abides with us still, never doubt only trust and obey.*" Ruth's godly mother had taught her to face life's trials with singing, but somehow it didn't seem to help her as much as it had helped her mother. "*Trust and obey, for there's no other way, to be happy in Jesus, but to trust and obey.*"

Her voice faltered as she remembered the strange mood Jack had been in when he left for school that morning. He had been so . . . so, vacant somehow. She sat down on her son's bed and smoothed the plaid bedspread with her fingers. He was such a troubled boy, sometimes loving, but too often brooding and hurtful. He was highly intelligent, or so the tests showed, but his grades were near failing. She worried about him constantly.

Her mother had always said that it was a sin to worry. "Leave it with The Lord," her mother had told her over and over. Ruth tried to leave it, tried to trust, but the frightening worry persisted. *I wish David would let me get some professional help for him,* she thought, *something is seriously wrong. I'm sure of it.*

"I'm not going to have some atheistic shrink playing around with his head, and that's final," David had said to her that morning after Jack left for school. "I know what's best for my own son. Trust me, Ruth, he's a teenager, he'll get over it."

There it was again, *"trust." I guess I should trust him, just like I should trust Jesus, but*—her thoughts were interrupted by the doorbell.

Opening the door she was alarmed to see the grim look on her friend's usually cheery face. She led Donna Schuster into the living room and listened with a sinking heart to what she was told.

Later, when the door finally closed behind her friend, Ruth leaned her head against the door and cried out to The Lord. "How could You let this happen? That sweet, lovely, young girl!" Rushing to the kitchen sink she vomited repeatedly until finally, drained and weak, she slumped down at the kitchen table, and with her head on the cool surface she cried. As she sat there sick with the realization of what was going to happen to Jack the words of her mother's favorite hymn came back to her in a taunting refrain, *Trust and obey, for there's no other way . . .* "Oh, God, there has to be another way," she cried, "please, please, help me find it."

Chapter 2

Jack saw the police car parked in front of his house as soon as he turned the corner. Driving slowly by the house he tried to see inside the windows but the blinds were drawn. He drove more rapidly then, speeding toward the outskirts of town. When he reached a large A & P supermarket he pulled into the center of the parking lot where his car would be hidden from the street by other cars. Leaning over the steering wheel, his face down on his crossed arms, alone and afraid, he thought about his life.

He knew something was wrong as soon as he got to school. In the hallway groups of kids stopped talking as he approached and turned to look at him after he passed them. He had a feeling that it was about what had happened with Mary Lou when he saw two policemen go into the principal's office. When the office secretary came out, started down the hall and went into his homeroom he knew they were after him.

Running down the hall in the opposite direction, pushing aside anyone who happened to be in the way, he rushed out of the school. The startled looks of his classmates followed him as he ran to the school parking lot, got into his battered 1934 Ford and drove away.

Jack could feel his heart thumping even now as he thought about it. *What if the police had caught him right there in school—in front of everyone! They'd all laugh.* He tried not to think about what had happened the night before. He especially didn't like to think about Mary

Lou's frightened screams. *I didn't want to hurt her.* He thought about Mary Lou's pretty pixie face framed with curly brown hair. *If she had just let me do it. It was all her own fault.* He remembered the velvety feel of the skin beneath her dress and the desire to feel her again was almost more than he could bear. *If she had just let me do it,* he thought again, *I wouldn't have had to hurt her. Now the police are after me and I can't go home. She'll never go out with me again. She probably hates me. Everybody hates me. Nobody wants me around. The guys at school, the girls . . . my dad is ashamed of me. Nobody wants me.* The thoughts kept churning around and around in his mind. *My dad's right, I am a sissy. I wish I was dead. They'd be sorry then—maybe. Maybe they'd be glad. They don't want me anyway, nobody wants me.*

Occasionally shoppers would glance at him as he sat hunched over in the car, but he kept his eyes averted. After awhile, his head on his arms, he slept. He awoke when a clerk from the store knocked on the window and mouthed the question: "Are you all right?" He straightened up and nodded. Looking around he saw that it was beginning to get dark and all the other cars in the lot were gone. Frightened that the police might see him now he started the car and drove away. As he turned the first corner he passed a large warehouse plastered with advertising. The large red, white, and blue poster caught his eye. UNCLE SAM WANTS YOU, said the figure on the poster. His finger was pointing straight at Jack.

The next morning

Staff Sgt. Barry Golden looked at the disheveled young man sitting in front of him and wondered briefly whether or not he should sign him up. *They said to sign up anyone who walks through the door, but this kid looks awfully young . . . and sad. Prob'ly running away from home or somethin'. Oh well, they'll sort it out at camp. They can always send him home.*

He hesitated, squinting at Jack, then he asked, "You sure you're eighteen?"

When Jack stuck to his lie the sergeant shrugged and pushed the form across the desk.

Three hours later, his car abandoned in the recruiter's parking lot and with only the clothes on his back, Jack boarded the bus for basic training and a raging European war.

Chapter 3

January 15, 1942, 8:30 A.M.

Somewhere near London, England

"Corporal Jack Stevenson reporting, Sir. I'm your new aide. I'll be driving you until an English driver is assigned. Your car is ready, Sir." Standing at attention, his hand in a crisp salute and his eyes forward, the dismay on his face was barely hidden as he opened the door.

Major General Anthony J. Williams settled himself into the back seat of his staff car and smiled to himself. *Just as I suspected. He hasn't changed much at all . . . still beautiful, still a delicious child. Too bad they have to grow up.* His body responded to the memory of their times together with erotic quivering.

His staff car, a new Lincoln just off the boat from the states, purred to life as its engine was started. He sniffed the rich new-car smell with satisfaction and glanced again at Jack's thin shoulders. *This war may bring me some pleasure after all,* he decided.

"Stop by my private quarters before taking me to HQ, Corporal."

"Yes Sir. Where are your private quarters, Sir?"

"It's your business to know these things Corporal," he barked, "I don't have time to do your job as well as my own."

"Yes Sir. Begging your pardon, Sir, I was just given this duty 15 minutes ago, Sir."

"Then you should have asked someone 10 minutes ago. Turn right here and follow the signs to Highgrove. I'll show you from there."

"Yes, Sir."

The general's personal quarters, formerly a large Tudor-style private home, were hidden from the street by high hedgerows. Even in winter the large trees and deep lawn that surrounded the house gave the grounds a park-like look.

When they arrived at the house, the general motioned for Jack to follow him inside. As they entered the door they were met by the joyous barking of the general's small pedigreed dog as she jumped and cavorted around his legs. General Williams scooped her up in his arms, nuzzled her head and handed her to Jack.

"Making sure that this little lady gets fed, watered, and walked will be one of your duties, Corporal," he said with a wink at the two WACs standing at attention by their desks in the former parlor of the old house. "That means you're off the hook, girls."

The two women continued to stand at attention while they covertly eyed Jack standing behind the general, the little dog licking his face. "At ease girls," General Williams said, "This is Corporal Jack Stevenson, my new aide. He'll be billeted here with us for the duration."

"Corporal, meet Kali and Angela, the two best secretaries in the Army." The two women, bundled in heavy sweaters over their uniforms against the damp cold that permeated the house, nodded and smiled at Jack. "As you were, girls," the general said. The two women sat down and turned back to their typewriters.

"Follow me Corporal, I'll show you where you'll bunk. Hope you brought your long johns. We can't seem to keep this place warm enough to be really comfortable."

With the little dog still in his arms Jack followed him with dread. Each step of the stairs sharpened the abhorrent memory of those steps that led down to General William's basement room back home in Maryland. The old familiar fear tightened his gut and, in spite of the cold, he could feel himself begin to sweat.

Downstairs Kali and Angela exchanged looks and raised eyebrows as they glanced toward the stairs. The general's predilection for young men was well known to them.

At the top of the stairs General Williams indicated the open door to a large front bedroom. "This room is mine." He paused and looked at Jack. "The one next to mine is yours." While he stood looking at the room he had indicated as Jack's he reached out, touched Jack's shoulder and slowly rubbed it in a provocative way. "No central heat here, Jack," he said with a smile, "but, we find our own ways to keep warm."

Jack jumped back away from the offensive hand and an involuntary shudder of revulsion passed through his body. "This assignment was not my choice, Sir," he mumbled.

The general laughed. "Of course it wasn't. It was mine. Oh, and by the way, your father sends his regards."

Jack looked at him in astonishment. "My father, Sir?"

"Yes, he wrote to me as soon as he learned you had signed up. They searched for you for days before they found out where you were. Anyway, he's hoping that I'll help you in your, uh, *chosen career*, and, of course, at the same time keep you from getting shot."

"Sir, with all due respect, those may be my father's wishes, but they are not mine. Please, Sir, I would like a transfer to get into the fighting."

"Corporal, from now on your 'fighting assignment' will be to do whatever I say." He looked at Jack with a smirk. "*Whatever*. You got that?"

"Yes Sir," Jack answered, eyes downcast, his voice a mutter just barely audible.

"Don't look so grim, Son. You'll find that being my aide has its rewards. How do you think that you, a kid still wet behind the ears, became a Corporal so soon? Just follow my orders—implicitly—and you'll find I can be very generous." He moved his face closer to Jack's and his eyes narrowed as he added, "on the other hand, one word . . . even a hint, to anyone at all, and . . . well, that's just not going to happen, is it, Corporal?"

"No, Sir," Jack mumbled.

Later that afternoon

Waiting beside the general's staff car in front of Army Headquarters, Jack shivered with the cold and from thoughts of what the general had in mind for him. As he stood there another driver sauntered over and offered him a cigarette.

Jack just shook his head and looked away.

The soldier shrugged and put the pack back into his pocket. Then, looking at Jack with a knowing smile, he asked, "How duhya like ole man Williams?"

Startled, Jack looked around. "I just started today. Why?"

"I hear he's tough to work for; treats his aides like they're his personal slaves. I heard one guy wouldn't do what he asked and the next day he was on his way to the front."

"What did he ask him to do?"

"Aw, I don't know," he shrugged, "it was probably just a rumor anyway."

Chapter 4

Two weeks later

Office of the Chaplain

Jack hugged his arms around himself shivering from the cold and from nervousness as he stood waiting just inside the door to the Quonset hut that served as a base chapel. The small office was strictly utilitarian with only a bookcase against one wall and a large picture of Christ behind the chaplain's desk. The picture was reassuring; it reminded him of Kali's whispered advice, "Go see the chaplain. He, and God, are the only ones who could possibly get you out of here."

When the chaplain looked up Jack stiffened to attention. "Sir, Corporal Stevenson reporting, Sir."

"At ease, soldier. Sit down. What can I do for you, Son?"

"I'd like to request your help with a transfer, Sir."

"Why's that Corporal? You have an assignment that most would envy. I understand that General Williams specifically requested you for his staff."

"Yes, Sir. I know that, Sir. He was a neighbor of ours at home, but I'd like to get in the fighting."

"Have you spoken to General Williams about this?"

"Yes, Sir. He denied my request, Sir."

The Colonel nodded, rubbed his left eyebrow, then crossed his arms and leaned back in his swivel chair. He looked at the young man sitting in front of him for several seconds in silence. *He looks very young, maybe only fifteen or sixteen; certainly not eighteen. He looks like a frightened child.* Then he leaned forward and asked, "What reason did the general give you for refusing your request?"

Jack hesitated for a moment then mumbled, "He said I was indispensable to him, Sir."

"Hmmm, I see. Corporal, is there perhaps another reason you want to be reassigned? Something you're not telling me? You can be honest with me, Son. Whatever you say in here is strictly confidential."

"I just want another assignment, Sir."

"Hmmm, I see. Tell me, Son, has General Williams ordered you to do something against your conscience? Something illegal, or . . ."

"Uh, well, I'd rather not . . . uh, no, Sir. I'd just like to be transferred. Anywhere at all, Sir. Just away from here."

"Perhaps if I spoke to General Will—"

Jack turned pale. "—oh, please, don't, Colonel. I know . . . well . . . that would not be a good idea, Sir. Please don't say anything to him."

"All right, Son. I won't. Not unless you ask me to. Now, how do you think I can help?"

"I don't know Sir, but I didn't know who else to go to, the general bein' so important and all. I thought you might know some way to get me transferred."

"I see." He rubbed his eyebrow again and leaned back in his chair. Tell me about yourself, Corporal. Where you from?"

"Silver Spring, Maryland, Sir. That's near Washington, D.C."

"Do you have brothers and sisters at home?"

"No, Sir. There's only my dad and mom and me."

"And your folks? What does your father do for a living?"

"He's an ordained minister, but mostly he does administrative stuff."

"Oh? What church does he work for?"

"He's with the End-Time Christian Church, Sir."

"Really?" the Chaplain said, leaning forward smiling, "Then your father must be Rev. David Stevenson of the General Assembly."

Jack looked at him in surprise. "You know him, Sir?"

"We were in the seminary together. I haven't seen him in years. How is he anyway?"

"He's fine, Sir." Jack's hands gripped the edge of the Chaplain's desk until his knuckles turned white. His voice was husky; "Do you think you can help me, Sir?"

"I'll try, Son. I'll do my best. But, first, I'm curious. Do you consider yourself a member of the End-Time Church?"

"Yes, Sir."

"Then, why did you enlist? Surely you were counseled to wait until you were drafted and then to request non-combatancy service?"

Jack looked down at the floor and his voice was low. "I guess I joined up in a hurry just to get away. I didn't think about asking for medical duty until I was in basic, then it was too late." He looked up at the Chaplain with fear in his eyes. "Does that mean you won't help me?"

"No, but it does make it harder. I'll do what I can. But, as I'm sure you realize, the general is a very powerful man and well . . . with the war going on . . . I may not be *able* to help you." As he was saying this he noticed that Jack's hands had begun to tremble.

"I know, Sir, but if you can think of any way at all—"

"—I'll do everything in my power to help you, Son. I know the general keeps you busy, but I want you to come see me again as soon as you can get away."

"Yes, Sir, I will, Sir, and thank you."

"Let's pray about this matter before you go. It may be our only hope."

Walking away from his office in the makeshift chapel, Colonel Robert Fredricks saluted absent-mindedly as he met other officers along the walk, his mind occupied with the problem of Corporal Jack Stevenson. *Strange I haven't heard of him before. He apparently didn't put a religious preference on his forms. Too bad; this boy clearly needs a friend. I hope I can get him away from Williams. I don't like the ugly hints that are circulating about him. Jack's clearly afraid; he may have already propositioned him. Humm, there is one possibility.* His step quickened with the new idea.

February 15, 1942

It was nearly two weeks before Jack was able to return to see the chaplain. As he stood waiting for the chaplain to look up his eyes were drawn to the picture of Christ.

"Please, God, please. Help me get away from him. I'm sorry for everything. Please help me."

He's lost weight, Col. Fredricks thought as he beckoned Jack to enter. *I hate to tell him the news.* "At ease, Corporal. Come, sit down."

Jack's face brightened and he quickly moved to a chair in front of the desk. "Did you find a way to get me transferred, Sir?"

He shook his head, "I'm sorry, Son. I tried, but Army Personnel tells me there's a directive that until the war's over no member of a senior officer's staff can be transferred without a specific request from the officer." He looked closely at Jack. "Are you sure you don't want me to speak to General Williams?"

Jack's face showed immediate alarm. He jumped up, panic in his voice, as he pleaded, "no, no, please don't. And, please, Sir, ask the person you talked to not to tell the general about me wanting to be transferred."

"Relax, Corporal, sit down. I didn't use your name. No one will know about this. I also went to see Colonel Joe Marques who, in other circumstances, could have made this happen. Did you know that Colonel Marques is a fellow believer? He also knew your father; worked with him in the Southern New England Assembly. We tried to get you transferred into the medics with the other End-Time boys, but . . . I'm truly sorry, Son, but it's not going to happen."

Jack sagged back into his chair, disappointment clouding his face. "I understand, Sir. Thank you for trying."

"Jack, we have a few End-Time families here in England who have opened their homes to our boys. I'd like to introduce you to one of them—the Thompson family. I've told them about you and they want to meet you. They're fine people, you'll like them, and by the way, they have two very cute daughters."

Chapter 5

February 28, 1942

The Thompson home

The chaplain was right. The Thompson girls *were* cute, Jack admitted, as he sat between them for a Friday night supper of potato soup and homemade bread. The chaplain had neglected to mention, however, that Amy and Andrea Thompson were only four and six years old. The little girls kept up a lively chatter on either side of him as the meal progressed, but Jack's attention was riveted across the table where sat the most beautiful girl he had ever seen; a visiting cousin named Patricia.

William and Fern Thompson watched in amusement as the two young people covertly eyed other with obvious interest. As soon as the simple supper and their evening worship were finished, the Thompsons excused themselves to put their daughters to bed.

By the second month the general's nightly assaults had become almost bearable to Jack. The once excruciating pain was mostly gone and Jack no longer came downstairs with bruises on his face and arms from resisting the general's advances. Many mornings Angela and Kali had looked at each other with sympathy in their eyes knowing what was happening and knowing that they were unable to help Jack.

The general's threats continued whenever Jack objected. "You stupid queer, stop fighting me and do what I want, or I'll have you killed; and, don't think for a minute that I won't!"

The general's repulsive groping, his grunts of pleasure and loud sighs of satisfaction continued to disgust Jack, while thoughts of Patricia helped push the humiliation ever deeper into the dark recesses of his mind.

During the day General Williams was correct and professional in all his contacts, his mind occupied with the serious business of war.

After a few unsuccessful attempts to make friends with Jack, Angela and Kali had given up trying to talk with Jack and he had no friends among the other soldiers. The persistent rumors about General Williams and his hand-picked aides made the men leery around him and he was generally ignored or laughed at behind his back. Jack pretended not to notice but the humiliation added to his anxiety.

As Jack worked on the general's schedule, took care of the general's dog, or ran his errands, he did his job mechanically and without interest his mind focused on Patricia's face, her eyes as blue as the sky back home, her pink lips so sweet, so innocent of artifice, her soft hand as it touched his arm.

Two weeks later

At last! While keeping a straight face Jack was jubilant when General Williams informed him that he would be attending a top-secret meeting at which Jack's help would not needed. Jack was given personal leave and advised to see London while he could. As soon as General Williams had gone, driven down the long driveway by his female English driver, Jack left for the Thompson home, worried that Patricia's visit with her cousins might have ended, worried that he might have lost her forever, worried that he would never again meet anyone as beautiful, as sweet, as *wonderful* as Patricia. Pa-trish-ah, Pa-trish-ah, her name reverberated in his mind as he hurried to the subway that would take him to her.

She was still there! As soon as he saw her he was struck with shyness and all the witty comments he had practiced left his mind. He felt awkward and clumsy; too embarrassed to even look at her. Only his eyes, which followed her when she wasn't looking, betrayed his avid interest.

After supper Jack joined the family in the parlor for evening worship. Surreptitiously he watched Patricia as Mr. Thompson read a passage from the Bible. After the Bible reading Amy and Andrea, who had quickly lost their initial shyness, climbed into Jack's lap and demanded a story. Across their heads Jack appealed silently with helpless eyes to Patricia. Smiling at his discomfort, she picked up Uncle Arthur's Bedtime Stories, a favorite of End-Time families, and moved across the room to sit beside him on the small love seat.

The story she read, about a naughty boy who always took the biggest piece of pie, was a familiar one to Jack. All through his childhood his mother had read stories to him from "Uncle Arthur." Now, with Patricia's warm shoulder touching his and the scent of her filling his nostrils, the childish story took on an exciting new dimension.

After the story was finished everyone gathered around the piano to sing "Onward Christian Soldiers," clearly a favorite of the little girls. Then they knelt in a circle to pray. Suddenly waves of homesickness overcame Jack, and without being aware of it, he began to shake with silent sobs.

Mr. Thompson's voice hesitated for just a moment, and then he went on with his prayer. He prayed for Jack's family at home, for the safety of all the young men, for England, and for special wisdom for their leaders. Then Jack felt a soft warm hand inserted into his with a gentle squeeze. He glanced up to see Patricia smiling at him, her eyes soft and loving.

As the prayer ended Jack's homesick feelings left him and his mind filled with love for this beautiful girl whose hand had held his in prayer.

This must be love, he thought in awe. He felt warm all over and safe and peaceful, just like he had when his mother had hugged him at home.

After the children had climbed the stairs to go to bed, waving and blowing kisses all the way, Patricia turned to Jack. "Would you like to take a walk?" she asked.

In the general's absence Jack visited the Thompson home each evening. The home-style food, so simple, so reminiscent of his mother's cooking, the sweet chatter of the little girls, the evening prayers for his safety, all filled him with a warm pleasure he had never before known. But, as he eagerly anticipated each evening, it was the thought of Patricia that overshadowed everything else.

It was during the second week of nightly walks that she said it. The night was cold, very dark, and moonless; the blackout complete. It was after they had laughed and whispered together, after he had confided his dream of one day being in The Lord's Work, like his father, after he had awkwardly, shyly, put his arm around her and pulled her close to him, and after she had rested her head against his shoulder that she said it. "I love you, Jack" she said softly, lifting her face to him.

He knew he should kiss her now. He wanted to, but still he hesitated. It wasn't until she reached up to pull his head down that his lips touched hers. It was a tentative kiss, soft, and brief. His heart beat drummed in his ears and he felt stirred like never before. "I love you too," he said, his voice hoarse with the wonder of what he was feeling.

Just as he began to kiss her again, the air raid siren sounded. Startled, they pulled apart and jumped up. The street immediately began to fill with the sound of people running to shelters and hand in hand they followed the shadowy figures through the dark streets.

Deep inside the subway shelter they could hear the thunder of bombers flying overhead followed by the whine of falling bombs and finally the blasts. Each new explosion seemed closer than the last and sent shock waves of fear through Jack and Patricia as they clung to each other in the cold, musty darkness. Around them little children cried out in terror as they huddled close to their mothers and strangers clutched each other in panic.

After what seemed like hours to the frightened, exhausted people in the shelter the bomb blasts were heard less frequently and the noise of the planes receded into the distance. Still the all clear had not yet sounded and soon muffled sleeping sounds could be heard throughout the shelter.

After a long while, in the dusty darkness Patricia lifted her head from Jack's shoulder, freed her hand from his and opened the top buttons on her coat. When she touched his hand again it was to lift it to her cheek. He had never touched her face before, and in wonder at the soft smoothness he traced the outline of her jaw and the smooth column of her neck. As his hand lingered on her neck Patricia put her hand over his and guided it down inside her coat. Suddenly his breath caught and he began to shiver as he pulled his hand away.

His voice, too loud in the crowded shelter, cried out, "No, no, I don't want to hurt you."

"Shhh, shhh, it's all right," she whispered, "you can touch me, it won't hurt me. Please, I want you to." She took his hand then and placed it against the skin beneath her blouse.

Jack's hand moved then, as with a mind of its own, feeling the satiny smoothness of her. He gasped aloud as he felt the soft mound of her breast.

"Kiss me, Jack," she whispered. "Please, I love you so much."

As Jack bent his head to do as she asked a surge of tenderness flowed through his body. She loved him! She wanted him! The wonder of it filled him with awe.

As the night went on, their kisses became more fervent, and then, led by Patricia's loving encouragement, they made love on the cold, hard, dirty floor of the subway. At first Jack was awkward, unsure of himself, but as his confidence grew, his early fumbling became passionate abandon. In the darkness the people around them, oblivious to all but their own sorrows and fears, simply ignored them.

In time they dozed and finally Patricia slept, her head cradled on Jack's chest, his arms supporting the precious burden.

When morning came and the all clear had sounded they stumbled with the others out of the shelter disheveled, dusty, and tired. A strong smell of smoke filled the air and two buildings across the street were now only rubble. In front of them struggled a weary-looking woman carrying a baby and a heavy bundle while a crying toddler pulled on her skirts. "Let me help you," Patricia offered. The tired woman nodded gratefully and handed her the baby. Patricia crooned softly to the little one as Jack watched her with loving eyes. "Wait for me here" she whispered to Jack as she turned away to follow the woman toward a nearby building. "I'll be right back."

Jack watched her go, unsure of what to do. Then, taking his eyes off Patricia for a moment, he offered to help an elderly man who was all alone and stumbling over the rubble in the street. When he turned his head again to look for Patricia she had disappeared.

After the elderly man was safely in his flat he ran back to find Patricia, but she was nowhere in sight. As he stood on the street corner trying to remember which building she had gone into he was approached by two MPs.

"Corporal Jack Stevenson?"

"Yes, what—?"

"—General Williams has been looking for you. He sent us to find you. You're to come with us. Now."

Jack had never seen the general so angry. The veins in his neck were prominent and his face was red with rage. When the shouting, the threats, and the tirade were finally over, Jack realized that he would survive—this time. He also realized that the general meant to make it impossible for him to see Patricia ever again. *When the war is over—then,* Jack vowed to himself, *I will leave this hateful man, I will find Patricia and I will marry her.*

"I feel sorry for Jack" whispered Kali to Angela after the general had stalked from the room. "No letters, no phone calls, no contact at all. He's really in love with her. I can tell, can't you? Do you think we could . . ."

"Don't be crazy! No way am I going to be court-martialed for disobeying a direct order. He'll survive. After the war he can look her up again."

April 23, 1942

Silver Spring, Md.
Dear Son,

We received a kind letter from the general yesterday. He told us about his intervention in your romance with the English girl. We know that must have been difficult for you, but in time you will come to thank God that you had this godly man watching over you. We know now that God in His plan for your life arranged for us to live next door to the general so that one day he would save your life. We thank God daily that he is there as your protector in this terrible war.

We keep hoping to hear from you. Please write. Your mother worries. Give the general our regards. Remember you're a Stevenson and make us proud, Son.

Love,
Dad

Every night of his life Jack had prayed before he went to sleep; now he was in a quandary; he wanted to pray. He *needed* to pray. He was afraid *not* to pray. What if they were bombed and he was killed before his sins were forgiven? Could he still go to heaven? It worried him. He just wasn't sure what to do. The general had caught him kneeling once and his scorn had been swift and hateful. He had tried praying after he got into bed, but, he was pretty sure that God wouldn't listen to him while he was doing what the Bible called an abomination. Maybe it was just better not to pray at all. To pray or not to pray; it was a nightly dilemma.

In bed at night, beside the sleeping general, he worried. He worried about his future; what if he were becoming what the general called him, a queer! He hated that word. *I hate this man, I hate what I'm doing, but You know what will happen if I don't. Make him stop, please Lord, and forgive me. I want to work for You someday. Please make him stop. Please, oh, God, please.*

"Just do it, or you'll die, but first I'll tell your holier-than-thou father what you've become." Jack had heard that threat so many times that he no longer doubted it would happen if he resisted.

Is this what You want God? I guess You just aren't listening to me any longer. You've given up on me, haven't You? Is it this or death? Oh, God!

The general stirred in his sleep, turned over and continued to softly snore.

Chapter 7

The pressures of the war increased as plans for the coming invasion of the continent filled the officers' days. The Supreme Commander General Eisenhower wanted General Williams at his side each day; and General Williams, after each stressful sixteen-hour day, wanted Jack.

Evenings as he entered his staff car to be driven to his quarters his hungry thoughts turned to Jack's boyish face and his tantalizing young body. Recently he had become aware that he no longer thought of Jack as merely a nightly release of stress and sexual tension. In surprise he wondered if he might actually be falling in love with the boy—a boy who was becoming a man! In love with a man? It was a new and disturbing thought. He began to think of ways to make Jack stop hating him; maybe even cause him to care for him.

Hmmm, I wonder, another promotion? Some Scotch to loosen him up? Too bad he's not a drinker. If this miserable war didn't take all our time maybe a weekend in Scotland or . . .

The shock of learning that Jack had been seeing a girl had unnerved him; especially as Jack's reluctant acquiescence during the last few weeks had lulled him into thinking that Jack might be starting to enjoy their time together.

"He'll forget her, I'll make him forget her," he muttered to himself in the back seat of the car.

His driver looked back over her shoulder at the general hunched in the back seat. "I beg your pardon, Sir. Did you say something to me?"

"No, no. Just thinking out loud," he answered as the car wove through the rubble-littered streets on the way to Highgrove—and to Jack.

June 1945

Kali looked up from her typewriter and watched Jack as he sauntered into the general's private office. Then she turned to Angela. "Have you noticed how muscular Jack's become? Remember what a skinny little kid he was when he first moved in?"

Angela laughed, "must be that exercise the general puts him through each night. He's finally transformed that cute little boy into one of those 'real men' Jack likes to talk about."

"Did you get a whiff of the general's new after-shave? Looks to me like he might be looking around for a change. I watched him eyeing that good-looking Corporal from Kentucky that was in the office yesterday."

"Well, frankly, I hope he does make a change. Jack's constant bragging gets on my nerves, and have you noticed how bossy he's become? He thinks he's sooo important being the general's favorite."

"Yeah, and he's started to use the same after-shave as the general. You can smell them both coming."

Angela laughed and glanced toward the office where Jack sat working. Lowering her voice she said, "Didya hear what Jack did the other night?"

"No. What?" Kali leaned forward in her chair.

"You know that GI I went out with last week? Well, I was in the mess hall yesterday and I overheard him and some others talking about Jack and a prostitute."

"Jack? With a prostitute? You sure? I thought the general had converted him into a you-know-what."

"Well, maybe, but don't forget Patricia. He sure liked her. Anyway, I heard one of the men say that Jack was hurting this girl so bad they had to pull him off her."

Kali shuddered. "Ooh! That gives me the creeps. I hope they told the MPs. Ya know, come to think of it, I thought there was something weird about Jack lately."

As Jack walked into the room the two women hurriedly turned back to their typewriters.

The little dog wiggled and squirmed as she waited for Jack to get into his poncho to take her for her daily walk in the garden. A steady, cold drizzle had made the path so muddy that Jack picked up the small dog and put her under his poncho. She had recently been bred and as Jack's hand cradled the belly of the dog he noticed that her teats had enlarged. Suddenly an overpowering urge surged through him and his body ached with desire.

The little dog's dead body lay beside the garden path when the general returned that night, its belly bruised and swollen, its head at an unnatural angle.

August 1, 1945

Jack's cocky, arrogant bravado had dissolved into self-pity as he sat on a barracks bunk awaiting orders to move out. *I didn't want to kill the dumb ole dog, but she kept trying to bite me. It was only a dog! Why can't he understand that? He prob'ly was trying to get rid of me anyway. He didn't want me anymore. I bet he wants that Corporal from Kentucky. Yeah, that's it. He must be the new "aide". Good luck! He'll need it.*

Jealousy rose in his throat like bile. He pictured General Williams giving his new aide all the perks that had once belonged to him. He hated that Corporal from Kentucky, but most of all he hated General Williams.

At least I'll never have to sleep with him again! I hate him. I really hate him. I'll prob'ly get killed now, then he'll be sorry. Huh! That's a joke; he'll prob'ly be glad. He prob'ly hopes I'll be killed right away. He's just like all the others. They all hate me. OK, God, I'm through with You, too. You could have saved me, but it's too late now.

He looked around the barracks at the other soldiers who were laughing and talking to each other, their gear, like his, on their backs. None of them had even spoken to him. *They all know why I was demoted. They're laughing at me. They all hate me. If I get a chance while we're fighting I'll pay 'em back, maybe I'll just kill 'em all.*

He looked at his shoulder where his Corporal's stripe had once been. He was a private again; busted by the man who had told him so many times that he loved him. *I'm going to get killed, and I hope I do. The general's getting his revenge. God, too, I guess.*

Chapter 8

October 14, 1945

Silver Spring, Maryland

The maple tree in General Williams' back yard was like a bright flame against the cool blue sky. It was a beautiful, brisk, fall day; perfect for drying clothes. Mrs. Williams watched the white sheets flapping in the breeze and smiled to herself. Her bed would have a delicious fresh-air smell when her husband got home from England. Her heart skipped a beat at the thought. It had been a long time since they had shared a bed. Maybe, after all this time apart . . .

She was hanging the last piece of wash on the line when she saw her neighbors drive in next door. She dropped the clothespins she was holding and hurried across the lawn to welcome Jack Stevenson home from the war.

"Welcome home, Jack," she said reaching up to hug him.

"Thank you," he muttered, abruptly pulling away from her embrace.

Taken aback she looked surprised and hurt. Jack's mother, embarrassed by her son's rudeness, quickly stepped between them. "Mrs. Williams, please forgive us. Jack is exhausted from his long trip. I know you understand. We'll have you over soon so Jack can give you the latest news about your husband."

"Of course. I'm sorry. I should have realized" . . . She turned away, and glancing occasionally over her shoulder, she walked across the lawn. Somehow the day didn't seem quite as beautiful as it had before.

David Stevenson watched all this in silence. Was this his son, muscles bulging beneath his uniform, his walk confident? *Why, he looks like a real man at last; not like the weakling he was before. Maybe the war did him some good. Thank God for the general.*

Jack had written home only three times in the three years he had been gone; always to his mother and always on her birthday. His parents' letters to him went unanswered; their only source of news an infrequent letter from General Williams. Jack's lack of courtesy to Mrs. Williams, their gentle neighbor lady, the wife of the man who had done so much for him—possibly even saved his life, surprised and angered his father, but he said nothing. *Later,* he thought. *I'll deal with him later.*

October and November were difficult and confusing months for the Stevenson family. Jack's travel fatigue had dissipated quickly and he began a vigorous body building program at the local YMCA. By late November it was obvious that he was strong enough that no one could ever again force him to do anything he didn't want to do. Often, during a workout, he remembered those early days in England when General Williams's strong arms had held him down against his will, forcing him to submit. At times he would catch himself looking down at his hands, now much larger and stronger, and then he would remember the general's powerful fists slamming into him when he resisted. *Never again,* he vowed, *never again!*

His parents knew that he needed time to adjust to civilian life, but it was a disquieting time for them. Their questions were answered in monosyllables. He volunteered nothing, he mentioned no plans for his future, and he asked no questions. At home his time was spent alone in his room, his activities and interests a mystery to them.

Sabbath mornings he habitually "wasn't feeling well" or was "too tired to go to church" and he simply walked out of the room whenever his parents began their long-established morning and evening worship. When his father was away traveling for church responsibilities, Jack disappeared with the family car refusing to tell his mother where he was going or where he had been.

Occasionally his mother noticed scratches or bruises on his face in the morning. "I'm OK, it's nothing, I cut myself shaving," was his stock answer to her worried questions. Alone in his room in the early morning hours he would relive his latest skirmish. When the women he picked up submitted to his advances without a struggle, as sometimes happened, he often found himself bored and sometimes unable to perform. It was the feisty ones who excited him. As soon as a woman resisted him a frenzied surge of desire and power would sweep over him. It was exhilarating. If scratches resulted from the struggles he wore them like badges of courage. He was a "real man" finally, and it felt *so* good.

At home his mother fussed over him, cooked the foods he liked, and kept his room and clothes spotless. He accepted her loving care without comment or thanks.

The thin walls of his home and his father's loud voice were still the same as he remembered them. Nights when his father was home from his many trips Jack lay on his bed listening to his mother's worried murmurs and his father's loud baffled responses. He felt no love for them, no connection to their life, no obligation to discuss his bitterness toward what had happened to him.

In December Jack began, tentatively, haltingly, to talk to them. He asked about local universities and whether they had the money to augment his GI bill. They were eager to discuss it with him and they assured him that they would help. They urged him to consider the nearby End-Time Missionary College. He sneered at their suggestion and said, to himself, *no way! I'd make some missionary!* His choice was the University of Maryland.

"I'm sorry, Mr. Stevenson, the Assistant Registrar at the University of Maryland told him. "We always give veterans the benefit of the doubt, but without a diploma, and with your poor high school grades . . . well, I'm afraid we really can't admit you."

The other area universities and colleges were unanimous in their opinions. "Finish high school, then reapply; and study this time." Anything to get away from home, he agreed to try the End-Time Missionary College; his parents' alma mater.

After a few pointed telephone calls from his father the administrators at the End-Time Missionary College reluctantly agreed to accept him under a "Provisional Admission," if his entrance tests at least showed promise.

His parents were thrilled. At night in their bedroom, while Jack listened through the wall, they assured each other that now Jack would surely find The Lord once more and perhaps a godly mate as well. Their prayers, they told each other, would now be answered.

But alone in the daylight hours his mother still worried. *Jack brags so much about how strong he is, how he can beat up anyone he wants to,* she thought, *why should he want to beat anyone up? The war is over.* She prayed for him all during the day and each evening before she slept.

Chapter 9

February 13, 1946, 7:15 A.M.

End-Time Missionary College

Nineteen-year old Wayne Dority sat up in bed with a start. He was still shaken from the dream he had been having. In the dream he was with his new roommate and they were doing really sick, bizarre stuff with two women. Then it hit him. They were doing the same things in the dream that Jack had described to him the night before. *Good thing Sandy doesn't know what I'm dreaming about; she'd drop me in a heartbeat.*

Wayne looked across the room where Jack was on the floor doing his daily one hundred push-ups. *OK, I know he's really strong, but the way he struts around campus showing off his muscles is disgusting. He looks like the beach bully kicking sand in the little skinny guy's face.*

Wayne leaned back in bed and stretched while Jack continued his routine. *He's sure had a lot of experience with women; that's if he's telling the truth, which I doubt. If it is true the girls on campus must look pretty tame to him. Of course, he's been in the army so maybe he really did do those things. He's probably just bragging to impress me.*

And, there were some other things about Jack that bothered Wayne; his contempt when he talked about the church—even about his own father who was ordained by God. *Maybe after he goes through Rev. French's Bible class . . .* Wayne yawned and swung his legs over the edge of the bed. *Think I'll ask Tom Green to add his name to their prayer group list.*

51

Later, while he was dressing for class, Jack surprised him by asking if he wanted to double date with him. "You didn't believe what I told you last night, did you?" Jack asked him. "I could tell. Get your girlfriend and come along with me and a date next Sunday night and I'll show you how easy it is."

Wayne just listened as Jack outlined his plan. "We'll go into D.C. for dinner, then on the way back . . ."

February 14, 1946, 4:30 P.M.

The Women's Dormitory

Katherine Landers burst into her dorm room in Halcyon Hall, breathing hard from running up three flights of stairs and down to the far end of the long hall. Her roommate, propped up in bed studying, looked up as the door opened.

"Roommate, wait 'til you hear what just happened! Jack Stevenson just asked me out for a date on Sunday night!"

Her roommate, Karis, covered her mouth and yawned. "Who's Jack Stevenson?"

Katherine threw her books on her desk and plopped on the end of Karis' bed. "You know, he's that new guy I told you about; the one who just started this quarter . . . you know, that cute guy who smiled at me when I came out of Bible class yesterday?" she said, excitement making her words run together.

"That's great, roommate. Where's he taking you? There's nothing good going on this weekend."

"Listen to this! We're going *out to dinner* at some fancy restaurant in Washington. We're going to double with Wayne Dority and Sandy Alexander. D'ya think the Dean will give me permission?" Without waiting for an answer Katherine jumped up, opened her closet and grimaced. "I don't have anything decent to wear and Sandy has such gorgeous clothes."

"How about that lacy new blouse your Mom just sent? You can borrow my black skirt to go with it."

"Thanks, but I think I'll wait 'til I see what Sandy's going to wear before I decide. Roommate, don't you think it's significant, I mean today being Valentine's Day and all?"

Karis looked at her thrilled roommate and smiled.

It was after "lights out" before Katherine was able to find Sandy Alexander in her room. Sandy's roommate, her mouth full of bobby pins, rolled her hair in pin curls in front of the dark mirror while Sandy and Katherine huddled on the bed whispering.

"I haven't decided yet," Sandy confessed, "Wayne sometimes tells me what he wants me to wear; once he even went shopping with me to show me what he likes. You should have seen him," she giggled. "He looked so serious looking through the dresses for just the right one."

Katherine didn't respond to Sandy's happy memory. "Do you think this would be OK?" She asked, spreading her new blouse on the bed and softly touching the silky fabric. The cream-colored lace bodice looked lustrous in the light from Sandy's flashlight.

"Oh, yeah, that's beautiful. Guys like lace."

Relieved, Katherine leaned back on the bed trying to imagine what Jack might say when he saw her in the blouse. Then she sat up again and asked, "did Wayne tell you anything about Jack, you know, what he's like?"

"Yeah, he talks about him a lot. I think he's kind of in awe of him."

"Why?"

"Well, promise you won't tell him I said anything?"

"Yes, yes, I promise, tell me."

"Well, Wayne said that when Jack was in the Army he had lots of dates. Usually with women he didn't know. He didn't say it but I think he meant—you know, bad women."

Katherine could feel her heart beat a little faster as apprehension began to color her excitement. "What else? Did he say anything else?"

"Let's see. He told me he does a lot of body building stuff—he's very strong—oh, and that he's not very religious."

Katherine felt her elation cool a bit more. "He's an End-Timer isn't he?"

"Oh, sure, his father's a big shot in the General Assembly, but Wayne says . . . shh, the monitor's coming. Here get under the comforter. Sandy turned off her flashlight and sat on the edge of the bed while Katherine pulled the fluffy pink comforter over her head and tried not to breathe. She could hear Sandy and her roommate assuring the hall monitor that they were almost ready for bed. After the monitor's footfalls faded away Katherine sat up. "D'ya think she guessed I was here?"

Sandy giggled, "No, she probably thought you were part of my unmade bed. She's always telling me how messy my room is."

"I better go before she gets to third floor and finds me gone," whispered Katherine slipping out into the hallway, "I'll talk to you tomorrow. Let me know what you decide to wear, OK?"

Wayne thinks Jack's not religious. Maybe he's just shy about showing it. Lots of guys are like that they say. Maybe I can help him.

Even before she reached her own room Katherine's prayers were ascending for Jack Stevenson's soul.

Chapter 10

Sunday evening, 8:45 P.M.

Coming back on the No. 231 bus from downtown Washington, D.C. Jack sat close to Katherine, his hard muscular shoulder pressed against hers. His body felt warm and strong against her and his masculine-smelling cologne added a pleasant fragrance to her euphoria.

They didn't talk much, but he often smiled and looked into her eyes while with his hand he drew slow circles on the back of her hand and wrist. Katherine found it strangely exciting and soon unfamiliar sensations began to course through her body. Sitting behind them Wayne and Sandy, engrossed in each other, softly laughed and whispered.

As the bus pulled up at a stop two blocks before the college Jack suddenly stood up, turned around, winked at Wayne and said, "We're getting off here. We'll walk the rest of the way. See ya later at the dorm."

"OK?" he asked Katherine as he took her hand and pulled her up. Without waiting for her answer he signaled the driver to let them off.

Outside the bus they walked slowly along the sidewalk toward the college, not talking, the streetlights casting a soft glow on their faces, their arms linked. For the end of February the night was unusually warm, almost balmy. It was Katherine's first real date. *I'm going to remember every bit of this magical night for the rest of my life,* she thought.

Sligo Creek, a languid little stream, meanders in a narrow, steep-sided canyon behind the End-Time Sanitarium and Hospital. Along its rocky banks young hospital employees and students from the nearby college have for many years pledged their young love in its leafy solitude. Just before Jack and Katherine reached the narrow bridge that crossed the creek Jack gently steered her toward a path that led down to the creek bed.

"Come," he said quietly, "I want to show you something."

Propelled along by his hand on the small of her back she tried, but not too hard, to protest. "Jack, we aren't supposed to . . ." Silently they made their way down the dark ill-defined path toward the creek with Jack leading Katherine by the hand. Suddenly she stumbled on a protruding tree root and began to fall. Jack turned and caught her before she reached the ground. As he helped her to her feet he pulled her close and kissed her. The kiss was nothing like the chaste first kiss she had so many times imagined. His mouth was hard on hers, grinding and demanding. After awhile he forced her lips apart and thrust his tongue into her mouth while one hand pulled her skirt up and began to grope toward her panties. Panic overwhelmed her.

Pushing on his chest with both hands Katherine was finally able to pull away. "No! No!" she gasped. "Please. Stop. You're hurting me." Without a word he grabbed both her hands and pulled her back to him. Struggling to get away she stumbled again and fell down the slope pulling him down with her. Jack fell on top of her, his weight pushing the breath from her slight body. Instead of getting off her he shoved her head back into the cold, hard ground and then pinned her hands above her head. Rocks dug into her back. She twisted and struggled to get out from under him screaming for help. His hand quickly covered her mouth as he growled, "Shut up and stop struggling. I'm not going to hurt you." He kept holding her down, pushing her against the hard ground for what seemed an eternity to Katherine. Finally, when she stopped struggling to gather her strength, he asked, "All right then, are you ready now? I didn't think you would be such a spitfire. You like it rough, huh? Good. So do I and that's the way you're going to get it."

His handsome face was twisted in a lurid smile, his eyes had a wild look, and Katherine cringed in horror as she realized what he was planning to do. Then, sitting astride her, while holding both her hands above her head with one hand, he began to open the buttons on her blouse. As she started to twist and to scream again he slammed his fist into her cheek and then ripped the buttons off and pushed the blouse aside. *My new blouse,* she thought irrationally, *he's tearing the lace. What is Mom going to say?* Her blouse open and torn, he ripped her flimsy slip open and thrust his hand into her bra. His fingers locked onto her breast and he squeezed. Hard.

Between the waves of excruciating pain shooting through her body she tried to scream against the hand that was once more covering her mouth, but her efforts appeared to excite him further and he continued to squeeze first one breast and then the other, his face filled with a lewd smile of satisfaction.

"Stop fighting me," he growled in her face, his hand still over her mouth. "Just do as I say. You'll like it. You all pretend, but you all like it."

Finally through the shattering pain she was able to move until she had the edge of his palm in her mouth. She bit down as hard as she could into the hand that held her mouth captive.

Snatching his hand away he doubled up his fist and struck her in the face again as she screamed in terror. Her cheekbone crunched. She tasted blood. He hit her over and over.

Later, when she lay bloody and silent and broken he looked down at her and said, "You should have let me do what I wanted; I didn't want to hurt you."

Later that night

When she opened her eyes she was alone; alone and cold and disoriented. She tried to move, to sit up, but the pain was so great she cried out and fell back down. She began to remember then and the horror of her ordeal came flooding back as she screamed again and again for help. Finally, exhausted, she lay still and tried to pray believing that she would die there alone in the dreadful darkness.

After awhile she heard a rustling in the bushes beside her and opening her eyes she saw a man looking down at her. She screamed and cowering behind her upraised hand she tried to roll away from him.

"Don't be afraid, I won't hurt you," the man said as he knelt beside her. Taking off his jacket he covered her chest and pulled up her skirt.

Still shrinking from his nearness and touch she cried out in fear, "Don't hurt me. Please, don't hurt me."

"I won't hurt you, I promise." He said in a quiet, gentle voice. "I'm going to help you. Do you think you can walk?"

"Who are you?" she stammered, her lips swollen and the pain in her face increasing in intensity as she tried to talk.

"My name is Don Scott. I'm a doctor. I work at the hospital. I heard you screaming as I was taking a walk. Here, let me help you get up."

He eased his arm under her shoulders and lifted her to her feet, but as she tried to stand her legs buckled under her and she fainted. He caught her up in his arms and began the steep climb up the path to the hospital.

The intake note in Katherine's medical chart was brief: Patient admitted in generalized pain, disoriented and frightened. Broken nose. Multiple contusions and cuts on face. Rule out concussion. Abrasions on lower extremities. 5 cm laceration on level L1 and L2, Multiple deep contusions on breasts. Two broken ribs. Contusions and bleeding surrounding genital area. Patient claims she was raped. Donald Scott, MD

4:30 A.M., the next morning

End-Time Sanitarium and Hospital

In a haze of drugs and sleep and pain, Katherine was vaguely aware that someone had quietly entered her room. She moaned in pain as her pillow was adjusted and the sheet beneath her was straightened. The nurse's starched white cap shone like a bright halo in the darkness of the hospital room; her face, at first off-center and blurred, slowly came into focus. To Katherine she looked so loving, so beautiful, and so caring. She wondered if she were dead, if she were in heaven, and if this was an angel.

As the nurse turned and left the room Katherine's awareness sharpened. She wasn't in heaven, but she knew she had been in hell.

Awake now her tears came silently sliding down her face into the bedding and down the neck of her hospital gown. *I'll never be pure again. I won't be able to wear a white wedding gown. No one will want to marry me. I wish I were dead.*

She didn't hear him come into the room, but even without turning to look she sensed evil in the room. She stiffened with fear and horror knowing that he was there looking down at her.

Then she smelled him; his cologne a distinct signature. He leaned over her, whispering something. In her terror she couldn't understand his words but the threat was clear. She tried to roll away from him, to get up, to get away, but the pain, the terrible pain, kept her a prisoner. All she could do was to scream through her swollen lips.

"No, no, please. Help! Help me!" Her frantic cries echoed through the quiet night hallways of the hospital as he disappeared into the darkness.

Soon strong hands held her arms and she felt a needle prick. A voice, quiet and reassuring, "Shh, shh, Katherine," it said. "You had a bad dream, that's all. We're here with you. We won't let anyone hurt you." Through the haze of drugs the kind voice and the strong hands seemed faintly familiar. Her eyes closed and she slept.

Later that morning

The sedative was wearing off and Katherine was just beginning to awaken when Mrs. Olive Gallagher, Dean of Women at the End-Time College, walked into her room.

Looking down at Katherine's bruised and swollen face she thought, *Poor foolish girl. They never seem to understand that the rules were made to protect them. She was such a promising student; it's a shame.*

She touched Katherine very gently on the shoulder, "Katherine? It's Mrs. Gallagher. Can you hear me?"

Katherine started as she felt the touch and opened her eyes in abject fear. When she recognized who it was she turned her face toward the wall and began to softly cry. "I'm sorry," she whimpered, "I'm so sorry."

"It's all right, Dear. The important thing now is for you to get well. We need to decide how we can help you. Have you spoken to your parents yet?"

"Yes . . . well no, the hospital called them," her sobs increased, "they, they, they're coming to take me, take me, home."

Mrs. Gallagher waited until Katherine's sobs had subsided a bit before she spoke again. "I think that's wise, Dear." When Katherine began to cry again she added, "Maybe in a year or two you can choose another college and finish your studies."

"Please don't tell anyone about this, Mrs. Gallagher," she whispered through her tears, "Please. I'm so ashamed."

"Katherine, these unfortunate incidents are very hard to hide I'm afraid. You can take some comfort in knowing that the other girls will understand now why they're not to go down to Sligo Creek unless properly chaperoned."

"Mrs. Gallagher, what's going to happen to . . . to him?"

"He will be disciplined, Katherine. I will personally see to that. You can rest assured on that score."

Katherine started to cry again, great sobs that wrenched her bruised body. Her words were muffled and her voice was hoarse when she said, "He came into my room last night. He's going to try to hurt me again."

"Katherine, you had a bad dream, that's all. I talked with Dr. Scott this morning and he told me about your fright."

"But, but, he was here. He said he would kill me if I told."

"You have had a very frightening time, but it's over now. The important thing is for you to get well and to learn from this terrible experience."

Katherine looked up at the Dean's kindly face. *She doesn't believe me. He was here, I know it, but she doesn't believe me; no one is going to believe me.*

"You think it was my fault, don't you? I tried to stop him, I really tried."

"I'm sure you did, my Dear, but when we choose to break the rules we must also suffer the consequences. Unfortunately as women we often bear more than our share of those consequences."

Katherine sighed and wiped her eyes with a bandaged hand. "Is it all right if my roommate cleans out my room? I don't want anyone to see me like this."

"Of course, Dear. We want to make this as easy for you as possible. All the girls will be praying for you. Would you like me to pray with you now before I leave?"

She nodded and obediently closed her eyes as Mrs. Gallagher prayed, but to her surprise her mind refused to listen to the familiar words. Without her permission her mind was praying its own prayer. *Lord, how could You let this happen? Where were You when I needed You? You knew what was going to happen and You let it happen.* It was the first time she had ever questioned God.

At that moment in the men's dorm

Wayne Dority was struggling with his conscience. *I knew that Jack was planning to do something bad to Katherine and I let it happen!* He remembered how Jack's face had looked when he returned to the dorm; twisted and ugly, but somehow proud and satisfied with himself. And, he would never forget Jack's words to him. "If you ever, ever tell anyone what I did I'll kill you. Don't ever doubt that I can and I will."

Chapter 12

The next morning

Office of the College President

The Executive Committee members of the End-Time Missionary College were already sitting around the conference table talking among themselves when the College Business Manager, Homer Alexander, arrived. "Sorry I'm late; I just got off the phone with Rev. Stevenson."

The others raised eyebrows and nodded knowingly.

"He wanted to let me know how sorry he was that this happened."

"What else did he say? Wait, let me guess," President Dennis said, "First, the girl had been shamelessly chasing Jack. Then, Jack is sorry he got carried away, and third, they're all praying for the girl."

President Dennis looked thoughtfully at each of the four men and one woman who sat nodding their heads around the table. "Looks like we each received a call from his father pleading his case. Right?"

Again there were five nods. President Dennis continued, "I also received a letter from the boy himself saying he was teased and goaded into it by the girl. He claims he was surprised to discover that she was 'that kind' of girl."

Homer Alexander looked uncomfortable for a moment then said; "I'm inclined to believe that. My daughter, Sandy, says that Katherine had a big crush on Jack and that she was very excited about going out with him," he hesitated and looked around before continuing, "Sandy did mention though that Katherine was a very shy and reserved girl and that this was her first date."

Larry Lowell, Dean of Men, held up a letter that Jack had written to him. "Jack says in this letter to me that being in the war changed him and that he wants to go into The Lord's Work. He says he's asked The Lord to forgive him and he believes that He has. He's afraid, he says, that this could jeopardize his opportunity to, in his words, 'serve The Lord.'"

Homer Alexander leaned forward to speak, "He's right about that. If this gets out it'll ruin his chances for a ministerial call, and—"

"—I'm not so sure about that," interrupted President Dennis, "I have a letter addressed to this committee from the General Assembly President himself asking for leniency for Jack."

Mrs. Gallagher, who had been listening without comment, raised her hand to get her colleagues' attention. "Aren't we forgetting someone? He wasn't even hurt, but Katherine was brutally beaten. You should see her; cuts and bruises all over, her clothes ripped, even some broken bones. Remember, he's a very strong young man and she was no match for his strength. He—"

"—Mrs. Gallagher, with all due respect," Larry Lowell interrupted, "He's just back from the war; being provoked was bound to make him act rough. We have to cut some slack for these young men. After what they've been through—"

"—Mrs. Gallagher is right." The interruption this time was from President Dennis. "Of course we must be sympathetic toward the girl." He turned to Mrs. Gallagher. "Have you talked with her yet?"

"Yes, she was very upset, but mostly, I think, she was ashamed. She thinks it was her fault; that she should have stopped him."

"What does she plan to do? I hope you explained to her that there was no way she could stay on here." Larry Lowell looked around the table for confirmation.

"She's planning to go home, although I don't know why she should have to leave. After all, *she's* the victim, not Jack Stevenson."

"The reputation of the college will be the victim if this gets out. Have any of the newspapers picked it up yet?" asked Homer Alexander.

Five pairs of eyes turned to Dan Ray, Public Relations Director for the college.

"No. We'd probably have heard from them by now if they'd gotten wind of it. The hospital has agreed not to report it; they aren't anxious to have it known either. After all, many of their student nurses, and even some patients, go down to the Sligo from time to time."

The committee members looked up as the President's secretary opened the door.

"Your next appointment is here President Dennis," she said, "What shall I tell him?"

"We're almost finished. Just ask him to wait." When the secretary closed the door he continued, "All right, gentlemen, and, of course, Mrs. Gallagher. If the girl goes home, as you say she is planning to, we have only to decide what punishment we should consider for the boy. What do you suggest?"

Larry Lowell spoke up at once. "It seems to me he's been punished already. He's already missed three days of classes and will be out at least until Monday. Also I intend to give him a strong talking-to when he returns."

"I suspect he already got that from his father—you know Stevenson!" said Dan Ray.

"Yeah, he'd scare most anyone into obedience. I know he sure scares me," added Homer Alexander as the other committee members chuckled.

President Dennis gathered his papers together and stood up; a sign that the meeting was ending.

"I plan to write a strongly worded letter to this young man warning him that this kind of behavior will not be tolerated on this campus. And, unless you are strongly opposed, I'm suspending him from classes for another week. Any objections?" He looked around the table and when no one spoke up he said, "Are we in agreement that this matter will then be considered closed? All in favor?"

No one seemed to notice that Mrs. Gallagher did not raise her hand.

February 21, 1946

The drive from the college to her home in Front Royal, Virginia, was one that Katherine had always enjoyed. The gentle green hills and historic small towns had a benevolent and friendly look that made her feel privileged to live among them. Her father and mother had been born not far from where she grew up, and Katherine expected that she and her children would someday live nearby. Unless, of course, The Lord should call her to the mission field.

It was a cold, cloudy day when John and Beatrice Landers brought their only child, Katherine, home from college. The grass on the hillsides was brown from frost and the trees were gaunt and empty of leaves. Sitting in the back seat of her father's 1938 Chevy, surrounded by the detritus of her college life, Katherine quietly wept for the loss of her innocence, the loss of her parents' pride in her, and for the hopelessness of her future. There was no conversation in the car, and Katherine hid her face as they passed through the friendly small towns.

When they arrived home, Katherine carried her suitcases up to her room and lay down on her bed. On a shelf above her head her favorite girlhood doll, its painted smile fixed in place, looked down on her desolate form. Her father, looking grim, unloaded the boxes of books and college memorabilia her roommate had packed for him. He carried these reminders of his hope for her into the basement and stored them in a far corner.

The first weeks at home passed like a bad dream for the Landers family. During the day Katherine was silent, listless, unable to concentrate. She had no appetite and as her weight began to drop her usual clear complexion became red and blotchy; her thick brown hair looked greasy and lank. She was sometimes dizzy and nauseated and when she came down mornings to pick at her breakfast her pretty brown eyes were often red-rimmed and puffy from crying.

Her parents watched and worried and prayed. During the first two weeks her mother, Bea, had run to her room in alarm each time she heard Katherine's screams in the night. There she would hold her close until the dream faded. By the third week Bea stayed in her bed cringing until the screams ended and sleep had overtaken the horror. The frequency of Katherine's nightmares diminished gradually as the weeks passed and her parents began to think that she was recovering at last.

Spring comes softly in the beautiful Shenandoah Valley of Virginia. The air has a fresh, sweet smell, and the sun shining through the new green leaves casts lacy patterns on the sidewalks and streets. In front of the Landers' home the bright spring flowers along the walk lifted some of the gloom inside the house. John Landers, an elder in the local End-Time church, prevailed on the pastor to hire Katherine part time in the church office. Bea started a new quilt at the Tuesday afternoon Ladies Aid Society. Hope for the future once again seemed possible.

On the first day of May they found out, and their nascent hope turned to utter despair.

Chapter 14

May 3, 1946, 11:15 P.M.

Lying on her side of the bed while John undressed Bea could feel her heart beating irregularly fast, then slower, then faster again. Her body felt strange to her, almost as if it belonged to someone else. The pillow beneath her head was wet from the tears that kept sliding unchecked down her cheek to her neck and onto the pillow. John, his face anxious, looked at her, sighed, and began to pull on his pajamas.

"Bea, don't make yourself sick now. We'll get through this. We're not the only family that's had to deal with an out-of-wedlock baby."

"It's all my fault. I should have warned her, prepared her somehow. Now she'll never have the kind of wedding she's always dreamed of."

John turned away to hide his own tears and continued to get ready for bed. They had been silent for several minutes when Bea began to cry again.

"Oh, John," she sobbed, "What about her job? She won't be able to keep working in the church office when they find out. They may have guessed already; she's so sick every morning. I don't know why I didn't guess . . . I just never thought . . ."

In bed John pulled her close and rested his cheek on her head. His voice was low and comforting, "We'll find a way to help her. I'm going to call my Dad tomorrow and tell him. They love Katherine as much as we do and, uh, I thought I might ask him if, if uh, well, if he had any ideas. These things happen more often in a big city like Chicago."

Bea pulled away from him, "Oh John, you're not thinking of an abortion, are you? No, please, don't even think it. It's wrong; you know that! And besides, they're too dangerous. Your mother herself told us about a neighbor who bled to death. Promise me you won't even consider that for Katherine."

"I know, I know. I don't want to, but what then?" he said, his voice strained. "All right, you think of something. We can't have her stay here, pregnant, without a husband. She'd live in disgrace . . . and think of the child . . . you know what they'd call him. A child like that would never have a chance in this town."

"Maybe your folks would let her stay with them until—"

"—That's a great idea!" he said. "I'll ask them. We could tell people she'd gone there to help them out. Of course, she'll have to give the baby up for adoption. My folks are too old to keep both her and a baby."

"Oh, John. Do you think they'll let her come? Tell 'em we can help out with money."

"I'll call 'em tomorrow. Come on Honey, it's late. We'd better get some sleep." He turned over, his back forming a comforting wall for Bea to lean against.

Bea lay quietly thinking. *She's so determined to keep the baby; but of course she can't. She doesn't realize how hard it would be. She'll have to give it up.* She turned over and pulled the blankets over her shoulders. But sleep eluded her and she was still planning the logistics of moving Katherine to Chicago when the clock in the hall downstairs struck three A.M.

The next night, 10 P.M.

A weary Bea sat on the side of the bed, staring at the hooked rug at her feet. *What if they can't take her? What if she has to stay here? I never thought this could happen to us, to Katherine. Katherine was always so conscientious, so . . .* She looked up when John opened the door.

"Bea, they said no. Dad said that Mom was just too fragile to take the stress. He feels terrible about it, I could tell."

"Oh, John, what are we going to do?"

"Dad said he'd check into homes for unwed mothers in Chicago if we wanted him to."

"There must be homes like that closer to us where we could visit her. Maybe the pastor . . . no, I guess we can't ask him, can we?"

"Honey, I think there's something else we have to face. When this gets out Katherine will probably be disfellowshipped."

She looked at him, shocked. "Oh, no! We can't let that happen; it would break her heart. We have to find somewhere she can go to have the baby and then let some good family adopt it. What about Dr. Delmar? He helped Jim and Jeanine adopt their baby; maybe he knows someone."

"Yes, and everyone in town knew all about it, too. No, Bea, this is something we have to do ourselves."

"John, let's try to sleep. You look so tired. I'll talk to Katherine again tomorrow and try to get her to listen to reason. She still thinks she can have the baby and live here with us."

"All right, you try; she sure doesn't listen to me. Good night, Honey."

Their customary good night kiss was brief; they got into bed, their eyes closed, but each kept a sleepless vigil on their anguish.

The next night, 10:45 p.m.

Bea was lying awake in bed when John came home from the church board meeting.

"I requested prayer for Katherine tonight," he said quietly, sitting on the side of the bed while he took his shoes off.

"Oh, John, I thought we agreed not to tell them." She propped herself up on one elbow and looked at him in dismay.

"I didn't tell them anything; only that I hoped they would include Katherine in their devotions. There were a lot of requests; we aren't the only ones with serious problems."

"Who else did they pray for?"

"Well, one request was for Rick Radford. Remember him? He's that red-haired man whose wife died last spring. Seems her medical bills have bankrupted him and he's moving to California. How was Katherine tonight?"

71

"She won't come out of her room, won't eat, won't talk to me," her voice broke and she began crying softly. "Oh, John, what are we going to do?"

Sliding into bed beside her he said, "Bea, this may be a crazy idea, but I've been thinking. I wonder if Rick Radford might want a new young wife. You know his wife was sickly all the years they were married; prob'ly why they never had children."

"But, John, he's way too old for her."

"He's not that old, maybe 35 or 40. He's an End-Timer, and anyway, what choice will she have now? How many men are going to want to raise some other man's illegitimate child?"

"But, how do we know he'd be good to her . . . accept her child? And you said he was bankrupt."

"I know, I know. I've thought about that. We could give him Katherine's college fund; she'll never be able to use it now. It's not much, but it would give them a start; sort of like a dowry."

The light in their bedroom burned far into the night.

Two days later, 9:30 P.M.

"He was trying, Bea. You have to give him credit for trying. He tried to talk to her, remember? She wouldn't even look at him. You have to talk to her, get her to listen to reason."

Bea sighed, "I'll try, but I'm not sure it'll do any good. Maybe when he comes for dinner tomorrow night I can get her to fix herself up a little." She stood at the window looking out at the night sky. "John, she's so sad; I don't think I've ever seen anyone so sad."

John joined her at the window. Slipping his arm around her waist he said, "I know, Honey. I'm worried about her. Did you hide the medicines?"

"Yes, and your razor blades, and the knives. I don't think there's anything left that she could hurt herself with."

"Well, let's make sure she isn't left alone. Maybe you could ask her to help you more in the house or something—take her mind off things."

Through the partially open door of her room down the hall Katherine lay watching the strip of light shining under her parents' bedroom door. As the hour hand on the clock on her dresser moved passed 2 A.M., exhaustion finally closed her eyes and she slept.

One week later, 11:30 P.M.

They entered their bedroom looking much older than their forty years. Bea took off her good navy and white church dress and carefully hung it in the closet. Her face was drawn and pale.

John looked at her, compassion in his eyes. "We did the right thing, Bea. She'll be alright now. Rick promised me that he'd be good to her and the baby. We can't ask for more than that."

"I just hope he meant it."

"Honey, we have to put this behind us now. You're making yourself sick. Maybe we can save up so you can visit Katherine in California when the baby comes."

"I just hope she'll be happy. She didn't smile or even look at Rick the whole time the Justice of the Peace was doing the service."

"We'll pray for her every day, Honey. It'll take a little time, but I think she'll be alright now. He seems like a good man."

"I hope so. Good night, John."

Chapter 15

November 1, 1946, 1:30 A.M.

Visalia, California

"Hello, Mr. Landers? This is Rick. Sorry to wake you, but Katherine insisted I call right away. You have a beautiful baby granddaughter." . . .

"Yes, yes, Katherine's just fine. The baby was born at 12:30 this morning." . . .

"Yes, a girl. Seven pounds three ounces." . . .

"Yes, Katherine is thrilled with the baby." . . . "Oh, by all means have her come. Katherine's really looking forward to her mother's visit. . . .

"She wants to name the baby after her roommate at college. Karis Lynn."

. . . "Well, I have to get back to her." . . .

"Thank you. Congratulations to you, too."

Upstairs in her hospital bed Katherine looked down at the tiny pink face of her daughter and a soaring happiness at last muted the painful memory of her conception. She gazed thoughtfully at the dark blue eyes and the wispy black hair and wondered how long it would be before people began to notice that her child's eyes and hair were very different from either her own or Rick's. She thought about Jack then, for the first time without rancor, and put him out of mind. "I will always love you, my darling," she whispered to her little girl.

When the baby was six weeks old Rick Radford watched as Katherine undressed for bed. "I've been patient, Katherine, you know I have. I didn't want to bother you during your pregnancy, but now it's time." Katherine looked at him with dread and began to tremble.

September 8, 1953, 8:30 A.M.

"Come on, Sweetie, big smile for Daddy," Rick Radford said to six year old Karis as he focused his camera. Her hand held firmly in Katherine's, Karis smiled broadly exposing the empty space her two front teeth had recently occupied.

The camera was still clicking as mother and daughter climbed into the car and drove out of the driveway. Rick stood a moment watching as the car disappeared thinking that it seemed like only yesterday that Karis was a toddler on his shoulders. He never thought of her as belonging to anyone else; she was his. *She's growing up and I'll never have another, never a son—forget that dream—but at least I have Karis.*

Katherine. Ah, yes, Katherine. She's a good mother; I have to give her that, but, a wife? She's not a wife. She's my housekeeper and cook; and my friend, but Anne's my wife. He sighed as he remembered the few occasions early in their marriage when he had gently insisted that she let him make love to her. She had screamed in fear and loathing and begged him to stop. He realized then that she had been raped and that Karis was not the love child he had been led to believe. For years now he and Katherine had slept in separate beds.

Thank God for Anne. He thought with affection and delight about the attractive woman he had met four years earlier when he opened his second store in Armona. Their love affair began the same day they met. Although he could only be with her two or three days each week while he tended the Armona store, Anne was surely his wife as Karis was surely his daughter. He might have married Anne, he wanted to, but he would lose Karis if he did. If Katherine suspected his affair she never mentioned it. Rick figured she knew and was glad he didn't expect anything from her anymore.

Katherine ignored the busy interstate and chose instead to drive through the quiet agricultural roads to the three-teacher End-Time Elementary School. When she and Rick had first arrived the peaceful

76

country roads of central California reminded her of her home in Virginia. She was seldom homesick any more, but once in a long while, when something reminded her of home, she would be overcome with a deep sadness that might last for days. When that happened tiny Karis became her comforter, her little hands smoothing her hair and rubbing her back.

Katherine glanced at Karis in the seat beside her. She noted with loving pride Karis' long black curls shining in the bright sunshine and her heart filled with love for this beautiful child; her only reason for living.

Wiggling excitedly in the front seat Karis kept up a running commentary. "Do you think the teacher will like me? I can't wait to see what surprise you put in my lunch pail. Crystal and Paul will be there with me and the other kids from Sabbath School. I won't miss you and Daddy too much." She seemed satisfied to accept Katherine's nods and smiles as answers.

Katherine smiled again at Karis' happy expectant face as she parked in the schoolyard. She knew how important this first day of school would be. As she stooped to kiss her excited little girl good-by outside the classroom, two men watched the arrival of the new first graders with interest.

One of them, Randy Brekke, was the eighth grade teacher and principal of the little school. The other man was the newly appointed Education Supervisor for the End-Time elementary schools in central California. His name was Jack Stevenson.

"We have an increase of twelve first graders this year as well as several more children in the other grades," Randy Brekke was saying, "if this keeps up we'll need another teacher next year."

Ignoring him Jack Stevenson stared at Katherine and Karis as they approached the school. "Who's the little girl with the long black curls?" He asked.

"Oh, that's one of our new first graders. Her mother—"

"—I think I know her," he said, as he abruptly left the room and walked quickly outside. By the time he reached Karis, Katherine had turned away to walk toward her car. He stooped to speak to Karis and held out his arms toward her in invitation. Karis, surprised and frightened, shrank back and lowered her head. When Katherine reached her car she turned around for one last wave.

"Oh, no, no!" she screamed, as she rushed back and grabbed Karis up in her arms. "Get away from her!"

As she turned to run toward the car Jack caught her arm and held her firmly in his grip. "What's wrong, Katherine," he said in a mocking voice, "aren't you glad to see me?"

Terror flashed in her voice. "Let me go," she screamed, "Let me go!" Shocked eyes turned to look at them and suddenly the happy chatter in the school yard stopped.

"Not 'til we have a little talk, Katherine." His whispered voice, rough and menacing brought back all the horror of her experience with him. "Your pretty little girl; six years old the principal says. She looks a bit like me, wouldn't you say?"

Before Katherine could answer, Randy Brekke came running up to them. "Anything wrong here, Katherine?"

Jack loosened his grip on her arm then and Katherine fled toward her car, the frightened Karis clutched in her arms.

"See you later," Jack called after her.

"What was that all about?" asked the principal.

Jack laughed. "Oh, it was nothing. She's someone I knew in college. I guess I frightened her. Give me her address and I'll run over and apologize."

Katherine drove wildly, without thinking where she was going, her mind in a panic of fear. *He'll know my name. He'll find out where I live. He wants to take Karis. I have to hide her. He's been looking for me. He wants Karis. I have to get away.*

Karis in the seat beside her watched her mother in amazement, frightened at her unusual actions. "Mama, where are we going? I want to go to school." She began to cry then, soft whimpering cries of fear and confusion. She had never seen her mother act like this before. *It was that bad man,* she thought, *he was hurting Mama. I'm going to tell Daddy on him.* She hung onto the seat with both hands fearful of her mother's erratic behavior.

Her mind a maelstrom of fear and indecision, Katherine drove on without hearing Karis' cries. *Where can I go? He's going to come after Karis. I must get her away.* Looking in her rear view mirror she saw a black car approaching fast with a man driving. *It's him! He's coming! I have to lose him.* She increased her speed and turned, sharply, at the first corner she came to. The car behind her did not follow her into the turn and as the man drove by he looked back at her in bewilderment.

As her tires hit the gravel of the farm road, her car spun around and skidded into a muddy ditch beside the road. After the car jolted to a stop Katherine shook her head and realized that she was not hurt. Then, her heart pounding, she let out a strangled cry as she saw Karis lying crumpled on the floor.

Chapter 16

Two days later

Fresno, California

Rev. Forrest Boyd, President of the Central California Assembly of the End-Time Christian Church, had serious doubts about what he was hearing. Jack Stevenson, threatening a woman? In front of everyone? It was too bizarre to be believed. He was young and inexperienced to be sure, but he came highly recommended. He had just received his Ed.D. with honors, from an eastern university and his father was very influential in the General Assembly of the church.

"You're sure he *threatened* her, Brother Brekke? That just doesn't sound like Jack Stevenson."

"I'm telling you, Rev. Boyd, he did. Many people heard him, students and their mothers, even one of the teachers."

"What happened after Sister Radford left?"

Randy Brekke shifted in his seat and took a deep breath before answering. "Well, at first I believed Stevenson, that he wanted her address so he could apologize, and . . . his face flushed, "I gave it to him. I know now that was a mistake."

"Did you give him the child's name as well?"

"He was so insistent about the address and was in such a hurry to leave that I'm pretty sure he didn't even ask for it. But he probably got it when he went to her home. I'm just not sure."

"What happened at the home? Did you find out?"

"Yes, I did. Rick Radford, the little girl's father, told me later that he had just let Stevenson into the house when the police arrived to tell him about the accident. Well, apparently when Stevenson saw the police he quickly left by the back door of the house!"

"Incredible! Then what?"

"Radford was so upset about the accident—his little girl was hurt pretty bad—that he forgot all about Stevenson until later."

"How's the little girl doing?"

"It was touch 'n' go for awhile, but she's going to be all right they tell me."

"Well, Brother Brekke, this is a very serious matter and you may be sure we will consider it seriously. In the meantime please reassure Sister Radford that she won't have to worry about Jack Stevenson bothering her. I'll make sure of that."

"Thank you, I'll tell her you said that."

"Was Sister Radford hurt in the accident?"

"Only some minor cuts and bruises, but she was very frightened by Stevenson. Rick Radford told me that they're planning to move away now; afraid Stevenson might come back."

Rev. Boyd looked at his watch, stood up and stretched out his hand, a signal that the meeting was over. "Well, let's hope something good comes out of this. Thanks for coming in, Brother Brekke. You did the right thing. I will personally see to it that Jack Stevenson doesn't bother any of our students—or their mothers—ever again."

September 16, 1957

Hanford, California

Karis Radford was quite sure that ten and a half was too old to play with dolls, but, she told herself, *this isn't really playing; it's practicing to be a baby doctor.*

She crossed her long legs and hunched her shoulders a bit lower so she wouldn't be seen in her small, triangular hiding place behind the parlor davenport. There was a funny musty smell coming from the davenport, and when she leaned back she could feel the horsehair upholstery scratching through the thin fabric of her summer dress. It wasn't a very comfortable place, but it was better than being with all her father's relatives in the back yard. She didn't like coming to Grandpa and Grandma Radford's house. There were no other kids to play with, and her aunts and uncles just acted like she wasn't there at all.

The only one who paid any attention to her was Grandpa Radford. "You're my favorite little girl in the whole world," he told her each time he saw her. She always tried to remember that when her Grandma Radford was scolding her.

Still in her hiding place she was tenderly rocking one of her favorite "patients" when her Grandma Radford and her Aunt Veda came into the room and sat down on the davenport. Karis heard the springs groan in protest as they bent low under the impact of the two weighty women.

"Well, if you ask me, he wouldn't have had an affair in the first place if she'd been any kind of a wife to him. She's so cold she'd drive any man away."

"I know, Mama. Rick says she's no bargain . . . still, you have to admit that's no excuse—"

"—I knew that woman was trouble the first time I laid eyes on her. I never could understand why he married her—of course I think she tricked him into thinking that Karis was his child. Why, anybody with eyes in their head can see she's not a Radford."

"You're right about that; she doesn't look like anyone in our family. She's sure pretty though; those dark blue eyes, and that skin—"

"—Oh, Veda, she's no prettier'n any other child. If her mother didn't spend everything Rick earns on clothes for her you'd see."

"Is Katherine still going to that psychologist?"

"Far's I know. That's another thing. She's bleedin' Rick dry with that nonsense. I hate to say it, but some women just need a good—"

"—Oh, Mama, just look at the time. I think Tim and I better be gettin' on home. Is it OK if we take some of that chicken casserole home? It was sure good."

"Of course, Honey. Come on, I'll put some in a Tupper for you." The davenport springs, relieved, gave a happy ping as they resumed their upright position.

Karis sat motionless for a long time, her sick "patients" forgotten. *I wonder why Grandma says I'm not a Radford. I better ask Mama to show her my baby book. Maybe Grandma just forgot. And she said Mama was cold. Maybe she left her sweater in the car; I'll go get it for her.* Picking up her sick babies she pushed the davenport out from the wall just enough to squeeze through and went to find her mother.

Chapter 18

March 6, 1963

Bakersfield, California

Katherine sat in her cheerful kitchen sipping tea and thinking about the day before her. Her once slim figure was rounded now, matronly, and her brown hair showed streaks of gray. Beyond being scrupulously clean and neat, her appearance was of little importance to her. Her daughter, her job, and her garden, in that order; these three were important. It was enough she had convinced herself.

What had started as a four-hour-a-week volunteer stint in the gift shop of the community hospital had evolved into a paying position as buyer and manager of the small shop. Choosing and caring for the beautiful gifts in the shop was one of the few enjoyments she allowed herself outside of her home.

She glanced at her watch; still an hour before she needed to leave for work. Anticipation of her Wednesday routine made her smile with pleasure. Without realizing it she had begun to hum a hymn her mother had sung when she was a child. *What a friend we have in Jesus. All our sins and griefs to bear . . .* When she caught herself she thought, ruefully, *He sure didn't bear all my grief. There was plenty left over for me, but maybe, maybe, it's time to give Him another chance. Karis would be pleased. She's such a good little Christian.*

Her Wednesday routine began after her shift in the gift shop at the hospital. A drive to the Bakersfield End-Time Academy to pick up Karis, an hour or two window shopping together at the mall, then dinner at a favorite restaurant. Since Karis was in high school now and always so busy with homework or school activities Wednesday afternoons had become their special "alone time" together. Katherine looked forward to Wednesdays as the highlight of her week.

Sitting there with the morning sunshine streaming through the window that looked out on her garden, it came to her, with a clarity that surprised her; she had a good life. She had Karis who, at sweet sixteen, was loving, intelligent, and as good as she was beautiful. She had a job she enjoyed, a big garden full of beauty to care for, and a husband who provided generously for her and for Karis. That was more than most women had.

True, she didn't love her husband, but she was fond of him—as a friend. *I should be thankful for my good life. I am thankful. It's enough.* But, there were times when it wasn't.

Usually she felt contented, even happy, and so when "the sadness" descended on her it caught her unawares. It could be triggered suddenly by a couple holding hands, or a man looking at his wife with love in his eyes. When it came it captured her completely; her mind, her energy, her will to live, her very soul. She would take to her room then, her body aching with a longing that transcended reason.

She knew that Rick didn't love her, but he was good to her and he loved Karis unconditionally. That was all she required of him. Weekends and holidays they were a family, but during the week Rick stayed in the tiny rented apartment near his store in Armona with a woman he was in love with. He had never spoken of her, and Katherine didn't question him, but she knew. If she thought about it sometimes it was always with relief.

Katherine stood up to rinse her cup and saucer before putting it in the dishwasher. *Almost time to go. I should eat something so those candy bars won't tempt me so much.*

The ring of the telephone on the kitchen wall shook her out of her thoughts.

"Katherine Radford." She said into the receiver.

"Katherine? Hi, this is Randy Brekke."

"Oh, Randy, how nice to hear your voice." She liked this man, now the Education Supervisor for the End-Time schools in all of California. He had been a friend she could rely on ever since that frightening day in Visalia. "We haven't talked in months," she said. "What's up?"

"I have some news for you. Not good news I'm afraid." He paused.

"Randy, what is it?"

"I just heard that Jack Stevenson is back in California."

"Oh, Randy, no!" her voice faltered, and her hands begin to sweat. "Is he here? In Bakersfield?"

"No, no, don't be alarmed, he's nowhere near you. He's the principal of an academy near San Diego."

Katherine said nothing. Pulling the phone cord as far as it would stretch she sat down at the table again. The happy promise of her Wednesday routine evaporated.

"Katherine? Are you still there?"

"Yes."

"Katherine, it's all right; he can't get to Karis. It's just that I promised I would keep you informed. But, honestly, and I want to emphasize this, you have nothing to worry about."

"He'll find her. I know he will," she whispered.

"No, he won't. Remember, he doesn't know where you live now. Rick made sure of that when he moved you to Bakersfield."

"I know, but what if—"

"—No ifs, Katherine. He's not going to find her. Your phone is unlisted and we've alerted everyone who has any access to Karis not to reveal her name or address to anyone." When Katherine didn't respond he continued, "Oh, I almost forgot. The other thing is that he's married now. I'm told she's quite a young girl, the daughter of missionaries, and that they have a child of their own, a little boy."

A small glimmer of hope appeared in Katherine's mind. "Thank you for letting me know, Randy. You've been a good friend. When am I going to see you again?"

"Katherine, I, uh, I have some other news, too. Good news. I'm getting married next month."

When Katherine finally hung up the phone she sat for a moment picturing Randy's kind eyes and his warm smile as clearly as if he were there in the room with her. Then, without warning, "the sadness" descended upon her.

BOOK TWO

Chapter 1

August 23, 1967

End-Time Christian Church
General Assembly Offices

Inside the conservatively-decorated offices of the End-Time Christian Church's headquarters the air was cool and pleasant—very different from the air outside where Washington, D.C.'s hot, muggy weather caused ambitions to wilt and tempers to flare. Reverend David Stevenson had just returned to his office from a committee meeting when his secretary buzzed.

"Rev. Stevenson, your son is on the phone. Line two."

"Hello Son. What can I do for you?" . . . "A visit? Well, your mother will be happy to hear that, it's been awhile" . . . "Will Eileen and Davie be with you?" . . . "Good. Jack, uh, Son, sorry, I know you had good reasons for changing your name, but to me you'll always be Jack" . . . "All right, all right, I'll try. Jason then, let me be blunt; are you in trouble again?" . . . "Well, I'm sorry, but I had to ask" . . . "All right, all right, don't get upset. When will you be arriving?" . . . "Good. We'll look forward to your visit. Good by."

Rev. David Stevenson hung up the phone and turned to stare unseeing out the window of his office. *A visit from Jack. Probably means I'll have to drop everything and solve another of his peccadilloes. I'm running out of friends I can call for favors.*

His thoughts turned, as they did so often of late, to the years of Jack's childhood. *What could have happened to change the soft, malleable boy he had been into the hard, immoral man he's become? Ruth and I—we did our best—of course the war changed him, still, maybe if I hadn't been so—well, it's water over the dam now, all I can do is leave him in The Lord's hands.*

As he picked up the phone to alert his wife to the coming visit he muttered to himself, *I just hope this isn't another problem with a woman. I don't think Ruth could stand another fiasco like that last one.*

As soon as Ruth Stevenson hung up the phone she started her "to do" list for her son's visit. *Let's see, I should buy some new toys for Davie; he's too old for those baby toys in the closet.* She put down her pen and glanced at the latest picture of her grandson on the refrigerator door. *Four years old already! He looks just like Jack did at that age; those dark blue eyes and milky skin against his black curls. He'd make a pretty girl! And he's such a sweet child; I'm glad he has a good Christian mother.*

She turned back to the list and began to plan her meals. *It'll be hot. I think I'll have picnic food for Sabbath. Maybe we can go to Rock Creek Park. Eileen and Davie would like that.* Her thoughts turned to Eileen; *such a good wife to Jack and such a good woman. It couldn't have been easy for her to deal with Jack's many problems.*

Ruth and David Stevenson had been thrilled when their son fell in love with Eileen Nightingale. They were sure that a godly wife was just what Jack needed to straighten him out. But, it hadn't been enough.

Somehow a problem with a woman always seems to come up. Maybe it's not Jack's fault at all, she thought, *He's so handsome the women just throw themselves at him. That's what he claims, but, well, I kinda doubt that.*

She still thought of her son as Jack. He had convinced her that the name change to Jason Stevens was needed, but it hurt to remember why. *Oh, Lord, what did we do wrong? We tried, you know we tried.*

Ruth turned back to her "to do" list, but the joy she had felt was tempered now with a nagging worry. Was Jack in trouble yet again?

Two weeks later

David Stevenson sighed as he crossed off yet another contact and picked up the phone to call the next person on his list.

"T.W.? This is David Stevenson. How are you?" . . . "fine, fine. I'm calling because I just heard that you haven't found anyone yet for your temporary Dean's position. Is that true?" . . . "I may have a solution to your problem."

Chapter 2

Seven months later
March 23, 1968

St. Helena, California

"Tom, Tom! *Listen to me!* You promised you'd talk to Matt. He's turning into one of those awful hippies before your very eyes and you just ignore it."

Tom swallowed the last mouthful of coffee, wiped his mouth with the back of his hand, set aside the newspaper he had been reading, stood up, and nodded at his irate wife without answering.

"Tom? Please. I can't deal with him by myself." She was still speaking as the door closed. "He needs his father. That's you," she muttered at the closed door, "in case you've forgotten."

Tom had already tuned out her nagging about their only son, Matt, as he got into his car. Tom Whittaker, fifteen-year veteran of the Napa County Sheriff's Department, was due in court in forty minutes. Sometimes he was tempted to double the time he spent at work. *It's the only place I have any peace,* he often told his complaining wife.

That wasn't exactly true, he reflected as he shifted his substantial bulk more comfortably in the driver's seat of his Chevy. Backing out of the driveway, he realized that his most peaceful time was his daily drive through the valley.

He loved living in the Napa Valley; it was unfailingly beautiful. Today the mustard plants in the vineyards were like bright sunshine against the black vine stakes and the pale green velvet of the hills. By June most of the mustard would be plowed under but the hills would still be beautiful; no longer green, a golden beige he decided, with a counterpoint of dark green valley oaks. The valley looked unreal every season, as though it were a painting instead of just the place where he lived.

I should have been born an artist, he thought, then chuckled aloud picturing how the other cops would laugh at that idea. At six foot two inches and with massive arms and legs he looked more like a longshoreman than an artist. He had worked so hard to develop his cynical, hardnosed cop reputation that he was quite sure no one suspected his secret, soft, artistic underbelly.

He liked autumn in the valley, too. Autumn started in late August, in his opinion, when the first grape harvests began and the air was filled with the fragrance of the wine mash. He wasn't a wine drinker—his drink was beer—but he sure loved the beauty that the vineyards brought to the valley.

On this morning he headed toward the eastern hills. As he reached Silverado Trail, where he would turn south toward the city, he glanced up at the mountain that blocked a view of the End-Time Church's college. Waiting at the stop sign before turning south he watched a shiny red Mustang screech around the corner. *Fool kids. Their religion sure doesn't keep 'em from breaking the speed limits. Holy hill, my foot!*

The valley's benign and peaceful look masked crimes that filled his days, but their number and violence was a far cry from what he had had to deal with in Toledo where he had begun his career.

His biggest regret was that he hadn't bought some acreage in the valley when he first arrived. *But, the kids were little and we wanted a home of our own. Also, we didn't have any money.* The well-rehearsed justification came easily to mind. *Now we have to find college money for Joan. And, if Matt straightens out—big if—he'll need money for college the following year.* Tom shook his head in frustration and sighed. It struck him that he always sighed when Matt's name came to mind. *Maybe I should be paying more attention. With that long hair and straggly beard he sure looks like those traitors in Berkeley.* His thoughts turned to the new

96

riots he had read about in the paper during breakfast. *The government oughta ship 'em all to Russia. Maybe they'd appreciate what they've got here. They're being manipulated by Communists and they don't even know it. Now Matt's starting to spout off about how "immoral" it is to bomb Viet Nam—as if he knows anything about it.*

As Tom passed the Yountville crossroad he mentally filed Matt's problems away for later worrying, and his thoughts turned to the day's assignment; the arraignment of a man accused of attempted rape against a Lake Berryessa girl. He intended to find out if there was a connection to the attempted rape of a local girl he had investigated two weeks ago.

At that chilling thought his only daughter, Joan, came swiftly to mind. *What would I do if some creep tried to rape her? Kill him prob'ly. Grace was right, for a change, Joanie prob'ly is safer up at the End-Time College. Of course, they're not all angels up there either. They like to think they're ten miles from the nearest sin, but believe me, they're not. It really gripes me how they deny and cover up anything that goes wrong. But, at least they don't allow hippies.*

The courthouse parking lot was full, as usual, and even all the reserved places were filled. Blast it! He found a spot across the street near the library and parked under a sign reading PARKING FOR LIBRARY PATRONS ONLY.

The same day, 10 A.M.

Matt Whittaker came through the back door of his home and started up the stairs to his room. He held onto the banister with both hands as he climbed unsteadily to the second floor. His head was pounding with pain and his legs were rubbery beneath him. *They should be all gone by now. If I can just get some sleep and get out again before they get home I'll be OK.*

The telephone's unexpected ringing in the hall below the staircase startled him so much that he almost fell. He considered the risk of answering it and decided not to. Trying to hold his head still to ease the pain he climbed the last few steps. At last reaching the second floor he sank to his knees, laid his head on the carpet, and fell into a drug-enhanced sleep. He had been awake most of the night. His ruse of bunched-up bedclothes in his bed had worked again. The rest of the family had early schedules and no one expected him to get up until after they were gone. It was very convenient.

April 1, 1968, 7:15 A.M.

End-Time Christian College

Her first class wasn't until eight, but Karis Radford was already up. Actually she was on her knees beside her bed, praying. She needed an answer from God, and, she wanted it today.

Her application to medical school was in her desk drawer, all filled out, all ready to mail. Her 3.95 GPA, and her exceptionally high MCAT score made her acceptance almost a foregone conclusion in spite of her gender. It was what she had always wanted—wasn't it? But lately she had been having second thoughts. The problem was Paul Bradley. They had planned to marry—someday—ever since academy, and now he wanted to make it official.

He's been patient, Lord, he tries not to pressure me, but he's getting anxious. I understand, Lord, I do. I know you want your pastors to be married. I know he probably won't even get a call to the ministry unless he's at least engaged. Oh, Lord, please. Show me what you want me to do, she prayed, unaware that she had spoken aloud.

Her roommate, Joan Whittaker, in the twin bed on the other side of the room, lifted her head off the pillow and opened her eyes. "Did you say something, Karis?" she asked mid-stretch. She rubbed her eyes, swung her long legs to the side of the bed, and sat up. Her tousled reddish-brown curls framed a pretty freckled face with sleepy brown eyes.

"Oh, Joanie," said Karis, getting up from her knees, "I just don't know what to do. Paul's meeting me after Chem class and I promised him an answer."

Joan covered a yawn and stretched. "If you really can't decide maybe you should go talk to one of your teachers, or the Dean. Maybe one of the Bible teachers, like Rev. Harrald? You said you liked him." Yawning again she headed for the bathroom they shared with two girls who lived in the room next to theirs.

"Umm, maybe . . . someone, but not Rev. Harrald. I do like him but I know he doesn't approve of a woman having a career—especially a pastor's wife. *Hmm, talking to someone; that's not a bad idea.*"

Karis was sitting cross-legged on her bed when Joan returned from the bathroom. "You ready for your Bible test?" Karis asked. "You want some help?"

"Thanks, but I think I'm ready. It's funny but six months ago I dreaded the idea of studying the Bible and now it's my favorite class. The one I dread now is Speech. The minute I get up in front of the class I panic."

"Yeah, I know what you mean. When I took Speech last year I shook for two days before every speech. If I turn out to be a pastor's wife I'll be behind-the-scenes for sure."

Pulling up her socks Joan looked up and chortled. "Hardly! You're not the type. Anyway, why can't you be both a pastor's wife and a doctor? You'd make a terrific doctor."

Karis looked away for a long moment. "I'd like that, but Paul says being pastor's wife is a full time job and, well, I know he's right, but still . . . I'm just not sure it's right for me, or even if I'm right for it. It's not an easy role you know. The other day I was talking to Bonnie—you know, that girl on the third floor who's engaged to a ministerial intern—she told me that she had already been 'counseled' by the wife of one of the Assembly men."

"You're kidding! Counseled? About what?"

"Oh, her clothes, and how to act in church, and things like that."

"Gosh, I don't think our pastor's wife has those kinds of pressures."

"Well, Paul says that the special relationship a pastor's wife has with God makes up for the pressures."

"You know," said Joan, chewing on the granola bar she had brought from the cafeteria the night before, "it's funny but sometimes I feel like I'm in a foreign country. Everything's so different here. Even the language."

"Come on," laughed Karis. "The language? We do speak English."

"But End-Timers have their own code words and everyone seems to know what they mean except me."

"I guess you're right; we do have some 'insider' words, but we're pretty much like everyone else otherwise. OK, you're shaking your head. What else?"

"Well, it's hard to describe, but it *is* different here. People look different; no make-up or jewelry, they dress more professional-like—even the kids. Of course the guys are *really* different. In high school you could hardly tell what a guy looked like they had so much hair hiding their faces. Oh, other things, too, no dating certain people, or—am I offending you? I really love it here. You know that, don't you?"

Karis laughed. "No, it's OK, you're not offending me. I know we're different. I guess that's why we're called God's 'peculiar people'."

Joan took a bite of granola, chewed and looked at her watch. Oh, oh, look at the time. I have to run or I'll be late for class. Karis, you're sure I didn't step on your toes? I'm really sorry if I did."

"Don't be silly, you didn't. Run, run. I'll see you at the cafe. Save me a place, OK?"

Karis lay back on her bed and glanced at the picture of Joan's family on Joan's desk. *She's really a dear. Her brother Matt is pretty weird though, but, of course, he's only seventeen and I guess we're all weird at that age.* Karis smiled to herself remembering the tentative pass Matt had made when she visited their home the week before. *I wonder if his folks know he's smoking pot.*

It had been hard to study lately. There was that all-important decision; Paul vs. medicine. Recently there was something else, too; something serious. There was this teacher, Mike Rollin.

The sunshine filtering through the curtains on her dorm window made an interesting pattern on Paul Bradley's picture. Leaning back against her pillow, still in pajamas, she studied the smiling face of her almost-fiancé. He'd been her best friend since first grade, the first boy to kiss her—well, in fact the only boy to kiss her. He was her steady boyfriend all through high school. Now he was eager to take the next step. Marriage. Until recently it had seemed so right, so natural, to expect to marry Paul, but now—now there was his strong objection to her being a doctor. And, most confusing, there was Mike Rollin.

Holding hands with Paul during the Saturday night movie in the gym, and even while sneaking a good night kiss outside the dorm, somehow it had been the teacher's face, not Paul's, that had invaded her senses.

Back in the dorm after the movie she had tried to pray away the "evil temptation," as her mother had taught her to do. *Oh Lord,* she had silently prayed as she undressed for bed, *help me to stop thinking about him.* The prayer had continued while she brushed her teeth. *I know this is just a crush and it will pass, but I keep having these thoughts. Please God, help me.* Kneeling by her bed, eyes closed, hands folded, she had continued, *Lord, are you waiting for me to decide to marry Paul before you take these thoughts away? I know it's wrong to think this way about a married man. Dear Jesus, please help me get him out of my mind. Amen.*

As she fell asleep she was confident that her prayer was heard and would be answered. But she still had dreamed about *him* that night and thoughts of *him* had spoiled her study time on Sunday. Now it was Monday and the tantalizing thoughts remained. *What would it be like to kiss him, to feel his hands on my face, to be in his arms, to touch his hair, his lips?* The thoughts made her feel giddy and slightly faint.

Her thoughts turned to Joan. *What would she think if she knew I was day-dreaming about a married man? If I'm a stumbling block she'll never become an End-Timer. And, my folks! What would they think!*

She lay back against the pillow and pulled the comforter up to her chin. Her last thought, before she dozed off, was of her parents' proud smile as she and Paul drove back to school together after spring break.

When a door slammed in the room next to hers, Karis awoke with a start and looked at the clock. She had overslept! There was no time for breakfast; she had to get dressed. It was time for her favorite class, her senior elective, Introduction to Urban Studies. *His* class.

She dressed more carefully than usual, not admitting to herself that it was because she would soon see him. The dress code came fleetingly to mind and was quickly dismissed as her fingers smoothed her new red skirt down over her slim hips. The narrow skirt tended to slide up a bit too far when she sat down. *I'll have to remember not to cross my legs,* she told herself. As she pulled over her head a fuzzy white angora sweater that emphasized the swell of her young breasts another small guilty feeling tweaked her mind. *No, I'm not wearing this for Mr. Rollin. I'm not! It's for Paul.*

A bit of lipstick and mascara—so skillfully applied that the girls' dean wouldn't notice—and she was ready. Suddenly the need to get to his class became an urgent pull that pulsed through her body and propelled her down the hall and across campus to the Urban Studies classroom. *To him.*

Chapter 4

8:00 A.M. the same day

Office of the college president
End-Time Christian College

Dr. Terrance Wolfgang Patton, T.W. to friends and enemies alike, looked up from the newspaper he was reading, settled his ample backside more comfortably into his chair and glanced at the clock on his desk. His secretary, Peggy Kester, was just walking into her adjacent office. *Eight o'clock exactly! How does she do it? This must be her fifth year with me, and I can't remember even one day that she didn't walk through the door at exactly eight. Exactly! Amazing.*

"Good morning, Peggy, after you get settled will you get Dean Stevens on the phone for me, please?"

"Sure, T.W., I'll get him right now."

Through the open door he watched as she picked up the phone and began to dial. Her salt and pepper hair was combed neatly back and her navy blue suit fit both her position and her modest demeanor. *She's the perfect secretary*, he thought, *quiet, competent, and she keeps her mouth shut about confidential matters.* Across the hallway from Peggy's office he could see into the open door of the "Acting" Academic Dean, Jason P. Stevens', outer office. The Dean's new secretary, Susan Baker, had not yet arrived. *Too bad Jason's secretary isn't more like Peggy,* he thought. In his opinion Susan Baker was too pretty to be a good secretary and,

105

although he had no reason not to, he didn't quite trust her with confidential personnel matters.

At Peggy's buzz he picked up his phone. "Good morning, Jason. Do you have the latest figures on freshman applications for fall quarter yet? . . . Very good! If those numbers keep growing our budget may not be as tight as we had feared. Now, if we can just find enough dorm rooms to put them in. Hold on a minute, Jason."

"What is it Peggy?" . . . "All right, just give me a minute."

"Jason? Why don't you bring those figures to the Executive Committee today . . . thanks . . . yes, I know, we need to talk about the Rollin rumors as well, but Peggy's giving me the high sign for another call so I'll have to call you later."

"Who is it, Peggy?"

"It's Dean Stevens' father. Do you want to talk with him now, or should I ask him to call back later?"

"No, no, I may as well get it over with. Put him on." He glanced at the URGENT pile that Peggy had put on his desk and grimaced as he picked up the phone.

"Good morning, Rev. Stevenson. What can I do for you?"

David Stevenson's booming voice spilled out from the telephone. "Good morning, T.W. Just checking in on Jack, uh, I mean Jason. Is he doing a good job for you?"

"So far, so good, in fact I think he may have found his niche here."

"Good. Good. I want you to know that Ruth and I pray for you and for the college every day. We surely do appreciate your giving our son a chance to show what he can do."

"Remember, it's only—"

"—I know, I know, it's only a temporary position, T.W., but it's a chance. Ruth and I have put him in the Lord's hands. We're holding tight to The Lord's promise, 'raise up a child in the way he shall go, and when he is old he will not depart from it.' I know you believe that, T.W."

"Of course, but—"

"—I keep telling Ruth that she doesn't have to worry, but you know how women are. How are those pretty girls of yours?"

"They're fine, they—"

"—Good, good. By the way, your man, Granados, is very visible here at headquarters. I wouldn't be surprised if he were looking for a permanent place here. You may need Jack, uh Jason, longer than you thought. I still have trouble remembering to call him 'Jason Stevens' but I know it's for the best."

"Well, give my best to Ruth," said T.W. hoping to end the monologue.

"T.W., I want you to know that if the Lord tarries and you ever need a friend in the General Assembly, well, after what you're doing for Jack, you can be sure I'll be here for you."

"Thank you, I appreciate knowing that."

"Well, the Lord bless."

T.W. raised his eyes to the ceiling in mock horror. *Dear Lord, what did I get myself into? Please don't ever let me need a 'friend' like Stevenson at the General Assembly. No wonder Jack changed his name to Stevens,* he thought, *not that everyone doesn't know who he's the 'son of' anyway.*

He glanced at the piles of undone work that he kept in sight on the floor beside his desk and wondered—as he did every day—how he was ever going to get to it all. He picked up the top piece of paper on the URGENT pile and promptly put Jason Stevens' officious father out of his mind.

9:58 A.M.

It was nearly ten o'clock when Peggy told him that an insistent board member, Clayton Wolfe, was on the line.

"All right Peggy, put him through."

"T.W.? This is Clayton Wolfe."

"Yes, Brother Wolfe, how are you?"

"Well, to be honest with you, I'm upset. My wife and I were on campus yesterday visiting our daughter and we saw something that greatly disturbed us."

"I'm sorry. What did you see?"

"Two young girls, obviously students, wearing short dresses, without sleeves even, standing in front of the church flirting with a couple of hippies."

"Are you sure they were hippies?"

"Oh, yes, they were hippies all right, complete with beards and sloppy clothes. My wife and I were under the impression that this college was different from the others. Why is this kind of behavior being allowed?"

"Well, I'm sorry you were upset—"

"—you bet we're upset. We sent our little girl there precisely so she wouldn't be influenced by worldly fashion; and then to see those girls sleeveless, in front of the church even! And with hippies!"

"I'll look into it Brother—"

"—Well, I certainly hope you will. Our support of the college has been constant and generous, as you know, but it has been based on our belief, and your assurance, that the Lord's blueprint would be followed."

"Let me look into it, Brother Wolfe, and I'll call you back."

"All right. We'll expect your call."

Peggy rolled her eyes at her boss and turned to go back into her own office. "Want me to call the girls' dean?"

"No, let's let him cool down for a few hours and then I'll call him back. Unfortunately we need his vote on the board next week. Better call security and ask them if they've seen anyone on campus that could be confused with a hippy."

Now, back to the URGENT pile, he thought, as Peggy closed his door.

April 5, 1968, 7:55 A.M.

The Chancellor's office at U.C. Berkeley announced late last night that in concert with universities across the nation all university activities today will be suspended from 11 A.M. to 1 P.M. in memory of Dr. Martin Luther King. A silent vigil is planned at noon in Sproul Plaza.

Mike Rollin switched off the radio as he swung his red Mustang into a faculty parking spot behind Urban Hall. As he turned off the ignition and opened the door to get out he was still frowning about the news he had been listening to. Just then he noticed the "acting" Academic Dean, Jason Stevens, getting out of his car. He waited until Stevens caught up with him on the sidewalk.

"Good morning, Dr. Stevens, may I have a word with you?" Stevens stopped and looked at Mike without a smile, his dark blue eyes wary, "Good morning, Mr. Rollin," he said. What can I do for you?"

"I notice you're the Chapel speaker today, that right?"

"That's right," Stevens said, looking pleased.

"CBS has just announced that hundreds of colleges and universities are holding prayer vigils today as a memorial for Martin Luther King's death. I thought a minute of silence during Chapel might be a good time for us to show some solidarity with our black students. What do you think?"

Stevens hesitated, frowned, and then said, "the Executive Committee would have to authorize that, of course, but off-hand I don't think it's such a good idea. We don't want to do anything that might incite our students to riot."

"A silent prayer hardly seems a call to riot."

Stevens looked annoyed. "Well, I'll mention it to T.W." he said as he began walking away.

Mike stood for a moment looking at Stevens' back, then, shaking his head in disbelief, he entered the door to the Urban Studies building and began to plan for his upcoming class.

Three days later

Baltimore, Md. (AP) Gov. Spiro T. Agnew today called for federal troops to "suppress serious domestic violence". . . . In Pittsburgh hundreds of National Guardsmen patrolled to stop three days of looting and burning.

11:45 A.M.

The college cafeteria

Joan left for lunch early to get there before the line got too long. Her Dad had warned her that she probably wouldn't like the vegetarian food that the college was known for. But she did. Still, her mother insisted on sending her "care" packages of roast beef sandwiches every few days which she shared with Crystal, one of her bath mates.

The lunch line seemed longer than usual this day. The granola bar she had for breakfast hadn't lasted very long. On the other side of the cafeteria, at the end of the boys' line, she could see Paul and his roommate, Wally, having some kind of serious discussion. She thought it was probably about theology. She had the distinct impression that all they *ever* talked about was theology.

Joan looked around the cafeteria to see if she could spot anyone she knew. One of their bathmates was sitting with her boyfriend but they were so totally immersed in each other that they were oblivious to everyone else. In another corner three teachers from the Communications Department were laughing and joking together while they ate.

I wish Karis would hurry. I hate to eat alone. It seems like everyone here has known everyone else for years; they went to academy together, or their parents worked together, or they're related somehow. On the far wall the long-dead Dean of Women looked down sympathetically from her portrait.

Just then she noticed Karis come in the door and, feeling a bit guilty about it, she asked the girl in line behind her if her roommate could cut in. She agreed, but Karis motioned that she would stay where she was.

Going through the food line Joan chose the lentil roast, broccoli, and a container of cherry yogurt. The tapioca pudding looked good, but she reluctantly passed it by. *I wonder how Karis keeps so slim. She's so pretty, and she's smart, too.* She acknowledged the little pang of jealousy with an inward smile. *It's no wonder Paul loves her. What I don't understand is why she isn't crazy about him.* In Joan's opinion Paul Bradley was the best looking guy on the campus. For about the hundredth time she thought how lucky Karis was to have Paul in love with her. *He's just about everything a girl could want; handsome, sincere, and funny.* When the girl in front of her turned to look at her curiously she realized that she had said that out loud.

Near the end of the boys' line Paul's roommate, Wally, noticed her and waved as she carried her tray to a table. She nodded back and motioned with her head for Wally to join her when he came out. Feeling better now, she remembered that Wally was pretty nice, too, and he wasn't taken! She looked up at the dead Dean's picture and smiled.

She had just taken her food off the tray and was sitting down when someone behind her put his hands over her eyes.

"Guess who," said an unnaturally gruff voice.

"Matt, is that you? Why aren't you in school?" As he stood looking down at her Joan smelled the sweet-acrid smell of marijuana. She saw heads at a nearby table turn to look and realized that the smell of pot must be equally obvious to them.

She lowered his voice, "Matt! You've been smoking pot again. Are you crazy? Have you forgotten your promise to Dad? Come on, sit down."

"Aw, Joanie, you're starting to sound like one of these weirdoes up here."

"They aren't weirdoes, and anyway, you should talk. You look like some sloppy old hippie. And what about the pot? You did promise to quit you know."

"Aw, it's no big deal and you know it. Everybody smokes pot. All your friends from high school smoke and I bet you did too before you became so holy-holy."

"Shh, Matt. Not so loud. I don't think, uh, I'm pretty sure no one up here does." She could see that Karis had come out of the food line door and was headed her way. Wally and Paul would be coming out soon too and they would all come to her table. Suddenly she could see Matt through their eyes and she was aware of just how different her brother looked and talked—and smelled—from her new friends. *Matt's right,* she thought, *I am starting to think like one of them.*

"Well, just because you haven't seen 'em with pot doesn't mean— hey, don't tell Mom and Dad, OK? No sense gettin' 'em upset about nothin'. After all, it's not like I'm on acid or anything."

"Matt, please, sit down. You're making a spectacle of yourself and it's embarrassing." Matt's eyes looked unfocused as he continued to stand, shifting his body weight from one foot to the other.

"Joanie, are you coming home this weekend?"

"Why?" she whispered. "Since when is my being home important to you? You're never home anyway."

"Dad's on the warpath again, but he always mellows out when you're there."

"What's wrong now?"

"Just the usual, 'hippies are traitors.' 'Go get a haircut,' you know, the same old song 'n' dance."

"Well, did it ever occur to you that he might be right?"

"Oh, cool it, Joanie. Are you comin' home or not?"

"Matt, you know I come home every weekend. Why are you really here? What's going on?"

"Joanie, ya think your roommate might go out with me? I was thinking we could go to the city, maybe to the Haight. You could come too. It's real neat there. I bet you'd change your mind about the war if you could hear some of the speakers. Whaddaya think?"

Joan rolled her eyes as she pictured the fastidious Karis surrounded by the flower children of Haight/Asbury. "I don't think so, Matt. She already has a boyfriend, and anyway you're just a kid to her."

"Yeah, well maybe she likes younger men. Just ask her, OK?"

"Ask her yourself, she's just behind you."

Matt whirled around, disconcerted when he saw Karis grin at him, knowing that she had heard him. He flushed and smiled sheepishly at her. "Hi Karis. Gotta go. See ya."

Before she had a chance to answer he was gone, threading his way among the tables and bumping into chairs as he moved quickly toward the door. Joan saw heads turning and questioning glances surreptitiously sent her way. *I hope no one thinks he's my boyfriend,* she thought.

Just then Paul and Wally reached the table. Joan waited in silence, mortified, as Paul set his tray down and held Karis' tray while she put her food on the table. She joined them as they bowed their heads for the blessing, but her mind was on Matt, not the prayer.

"That your brother?" said Paul as he looked at her and smiled. "Too bad he didn't stay and eat with us. I've seen him on campus before and I'd like to get acquainted with him."

"Well, for obvious reasons, he doesn't feel very comfortable here," she answered with just a touch of defensiveness.

Karis, sensing Joan's embarrassment spoke up quickly. "I've wanted to ask him what he thinks about Viet Nam. We were talking about the war in Urban Studies this morning. Mr. Rollin said that the war is illegal and immoral, and he says that we're killing a lot of innocent people. Some of the guys in class got really mad at him, but I think maybe he's right."

Wally looked at her in amazement. "Karis, you can't be serious. How about all those unpatriotic cowards who burn their draft cards and move to Canada? Do you think they're right, too?"

"I haven't really thought about it much, but Mr. Rollin says that—"

"—You know, the trouble with people like Rollin is that they don't appreciate what a great thing it is to be an American." Wally's usual bland face twisted in disgust. "I bet Rollin is a secret pinko."

"Oh, Wally, just because he doesn't agree with you doesn't make him a communist. Lots of people think we should get out of the war. She turned to Paul who had been uncharacteristically quiet. "What do you think, Paul?"

"I think our job is to prepare ourselves to spread the gospel not to get involved in politics. That's why God chose this isolated spot for a college; so we wouldn't be distracted by worldly concerns."

Karis looked at him but said nothing.

To break the awkward silence Joan looked around the cafeteria at all the young men who were obviously over eighteen and asked, "Don't End-Time men get drafted?

Paul answered her, but his eyes were on Karis. "Of course they do. Most college students get deferred, but if we're asked to serve our country we do. God's people usually go into the service as non-combatants and serve as medics."

Before Joan could ask another question Paul spoke up again, his attention still focused on Karis. "I don't think that was an appropriate subject for Rollin to be talking about in class anyway."

Looking at Karis with speculative eyes Wally said, "Yeah, I agree. Rollin should stick to planning sewers or whatever it is he teaches. Why are you in that class anyway? Don't tell me it's part of your Chemistry major."

"You know it's not. It's an elective . . . and don't change the subject. Mr. Rollin says that every American has a stake in this war, and I happen to think he's right. Mr. Rollin says that he's surprised that none of us are demonstrating like they are in other schools—demonstrating for peace. Why shouldn't Christians be for peace?"

Wally jumped in to answer before Paul could speak. "That's all we need—a pinko teacher encouraging End-Timer college kids to demonstrate. He sounds like he belongs at Berkeley with all the other traitors. Come on, Paul, tell her. I know you agree with me, we've talked about this plenty of times.

Turning to Wally Paul said, "Do we have to constantly discuss the war? I'm getting sick of it."

"Well, Mr. Rollin says—"

"—Excuse me, Karis, but I think I've heard enough about what Mr. Rollin said for one meal," said Paul as he stood up with food still on his plate. "I have to go. Will I see you after your Chem class?" Her smile was forced as she nodded yes.

"You coming, Wally?"

Wolfing down the last bites Wally quickly gathered up his dishes, piled them on a tray he grabbed from the table behind them, and stood up to follow Paul. "See ya girls. And Karis, sorry if I sounded off too much, but guys like Rollin really burn me up. I'll tell you some stuff about him sometime."

Joan looked thoughtful as she watched them walk toward the door. Wally was gesturing as he said something to Paul who was looking upset.

Karis looked down at her plate and said in a low voice, "I can't imagine what Wally thinks he knows about Mr. Rollin. He's really nice."

"What's he like at home? You've been there baby-sitting."

"He's even nicer at home," her eyes brightened and she sat up straighter. "They live in this gorgeous house that he built himself. The living room is nearly all windows and his little boy's room is so cute. Joan watched Karis' face come alive as she rambled on and on about Mike Rollin's home and family. "Oh, did I ever tell you about Benji?"

She had, several times, but Joan just shook her head and said nothing. *She has a crush on Mr. Rollin! I bet she's going to turn Paul down.*

"Benji was hurt in a car crash when he was only three years old and now he's in a wheelchair. He's such a good kid! I just love talking to him. His Mom, however; she's something else. I think they must fight a lot because she always looks at me in this angry way. I don't think she likes me."

"I doubt she'd have you baby-sit if she didn't like you."

"It's Mr. Rollin who always calls me. Oh, did I tell you about their cat? She treats it like it was a child—and you should see the cat books and magazines everywhere. There's this one book entitled 'Why Cats

Paint.' You wouldn't believe it. There are pictures in it that they claim were painted by cats that sell for thousands of dollars."

"Wow, I never heard that before. Does she think that maybe her cat is a pussy Picasso?"

Karis began to giggle as she piled her empty dishes on a tray. "How about Cat Van Gough? Or maybe Muffy Mattice, or" . . . They were laughing together as they left to walk back to the dorm. *Mr. Rollin, however, is not a laughing matter,* thought Joan.

The same day, 3:15 P.M.

St. Helena Police Department

"Whittaker here"

"Captain Whittaker, this is Chuck Salah from the Calistoga Police Station."

"Don't think I've met you—"

"—No, Sir, I'm new on the force."

"What can I do for you?"

"Well Sir, the Chief had to leave on an emergency or he would have called you himself."

"Yes, well what is it?"

"It's about your son, Sir."

"My son? What about him? Is he hurt?"

"Uh, no, Sir, he's not hurt, but I picked him and a couple of his buddies up a little while ago and we're holding him until you can come and bail him out."

"Why did you pick him up?"

"I caught him and his friends smoking pot and drinking beer in a parked car on Tubbs Lane."

"I see. Well, lock him up 'til I can get there. I can't make it until later this afternoon."

"Yes, Sir. We'll hold him until you get here. The Chief thought I'd better call you instead of Mrs. Whittaker."

"Tell the Chief I appreciate it."

116

April 10, 7:30 P.M.

The women's dorm

Joan Whittaker closed her textbook with a snap and picked up the phone when it rang.

"Hello. Mom? Hi. I'm glad you called. Is it OK if Karis comes home with me this weekend? She has a big decision she's struggling with and she thinks a change of scenery might help."

"Sure, Honey, she's always welcome; just help me think of something to feed her. I never know what to fix for vegetarians; I'm sure she must be tired of my macaroni and cheese."

"Why don't you just make some corn bread and vegetable soup for Friday night? Saturday Karis and I will take a picnic and drive to Goat Rock."

"Why don't you take Matt with you? He needs to be around you more."

"I don't think so, Mom. Karis wants some time alone to figure out what she wants to do. Anyway, I doubt Matt'd be interested in just walking on the beach. That's hardly his thing anymore."

"Honey, you might as well know, Matt was picked up by the Calistoga police today. Your Dad had to go bail him out."

"What? Why?"

"Smokin' pot and drinking, and cutting classes. Honestly, Joanie, I don't know what's going to become of him."

"Oh, Mom, I think you worry about him too much. Lots of guys his age are going through this right now. Matt's a good kid. He just needs some time to grow up. Maybe it's good that I'm bringing Karis home for the weekend. Matt has a crush on her you know."

"I wish he did have a girlfriend like Karis. Tell Karis we'll be happy to have her."

"Try not to worry, Mom. See you Friday night. I love you."

"I love you too, Honey."

Chapter 6

Early Sunday morning

The Whittaker home

Karis, still in her pajamas, listened while her mother assured the long distance operator that, of course, she would accept a collect call from her daughter.

"Mom? I just called to let you know that I'm at Joanie's house for the weekend."

"Karis? You don't sound like yourself, are you OK?"

"I'm fine Mom, I just needed to get away for awhile to make a decision, you know, about Paul." Her voice faltered, "Mom, I'm really confused. I just don't know what to do."

"Would you like me to come up for a day or two so we can talk about it?"

"No. You know I love having you here, but I have to decide this by myself."

"Of course. I understand, Honey."

"Paul wants an answer right away, but it's really hard. Sometimes I think I love him, but then sometimes I'm not sure. And, Mom, there's something else, too."

"What is it?"

"It's, well, it's that I keep thinking about someone else. I . . . he's not someone I can be serious with, or even date, but whenever I'm near him I feel, well, different than I do about Paul."

"Karis, now you're worrying me. Are you sure you don't want me to come up for a day or two?"

"No, really, thank you. I just have to make up my mind. Once I make the decision I'll be OK. Paul is so wonderful and I know he needs a wife to get into the ministry, but, there's medical school, too, and, Mom, if I really love Paul enough to marry him, how could I have these feelings about someone else?"

"Tell me about this 'someone else'."

Karis' voice broke again and for a moment she couldn't speak. "I can't, Mom, he, he, he's married!"

"Oh, . . . Sweetheart, I'm so sorry. Don't cry. Tell me, have you been out with this person?"

"Not on a date, of course, but I see him in, uh, on campus, and yesterday he was at the beach where Joan and I had gone for a picnic and we talked for a long time, but Mom, nothing happened. Honest."

"Oh, Honey, be very careful. I know I don't have to tell you how much heartache an affair with a married man could cause."

"I know, I know. But, it's not ever going to be an affair. These feelings are only on my part; he doesn't pay any attention to me. It's just that I keep wondering what it means about me marrying Paul. Would you and Daddy be terribly disappointed if I didn't marry him? I know how much you like him, but I just hate to give up medicine."

"Daddy and I will never be disappointed in you no matter what you decide."

"I just wish I knew what God wants me to do."

"Don't cry, Honey."

"I'm not crying, well, maybe just a little. I'll be OK when I decide. I'll call you after."

"Remember, Daddy and I will be praying for you. Let me know if you want me to come up. I love you, Honey."

"I will. I love you too."

30 minutes later, The men's dorm

Paul's fingers drummed impatiently on the telephone as he waited for someone to answer at the Whittaker house. *Why is she avoiding me? Gone all weekend without a word . . . something's wrong. I hope Wally's not right about her being mesmerized with Mike Rollin. What if I should lose her? I love her so much.*

"Hello."

"Uh, hello. Joanie? This is Paul, is Karis there?"

"Paul, I'm sorry. She *is* here, but she can't come to the phone right now. She asked me to tell you, if you called, that she'll talk to you tomorrow. . . . No, really Paul, she's fine. She just needed to get away from the campus awhile to think, that's all. She'll talk to you tomorrow. Don't worry! Remember what you and Karis taught me; 'all things work together for good for those who love the Lord'."

For a moment no one spoke, and then Paul's voice finally broke the silence. "OK Joanie, I know you're right. But, will you tell her that I'm thinking of her and that I'm anxious to talk with her?"

"Sure Paul. I'll tell her."

9:15 A.M.

Max & Susan Baker's home

Susan Baker stood looking at the telephone rubbing her chin. *Should I or shouldn't I? Is my duty to my best friend more important than keeping confidential what I heard the Dean tell T.W.? I'd sure want to be told if someone saw Max running around with some cute little coed.*

Friendship won. She picked up the phone and dialed the home of Mike and Sydney Rollin.

"Sydney? Hi. This is Susan. Max just told me he saw Mike in his office this morning trying to meet some deadline, sooo, I thought, maybe, if you had nothing more exciting to do, you could bring Benji and come over for lunch. One of Max's students is coming over to talk to him, but we can stay out on the patio. It's really pretty now with the azaleas blooming."

"That sounds like a plan, Susan. What time?"

"How about 11:30? We can catch up and I have some news that you should hear. Oh, and another thing; wait 'till I tell you what they're saying about Milly Munsell."

Sydney chuckled, "Milly? Does she have another crush on someone? I can hardly wait to hear."

"OK, see you in a couple."

9:40 a.m.

Paul pulled the collar of his jacket up around his neck. The breeze was chilly, but it was undeniably spring. The pansies that lined the campus walks were in their colorful graduation-season regalia, and sunshine added a rich glow to the bright yellow broom growing along the road across from the campus. Entering the aging College Mercantile, already crowded with students and teachers, Paul approached a clerk, a girl he knew from one of his classes.

"Hi," he smiled. "What would you suggest that I could take as a small gift for Dr. Baker's wife?"

"Maybe candy?" she said, showing him a box of Whitman's, "Or, I know! How about a rose? Just a single red rose."

"Good idea! Maybe I'll stop in later and get another one for someone else, too. Save one for me, OK?"

She looked at him and smiled. "Sure," she said, "Karis will like that."

The footpath up to Clark Way, where some of the faculty lived, was steep at its beginning then leveled off to a gentle upward grade as it passed behind the large, impressive home of the college president. Paul knew that the homes of several other faculty members were hidden behind the thick screen of Manzanita bushes. Beside the path bright green new moss softened the outlines of partially buried rocks, and small barriers were formed by the exposed roots of the tall pines.

As he continued along the path, Paul's long legs dodging occasional clumps of red-leafed poison oak, he drew in deep breaths of the pine scent and listened to the wind in the trees. *God's music to heal my soul,* the words of a poem he had once read came back to him. Reflecting on the beauty that surrounded him, he thought, *this is a perfect place for prayer.* He considered kneeling right there, but a glance at his watch told him that he needed to keep going if he wanted to be on time for his appointment with Dr. Baker. A continuing "walking prayer" kept pace with his steps. *Oh, Lord, you know how much I need her. I will serve you always, but I need her beside me. Thy will be done, but please, Lord.*

A Diogenes Lantern growing beside the path bowed its yellow head as if in prayer and he smiled acknowledging its shared attitude.

Climbing up a steep branching path he finally emerged onto Clark Way. Down the street he could see Dr. Baker working in his yard.

I'm glad I told him I would help him with his yard work while we talk. It won't be so embarrassing if I don't have to face him. He would have made a good pastor. They say his classes in Urban Planning are more like Bible classes than some of those in the Religion Department. I wish Karis had elected his class instead of Rollin's.

The modest Baker home was surrounded by blooming azaleas and dogwood trees and as he approached the house Paul could tell that a lot of effort and loving care had been lavished on it. *This is what I want for us, for Karis and me. Not a big fancy house, just a loving and restful place to come home to. Lord, will you tarry long enough for us to taste life together? No, no, I'm sorry. Forgive me, Lord. Come quickly, I know You're preparing a mansion for us.*

Dr. Baker was no longer in sight as Paul entered the yard and walked up the steps to the door. Mrs. Baker answered Paul's knock dressed in jeans and sweat shirt looking more like a pretty student than a faculty wife. When he handed her the rose she looked up at him and smiled broadly, surprised and pleased. "Thank you!" she said.

"My husband tells me you're going to help him outside," she said as she opened the door and motioned for him to enter, "it's very muddy out there and you don't look like you're dressed for mud. Let's see, hmmm, you're just about Max's size. Come in, I'll get something of his that you can get dirty in." Before he could object she had ushered him into a bedroom and handed him an old pair of jeans and a long-sleeved plaid shirt. "Oh, and he says you're to stay for lunch."

As she closed the door and left him to change he looked around at the neat, comfortable room and wondered again if he and Karis would ever live together, sleep together, have children and, most importantly, do The Lord's Work together.

Behind the house on the sheltered patio the sun was warm—as long as you kept out of the wind. Sydney Rollin sat on a green-stripped lawn chair sipping a cup of tea. With the sun on her face and with her only real friend beside her Sydney felt relaxed for the first time in a week. Smiling she watched Benji as he squealed and rolled his wheelchair around and around the Baker's big dog. The dog seemed to realize Benji was handicapped and was obviously limiting his romp to match the little boy's ability.

"Who all were at the Bailey's party the other night?" Sydney asked. "I suppose Mike was 'the topic du jour' since we weren't there."

"Not really. I made sure the subject was quickly changed whenever Mike's name surfaced. Anyway, they *are* all your friends you know. Ginger and Larry Shephard and Heather and Chris were there in addition to the Baileys and Max and me."

For awhile the two women sat quietly watching Benji and the dog at play. On the far side of the house they could see the two men talking as they worked. Sydney finally broke the companionable silence.

"You know Susan, I don't blame the girl. I really don't. I know how charming Mike can be with coeds. After all it was only six years ago that I was the student he was flirting with."

"You've only been married six years?"

"Well, I don't like to advertise it, but I was already expecting Benji when we got married. My folks, bless their hearts, were so upset—you know, worried about me, and what the church members would say. But, I didn't care, I was just thrilled to be marrying him, pregnant or not. Oh Susan," she leaned forward and crossed her hands on her chest, "he was the most ardent lover you can imagine, and we were just crazy about each other." She looked away for a moment to hide sudden tears. "It doesn't seem possible that it's over." Suddenly the sun didn't seem so bright any more.

"It's not over, Sydney." Susan's voice was gentle. "Lots of teachers are tempted by students, you know that. Mike is a good guy and he loves you and Benji. Don't worry about a little gossip; gossip is like the poor—always with us." Leaning forward she covered Sydney's hand with her own and gave it a little squeeze. "You need to hang on to him if you love him. Fight for him."

"To tell the truth, Susan, I'm tired of fighting for him, I'm tired of worrying about him; I'm tired of holding my head up when I know everyone's talking. Maybe I'm just tired of dealing with him. I'm thinking of getting a divorce. Please don't mention this to anyone else, yet. OK?"

Susan caught her breath, "Oh, Sydney, Of course I won't say anything, but you must know this is just a flirtation. Surely that's not serious enough for divorce." Seeing Sydney's tears she was immediately sorry for her quick words. "I'm sorry, I shouldn't have said that, but it hurts me just to hear you say that ugly word. Isn't there someone you and Mike could talk to—the pastor, or someone in the Religion Department?

"Mike would never talk to anyone on campus, and anyway I think it's too late for talk. If this were the first time it would be different, but it isn't. Remember Synnove, that Norwegian exchange student? The summer Mike built our house Benji and I were gone for two months staying with my folks in Wisconsin. While we were gone he—well, I found out later that—you know. And I'm pretty sure there were others too. I just don't think I can face a lifetime of infidelity."

"Oh, Sydney. I'm so sorry. I didn't know. But still you can't just give up. Think about Benji."

"I know, but Susan, parents who fight all the time are hard on children, too. I do worry about Benji though; he's so crazy about Mike." Her voice softened as she watched Benji hugging the big dog. "He is wonderful, isn't he? He's so smart and so sweet and loving. At least I have him."

Susan said nothing in return, but when Sydney looked at her she noticed that now Susan had tears.

"Susan, that was thoughtless of me. I know how much you want a baby." Now it was Sydney who offered a hand squeeze.

"It's all right. I haven't completely given up yet." Her voice quivered as she asked, "Sydney, do you think the Lord wants any woman to go through life without children? Isn't that what we were created for?"

"Who knows what God wants from women. Susan, this is none of my business, but Mike told me once that the reason you have no children is because Max doesn't want any. Is that true?"

"Oh, no. No! That isn't true at all. I thought you knew. I thought everyone knew. Max was seriously burned when he was a teenager; he still has scars all over his body. He was trying to start a fire on a family camp-out when the lighter fluid exploded. The burns were extensive and as a result he . . . well, he can't have children. We've been trying to adopt, but—Sydney, this is confidential, OK?—Max started to have really scary anxiety attacks shortly after we were married and he's been in therapy ever since. Because of that the adoption agencies won't qualify us."

Susan brushed away her tears and stood up. "I guess we both should count our blessings—you have a wonderful child, and I have a faithful husband. Come on, enough gloom. Let's go make lunch. I thought we could have burgers and a salad. Everyone likes that."

"Sounds good to me. Hey, I heard that there was a 'streaker' in assembly the other day. I bet Dean Stevens had a fit. Did they find out who it was?"

"Yes, it was a sophomore named Jimmy Allen. He was suspended for two weeks. They're saying that the students enjoyed the streaker a lot more than the speaker—old 'Sour Puss' Moore—giving his usual harangue on the evils of beards and sleeveless dresses."

Susan suppressed a giggle, "I guess I shouldn't laugh, but you have to admit it's pretty funny to see these naked guys running across stages or down the street when you least expect it."

Susan, a dedicated vegetarian, opened a can of Vegeburger and took oatmeal and sage from the cupboard. "Dean Stevens sure didn't think it was funny, though. He's still getting phone calls from parents and a couple of the General Assembly officers telling him to put a stop to it. How about you making the salad?"

"Sure," Sydney replied as she opened the fridge for the ingredients. "You said you wanted to tell me something juicy about Milly Munsell."

"Well," she said with lifted eyebrows and a chuckle, "I have it on good authority that she has a crush on Dean Stevens. She thinks he's, quote, 'dreamy'."

"I thought Milly had more sense than to fall for that phony. Of course, she flirts with all the men so that's probably all there is to it. Anyway, she's a lot older than he is."

Susan stopped mixing the burgers and turned, spoon in hand, to look at her. "He's not a phony, Sydney. I can tell he's trying hard to do a good job. He's especially good with the students—really sensitive to their concerns—and he's the best boss *I* ever had."

"Whoa! Well, I admire your secretarial loyalty, but I still think there's something creepy about him. I don't like the way he looks at women. Mike told me that he's had problems with women in every job he's ever had, but his father always gets him out of it somehow. Any truth to that?"

"Not that I've heard. I doubt it. Anyway, I like him, and I need the job, so I hope he stays here for a long, long time."

When Paul realized that Mrs. Rollin and her son would also be guests at lunch he asked to be excused, pleading assignments to finish before the next day. He didn't feel up to facing Mr. Rollin's wife.

He decided to take the long way back to the dorm to think about his conversation with Dr. Baker. As he walked down Clark Way he looked with interest at the pleasant faculty homes that lined the street. When he passed the art teacher's home he remembered with pleasure the emphasis on spiritual values he had integrated into his classes. The next house belonged to Rev. Harrald. The distinctive Tudor-style home was almost hidden behind the trees. The Harrald twins, Sarah and David, were playing with their pet Basset Hound in the front yard and he smiled remembering Rev. Harrald's comments about the dog; "He's Bosco, the blessed Basset beast and he's beloved."

He walked by two other faculty homes with well-cared-for lawns wondering who they belonged to. On the next block he saw Dr. Elgen planting azalea plants in front of his house. Paul smiled and waved, but did not stop.

As he walked on his thoughts turned again to Dr. Baker. It was clear that the Lord was using Dr. Baker, a troubled man himself, if the gossip he had heard was true, to help him in this critical time of his life. His words of advice reverberated over and over in Paul's mind as he walked.

After he and Dr. Baker had finished cultivating and feeding the plants around the house they had knelt beneath a pink flowering dogwood tree, and prayed together. He had felt a sweet peace come over him during the prayer. He knew now that whatever Karis decided he could accept knowing that God was leading in her life as well as in his own. Dr. Baker's calm faith had been just what he needed. No more worrying, no more anxiety; he would leave it with The Lord.

Chapter 7

April 15, 1968, 7:45 A.M.

Department of Urban Studies

Professor and Department Chairman of the Urban Studies Department, Max Baker, didn't feel like teaching. He longed to go home, to work in his yard or on Susan's "honey-do" list, or . . . anything but teach. There had been a lot of days like that lately, he reminded himself, but somehow today was worse. He dreaded giving the lecture he had prepared; it seemed dull and uninteresting even to him. *It's not easy to interest students when even the teacher is bored,* he thought.

Once Urban Planning had seemed a challenging and rewarding field—an opportunity to improve human living conditions for millions of people through innovative and visionary planning. In his youthful idealism he had imagined himself helping to change blighted cities into havens of safety and rest without the problems that wither the human spirit. He no longer believed his chosen career could achieve those goals. There didn't seem to be anything about his field of study that challenged or inspired him anymore. He was happiest when discussing and thinking about sacred matters, yet there was only so much spirituality one could fit into the classes he had to teach.

After his counseling time with Paul Bradley on Sunday he had felt stimulated for the first time in weeks and had slept through the night;

something he rarely did anymore. But, when Monday morning came and he had to face a classroom, his mood had darkened again.

This nagging discontent about his chosen career had been with him for weeks now. Still, loyalty to the students who had chosen to major in his department was a strongly held commitment. *People are depending on me; I have to shake this off and be enthusiastic for them.* He looked at the charts he had so carefully prepared for the class and willed himself to be cheerful. *Maybe I'll see T.W. about a sabbatical, or maybe I should apply for one of the Administrative trainee spots, or . . . maybe the Lord is telling me I should start over and train for the ministry.* He squared his shoulders, picked up his class file and the new charts, put a determined smile on his face and walked through the door to his waiting class.

It was already 11:35 A.M.—five minutes later than usual—when Max Baker hurried from his office to the college library for his daily half hour with the New York Times. It was a time he carefully guarded and which, he firmly believed, gave him a certain cachet that set him apart from the rest of the faculty. He believed with a certainty that reading "all the news that's fit to print" each day was a must for the *truly* educated man.

This quiet interlude between student demands and his wife's lunch time chattiness also gave him some badly needed private time. The library was usually nearly empty at this time of day, the students either still in class or in the lunch line. He smiled pleasantly at Milly Munsell as he lifted the heavy paper from its rack and leaned back into his favorite chair.

Mildred Munsell, everyone's favorite librarian, smiled coyly at him as she did every day. Whenever Max thought about Milly, as she liked to be called, he remembered Fluffy, his childhood pet cat. Milly had hair that was, well, *fluffy.* It wasn't that she didn't try to reach the standard that the head librarian had mandated. Each morning, immediately after her shower, she carefully combed the wet mop back into its intended bun, only to have it soon escape into her trademark halo-like fluffiness. By noon she looked like a benign, slightly plump, middle-aged angel.

Milly's halo changed color from week to week. It had become a favorite campus game to guess which color Milly's hair would be on any given day. "It just depends on which Clairol color's on sale," she had confided once to a courageous friend who had asked. "And, it does seem to give me a bit of attention from the male faculty."

Milly Munsell definitely preferred males. She didn't dislike women, she was always polite and cheerfully helpful to the female users of the library, but there was no mistaking her preference. Max looked on now with amusement as dour old Professor Moore responded to Milly's seeming admiration with a wide grin. *She should be given a framed Certificate of Achievement for getting that old codger to smile,* he thought.

His half hour over he reluctantly replaced the Times to its rack, gathered up his jacket and the papers he was taking home to read, and walked toward the door. Milly looked up as he passed the reference desk. "Have a good lunch, Dr. Baker, I'll see you tomorrow." Her coquettish smile followed him out the library door.

Milly was immediately forgotten as his mind went back to the day's headlines in the Times, BOMBING CONTINUES IN SPITE OF PEACE TALKS. *The Lord needs to come, and soon,* he thought. *Such dreadful things are happening. That terrible bombing of innocent people in Viet Nam, unrest in all the universities, new calamities every day. All the signs of His coming are in place. It can't be long now. What am I doing here anyway? City planning won't hasten His coming. If I just had more time to witness and to talk with the students about The Lord . . .*

Usually he enjoyed his walk home and he especially liked the view of the new bell tower against the blue sky. Inevitably the slender pointed shaft led his thoughts to Heaven, as it had been designed to do. This day he paused to pray as he looked at the inspiring sight. *What about it, Lord? Is it too late for me? Could Susan be happy as a pastor's wife? Could she find relief from her disappointment by working for Your children instead of for one of her own?*

As Max walked on toward his home he met Paul Bradley and two other ministerial students leaving one of the classrooms. Motioning for his classmates to go on without him Paul stopped to talk with him.

"Dr. Baker, I wanted to tell you again that our time together yesterday was exactly what I needed. I won't keep you now; I know you're on your way home, but I want you to know that your prayer for me was very meaningful. Thank you so much."

"You're welcome, Paul, I enjoyed talking with you."

In the street beside the campus the glare of sunshine on a passing car's rear-view mirror flashed a momentary blinding light in Max's eyes. Suddenly Paul's earnest young face was obscured by a terrifying memory of bright hot flames and Paul's voice sounded like an echo coming from far away. Max felt his chest tighten and his hands clench. Perspiration rolled down his face and he began to tremble. *The fire! The beast! It's coming. I'm going to die!* Then, at almost the same moment, his therapist's words came to him, "Relax your chest and hands. Close your eyes. Now take a breath." As suddenly as it had begun the panic attack began to subside.

"Dr. Baker, are you all right? You looked like you were going to faint. Listen, I have my car up by the dorm. Why don't you sit down by the fountain and rest while I run and get it. I'll drive you home."

"No, no . . . I'll be fine . . . I sometimes have little spells like this. The doctor tells me they're nothing to worry about. I'll just rest here for a minute and then go on home. I need the exercise. Please. I'll be fine. You go along, Paul . . . but thank you for the offer."

But he wasn't fine. After Paul had gone, and he had rested for awhile, a deep depression accompanied him as he crossed the road and began to climb up the path toward home.

Another one. Just when I thought I was getting better. I won't mention this one to Susan; no need to start her worrying again. I suppose I'll have to start seeing the therapist more often.

When he arrived home Susan had everything ready for lunch. "You're late. We need to hurry and eat or I'll be late again, and Dean Stevens has been looking at me and then at the clock whenever I get in—like he's checking." Max washed his hands at the kitchen sink and sat down at the table without comment.

"You know what I heard this morning—well, overheard actually? Someone was telling Dean Stevens that he saw Mike Rollin at the beach last weekend with a college girl. This is the second time someone has reported Mike's flirting with a student. Do you think he's cheating on Sydney?"

"They're rumors, Susan, that's all."

"Well, Sydney is certainly concerned. She's even thinking about getting a divorce. But don't mention it yet, OK? She told me that in confidence. Anyway the person talking to Dean Stevens knew the girl. Her name is Karen or Kate, or something like that, and she's got a boyfriend who's a ministerial student."

"Susan, Honey, slow down. I hope you won't spread this any further. That kind of gossip could really hurt both Sydney and Mike. He could even lose his job."

Knowing his wife's propensity for repetition Max rarely reported gossip. Actually he heard very little as he rarely engaged in small talk with other teachers.

He had no plans to mention Paul Bradley's concern about Karis to anyone, but he was worried about it. He ate now in silence, his thoughts on Paul and on Mike as his wife continued to chatter. *I'll probably have to talk to Mike right away. If Mike is fooling around it could ruin his career, not to mention that it might break up his marriage—and break Paul Bradley's heart. Then again, if she's that kind of girl she wouldn't make a very suitable pastor's wife anyway.*

Not looking forward to his afternoon and the conversation with Mike, Max finished his spaghetti and salad while Susan put on her jacket to prepare to leave for work.

9:30 P.M. that night

A phone booth in Calistoga

"Hello? Mrs. Whittaker? May I speak to Matt?"

"Who is this?"

"Uh, I'm a friend of his from school."

"What do you want?"

"Well Mam, I, um, ah, just wanted to tell him about, uh, an assignment in class."

"All right, just a minute."

"Matt? Your old lady really gave me the third degree."

"Oh. Hi, what was that assignment?"

"Oh, I see, she's right there, huh?"

"Yeah, OK, what page?"

"Did you do your homework, Sonny? Did you eat you spinach?"

"Yeah, thanks. Anything else?"

"Sorry, uh, listen, if you can't get out now how about Dave and I bring you some 'tea' tonight? Can you climb out a window or something?"

"Well, thanks, I'll see you in class."

"I know you can't answer so let's just say we'll be back of your garage tonight about 11:30"

"OK, yeah, later."

1:55 P.M.

Office of Dean Jason Stevens

"Uh, oh," Susan Baker groaned softly as she looked furtively at her watch. Late again. She tried not to look too obvious as she hung up her jacket and went quickly to her desk. Across the hall, Peggy Kester, the President's secretary, glanced up, smiled, then looked down and continued to type. Susan grimaced, *perfect Peggy, always on time, always sooo proper. I bet she keeps notes on me for T.W.* A few minutes later when Susan looked up again Peggy was looking straight at her through the open doors of their offices. Susan smiled, innocently, in Peggy's direction and turned back to her desk.

Fortunately Dean Stevens had been inside his office with the door closed when she arrived. Just as she took the cover off her new IBM Selectric typewriter, her pride and joy, the Dean's office door opened and the tall, heavy figure of President T.W. Patton strode through her office toward the door. "—just too many rumors and complaints lately. Let me know what you find out," Susan heard him saying as he walked by without even a glance in her direction.

The shorter, more muscular figure of Susan's boss, Jason Stevens, had followed the president out of his office. He paused and holding his chin in his hand he looked speculatively at Susan. "Susan. Come into my office, please."

Susan followed him into his office, apprehension nibbling at the corners of her mind. He pointed to one of the big leather chairs that faced his desk.

She sat on the edge of the chair waiting while he silently looked at her now rubbing his chin between two fingers. He had just, finally, opened his mouth to speak when his private phone line rang. Susan squirmed uneasily as she waited for him to finish the call. *He must know I was late again.* She couldn't afford to lose this job. Max's therapy was only partly paid for by the college's health insurance, and there was the mortgage, and tithe, and all the other bills that piled up each month.

As she waited she looked around at the dignified office. On one wall there was a picture of Jesus praying and on the opposite wall a display of sailboat pictures, lingering evidence of the interests of Dean Herman Granados who was on sabbatical in Washington. Behind Dean Stevens, on a credenza, were pictures of his wife, Eileen, and their little boy, Davie. Susan felt a familiar pang of longing when she looked at the cute little boy. On one corner of the credenza was a big Grape Ivy plant that she was supposed to water every Tuesday and Friday. It was looking a little droopy.

Still waiting Susan thought about the students who sometimes sat trembling in the same chair she was sitting in. Dean Stevens was becoming known for his strict enforcement of the college rules and his lack of sympathy with those who tried to bend them, but she had also seen his kindness and even his generosity with students who were troubled about personal problems. She knew some of the faculty were intimidated by him.

Susan was more attracted than she was intimidated. *He's so forceful, so strong-looking, although . . . I think he's going to be bald someday, he already has that thin spot on top. Ahh, but those piercing blue eyes and curly black hair; I think he's really handsome. He smells good, too, manly and . . .* she could feel herself blushing at her thoughts . . . *I wonder what it would be like to . . .* the forbidden thought was pushed away by Dean Stevens's impatient voice.

"All right, Dad . . . all right . . . yes, Sir, I know this is a new start . . . I *am* taking it seriously . . . yes, you have my word." He rolled his eyes at the ceiling and winked at Susan, as she wondered at the impatience

136

and barely concealed anger in his voice. "Yes, I'll do it . . . yes, yes, I understand . . . I have to go, Dad, I have someone waiting for me . . . I'll call you next week. Give my love to Mom. Good by."

He replaced the receiver with a relieved look. Flexing his fingers he folded his hands together on his desk and smiled ruefully at Susan. "My Dad can be a bit demanding at times, but he means well so I try to humor him."

Susan took a deep breath, "Dr. Stevens, is there something special you wanted me to do?"

"Susan, I've been meaning to talk with you about something. You seem unhappy. Does it have anything to do with your work?"

"Oh, no. I love my job. I'm fine." Her voice faltered, "I'm sorry, I guess I sometimes let my personal problems show. I'll try not to let it happen again."

"Well you and I are both in The Lord's work—part of His family, so why don't you tell me what's bothering you?"

For just a moment she felt like laughing; his "Christian counselor" approach hardly fit the thoughts she had been having.

When she hesitated he picked up the phone and dialed the inter-office number of the president's secretary. "Mrs. Kester, will you answer my phone for a few minutes? We're in the middle of something that can't be interrupted for awhile. Thanks."

He looked at Susan sitting primly before him and wondered how much passion was hidden beneath the pretty façade. "Now, what's the problem that's been keeping you so glum?" he asked.

"Oh, Dr. Stevens. Thank you, but I couldn't. You have enough on your mind. I'm fine, really." Susan looked down to hide the discomfort she felt.

"What is it, Susan, I want to know. Maybe I can help."

Her embarrassment was complete now. She couldn't look at him. "Well, you may think that I'm just being silly, but . . . it's that when I look at the picture of your little boy, it always reminds me that I can never have a little boy or girl of my own, and . . ."

His face softened as his eyes followed Susan's to the picture of his five-year-old son and momentarily he forgot Susan. *Davie! The one person in the world that I couldn't live without,* he thought.

Looking back at her he said, "Susan, you're still very young and you look healthy. Are you sure you won't still have a baby?"

Susan looked up, her eyes suddenly flashing with irritation. "Of course I'm sure and it's not my fault!" She hung her head again, "I mean, Max, uh, I mean, we can't have one of our own."

"This is none of my business, but maybe you're trying too hard. They say if you just relax and enjoy loving each other you may be surprised."

His words felt like a blow. Caught off guard, she blurted out, "How can I enjoy something that he can't do?"

At his startled look she blushed again, looked down at her hands twisting in her lap, and said, "I guess you didn't know about Max's accident. If you don't you're probably the only one on campus who doesn't."

"You aren't going to let me continue to be the only one on campus who doesn't know, are you?"

It was the only time Susan had confided in anyone, except Sydney, and her words came haltingly as she told him about the accident.

When she was finished he took her hand across the desk. "Susan, I'm so sorry, I didn't know. Why don't you take the rest of the day off and let me give this some thought. Maybe I can help. The work can wait, and Mrs. Kester will answer my phone."

Without looking at him Susan nodded and stood up. "Thank you," she whispered as she left his office and shut the door behind her.

She drove home slowly, thinking about what had just taken place. *How could I have been so foolish? I'll never be able to face him again. He'll tell his wife, and she'll tell . . . Max is right; I talk too much.* Her thoughts turned to Dr. Stevens. *He's so good-looking . . . and so kind . . . Mrs. Stevens is so lucky; she has that big gorgeous man to sleep with and her own little boy to love. He said he wants to help, but of course, there's no way he can . . . NO! What a thought! I could never explain a pregnancy to Max!*

8:35 P.M. that evening

A telephone booth in Calistoga

"Hey, Matt" . . .

"I was talkin' to some of the others and I think we're gonna take off" . . .

"You know where" . . .

"No, the place we told ya about—where they all go. We think ya should come along" . . .

"Yeah, like, if you'd rather go to jail? Not me, Man. Think about it, Man, OK?" . . .

"OK, we'll see ya tonight, but then we're splittin' with or without ya."

Chapter 9

April 17, 1968, 8:55 A.M.

Urban Planning Department

SACRAMENTO, CA (AP) April 17, 1968. State Assemblyman Scott Landon today introduced a bill designed to give police an unprecedented extension of their already broad powers to rid California campuses of "undesirable elements." The bill makes it a crime for "a non-student to enter a campus to commit a disturbance" thereby allowing police to make an arrest even before an illegal act is actually committed."

Mike Rollin gritted his teeth in frustration as he reread the Oakland Tribune article. He could almost hear certain End-Time administrators latching onto this new police power to throw the occasional longhaired visitor off campus before they could "contaminate our youth with their godless ideas."

He leaned back in his chair thinking about how he could incorporate this latest political outrage into his day's lecture without getting himself in trouble yet again. The rumor mill was just waiting for another excuse to work him over about his "liberal" views.

The rumors didn't bother him particularly, but he knew Sydney hyperventilated every time anyone mentioned his name. *Oh well, might as well chance it. These sheltered plants need a little fertilizer if they're ever going to grow. This could even be fun.*

9:50 A.M.

The Mike and Sydney Rollin home

Sydney Rollin was having a bad day. She had a slight headache and her hands were beginning to tremble. She also felt chilly, a bad sign that the headache would probably develop into a full-blown migraine. Sitting at the kitchen table she slowly sipped her favorite cinnamon tea, breathing in its fragrance and holding the cup with both hands to warm her hands.

Sydney didn't worry about Mike's "liberal" ideas; she shared most of them. The gossip she hated was what Susan Baker had repeated about Mike and "some coed." She knew the gossip had spread all over campus when she overheard two faculty wives talking in the campus Mercantile. She was pretty sure the "some coed" was Karis Radford.

The more she thought about Mike and Karis, and about the campus gossips having a field day at her expense, the angrier she became and the tighter she gripped her cup. It wasn't until her cat, Ellie, rubbed against her ankle under the table that she was reminded of her coming trip and her mood lightened.

In a few days she was taking Ellie to the big cat show in Chicago. Her mom and dad were paying for her trip and would be meeting her there with their own award-winning Siamese. Her mom had been urging her to begin "showing" Ellie and this would be her first time. *Wouldn't it be great if Ellie was a winner? But even if she doesn't win the trip will get me away from this backwater for awhile and let me see my folks. Maybe I should prepare them . . . for what? For the unthinkable? For the inevitable?*

Picking up Ellie, who was continuing to rub against her leg looking for attention, she put her hand on the cat's head and absently smoothed the silky fur as she thought about what she would say to her parents. She had just left the kitchen, cradling the cat in her arms when the phone rang.

"Sydney? Susan here. I was just wondering if you and Mike were planning to attend the faculty dinner tonight."

"Yes, we're going, but I can't say I'm looking forward to it."

"Well, let's sit together. Heather and Chris want to join us. That OK?"

"Sure, whoever. Are you at home?"

"No, I'm at the office. Dean Stevens is in a meeting so I have a quiet minute for a change. It's been a zoo around here today. Sydney, I don't quite know how to tell you this, but I think you should be prepared because there might be some embarrassing questions tonight. People have been talking to Dean Stevens about Mike again."

Sydney could feel the migraine coming on strong now as Susan reported what she had overheard. *I'm really sick of listening to this,* she thought, as she held the telephone farther away from her ear and tried to think of a polite way to hang up.

"Susan, I see Mike driving in so I have to go. Thanks for filling me in on this. I really appreciate it. I'll see you tonight. Bye, bye."

It wasn't true. He wasn't driving in—not yet anyway. With the phone still in her hand Sydney dialed Mike's office number. He answered on the first ring.

"Mike, I need you to come home."

"Syd? What's wrong? What is it?"

"I just need you to come home. I know you don't have class this period."

"OK, OK, I'll come, but I wish you'd tell me what the mystery is all about."

"I'll tell you when you get here." She hung up, trembling.

Mike sat looking out his office window wondering just what Sydney was upset about this time. Probably already heard about my lecture on the war this morning. Finally he took his jacket from the back of his chair, locked his office door, and reluctantly left for the showdown he was sure was awaiting him.

The drive from the college to Terrace View Drive took most drivers five minutes; Mike's shiny, red Mustang, as usual, made it in two.

Sydney watched through the kitchen window as Mike got out of the Mustang. She hated that car. They couldn't afford it and he looked too much like a college student in it. *He's such a jerk. If it weren't for Benji . . .*

As soon as Mike walked into the house he knew they were in for another big fight. Sydney was standing in the living room just looking at him with a wet washcloth held to her forehead. *Oh, oh, not a good sign,* he thought.

He walked past her without saying anything and stood looking out the window at the valley below. The fog cover, which earlier had been like a thick, white layer of cotton batten, was breaking up now. He could see the pointed tips of trees poking up into the sunshine. In a couple of hours the lake would come into view.

He had always liked their living room. The four tall Southwest windows looked out over a view that changed hour by hour. He had designed and built this house himself, with a little help from one of his former students and a loan from the college.

The summer he built the house had been one of his best. The college had kept him on salary and Sydney and Benji had spent the summer in Wisconsin with her folks. Each night he had slept in his sleeping bag on the floor of the developing shell.

Still not looking at Sydney he smiled to himself as he remembered the last few nights when there had been a second sleeping bag zipped together with his. *She was something else. Beautiful, sexy . . . it must be true what they say about Scandinavian women—cool in the city, hot in the sack—beautiful Synnove—I was in love with her . . . I think.*

Reluctantly now he glanced at Sydney who was watching him with that superior knowing look of hers that always ticked him off. *I think I may hate this woman. If it weren't for Benji . . .*

"Mike," she said, moving toward him. "We need to talk."

"Now what have I done?" he asked, backing up, caution in each step.

"I've decided that we're not going to the faculty dinner tonight."

"That's it? You couldn't have told me that on the phone? I thought that—"

"—we have no baby-sitter, and—"

"—that's it? No problem," he said, "I'll call Karis and see if she's free."

Mike watched in surprise as Sydney's eyes narrowed and her face flushed. "Never!" she screamed. "She is never coming into this house again."

"Whoa. Calm down. We'll get someone else. What's going on here? Who's been talking to you this time?"

"Who? Who *hasn't*? The whole campus, that's who. I'm sick and tired of being the 'good little wifey' while everyone talks behind my back about what's going on with you and Karis."

"Aw, Syd, there's nothing going on between Karis and me. Where do you get this stuff, anyway?" Tears flowed unheeded down Sydney's face, already flushed with anger and pain. "I can't take this again, Mike." Her voice cracked, "you promised, after Synnove you promised me."

"Syd, I'm telling you, there is absolutely nothing going on with Karis. I swear! I bet Susan Baker has been stirring you up again. I wish that little witch would mind her own business."

Sydney wiped her tears with the wash cloth before answering. "Don't give me that 'I'm so innocent' routine. I know you too well. And yes, Susan Baker, who, don't forget, just happens to work for your boss, told me what she's been hearing all over campus. Just be thankful that she came to me instead of to the Dean. Are you ready for another scandal?"

The pain in her head was increasing and her eyes were not focusing. She needed to rinse the washcloth in cold water, but if she left the room Mike would be gone in a flash. "I'm not stupid, Mike. I see how you look at her, how you manage to touch her 'accidentally.' And anyone can see that she has a big crush on you."

"Sydney, this is really silly—"

"—I can't stop you flirting while you're at the college, but I don't have to watch you do it in my own home. I mean it, Mike. I won't be a laughing stock again like before."

"OK, OK. We won't use her again. Can we change the subject now? My Mom has agreed to stay with Benji while you're in Chicago. You still want to go?"

"Of course I want to go, why wouldn't I? You have plans for—"

But Mike had already left the room. Sydney could hear him muttering to himself as he fled down the hall. He barely noticed Benji as he passed him in the hallway.

"Mommy, is Daddy mad at you?" Benji's big brown eyes, so like Mike's, were serious and his lower lip was trembling as he came into the room.

Sydney took a big breath and wiped her face with the washcloth before she answered. "Well, yes, Baby, he is a little. But, he's not mad at you. Daddy and I had a grown-up argument, that's all. It's nothing for you to worry about. I'm going to the kitchen now to call Grandma Rollin. She's going to stay with you when I take Ellie to the cat show. Why don't you go out and play on the patio for awhile. I'll come get you when it's time for lunch."

Trying to ignore the throbbing headache she dialed her mother-in-law's familiar number.

"Mom? Hi, this is Sydney . . ."

Fifteen minutes later she had given Mike's mother her trip schedule and had described Benji's special needs—although his doting grandmother was already thoroughly familiar with them. She hung up with her head pounding from the migraine and from the encounter with Mike.

Suddenly Sydney felt nauseated and she hurried to the sink where she vomited until there was nothing more to come up. The pain was severe now and she let herself slide slowly to the kitchen floor and laid her cheek against the cool tile floor.

She lay very still letting the pain wash over her in waves. Ellie, who had curled up purring beside her on the floor, pushed her head against Sydney's hand begging to be petted. The soft fur felt good against her hand, comforting her.

The vomiting had signaled to Sydney that the crisis phase of her headache was nearly over, and she knew that, although it might be a day or two, the pain, like her marriage, would then end.

There on the floor of her kitchen she pictured Karis Radford. *She's so pretty . . . so young and sexy . . . like I was . . . he'll break her heart just like he did the others . . . like mine is breaking.*

She had loved him from her first day in a class that he was teaching in the junior college near her home in Wisconsin. When she found out that he was single and that he had been raised an End-Timer she was thrilled, sure that God had arranged for her to take his class so they would meet.

After the second class meeting they began to date and three months later she was pregnant. Her parents, resigned to the inevitable, gave their only daughter a hurried wedding. She remembered the soaring joy she had felt on that day.

It was Mike's roving eye that had spoiled it. But he was such a proficient "sweet talker," always so sorry, and so humble, that each time, after he told her how much he loved her and promised never to do it again, she had forgiven him. Over and over and over.

The migraine was finally beginning to subside a bit and when Sydney began to move her cat stood up, stretched, yawned, and began to wash herself.

Sydney sat up, carefully, and leaned her head against the cabinet door for a moment before she stood. *I have to stop thinking about Mike and Karis. I'll start packing for Chicago. I'll think about Benji, about my folks, about something else. Anything else.*

NAPA REGISTER, April 19, 1968. The light rain forecast for today is not expected to bring enough moisture to offset the abnormally dry conditions that prevail in the brush on the hills. Forestry officials are calling for citizens to take extra precautions, and burning regulations, unusual for so early in the season, have been imposed.

By afternoon the misty fog that had lingered over the college all day had developed into a persistent drizzle. As she left the rear door of the women's dorm Karis decided it would take too long to go back to her room for an umbrella. *My hair is going to be all frizzy,* she thought.

It wasn't far from her dorm to the Urban Studies building, but to Karis, nervous and excited, it seemed like a long way. As she walked past the rear windows of the cafeteria she could see people preparing the evening meal. Behind the Home Ec building she saw two teachers talking quietly together while through a basement window she could see a student cleaning one of the class kitchens. Seeing them reminded her that it was her turn to clean her shared bathroom in the dorm and she hadn't even started yet. She knew she should hurry, but her steps slowed instead; it surprised her to realize that seeing *him* was even more important to her now than getting ready for the Sabbath.

Only one car was parked in the faculty spaces behind Urban Hall—a shiny red Mustang. Her eyes lingered on the car, remembering how he had looked sitting behind the wheel as he drove her back to the dorm after baby-sitting. *He loves that car. He says he bought it for Benji, but he's the one who loves it, he's just like a kid.* She smiled at the idea.

I'll see him in a minute. The realization produced an unfamiliar jolt to her midriff; it felt like an actual blow! Surprised, she thought, *this is like some kind of disease. Maybe it's like the flu and I'll get over it in a couple of days, or maybe . . . maybe . . . could it be that this is what love feels like? No, that's silly, but why do I keep seeing him whenever I close my eyes. I look for him in a crowd, I know where he sits in church, I even know his license plate number. This is crazy. Lots of girls get a crush on a teacher. That's all it is, it's a crush and I'll get over it.*

The drizzle had stopped, but the wind felt cold. Pulling her jacket closer she decided to walk through Irwin Hall so she could stop in the Ladies' room to do something about her hair. It wasn't far now.

Her heels echoed on the worn wooden floor of the hallway. It felt eerie to be in the building when no one else was around. Her heart-beat sounded as loud to her as the big clock ticking high on the wall at the end of the hall. Past an empty classroom, where once she had sat dreaming of a medical career, past the History Department offices and the bulletin boards which offered research and job opportunities to history majors.

Where is everyone? It's not time for worship yet. I should have asked Joan to come with me. Forgetting her hair she opened the heavy doors at the end of the hall and descended the aging cement steps as she left the building.

The relatively new, and enormously popular, Urban Studies Department was housed in a small one story building between Irwin Hall and the Religion Department building. Its interior housed small offices for the chairman of the department, two other faculty members, and a small reception/waiting area. Mike Rollin's 10 x 10' office space was on the right in the corner.

As Karis walked into the department it was dark and it had a closed look. *This doesn't feel right; could I have misunderstood his message?* Her fingers touched the folded note in her jacket pocket. *No, this is Friday, and the note clearly says Friday at 5 P.M. in his office. What could he possibly want?* The reception area was empty, the student secretaries gone for the day. The door to the chairman's office was open, the late afternoon light coming faintly through his window dimly lighted the reception area. But, the chairman, Dr. Baker, was not at his desk and the doors to all the other offices were closed. No one was there!

Her courage suddenly failed her as she stood for a moment in front of Mr. Rollin's closed door uncertain what to do. She could hear religious music coming from a speaker inside his office. She knocked, lightly, hesitantly. Her chest felt light and shaky.

"Come in, Karis," she heard him say through the door.

His office was dim, a small desk lamp shone a cone of light on a newspaper he had been reading, the only other light was the pale illumination coming through a small rain-streaked window behind him.

"Sit down, Karis," he said in a low, quiet voice. His long fingers tapped a pencil rhythmically against the green pad on his desk. His eyes avoided hers. She waited.

"Karis, uh, there's something I need to discuss with you. I'm sorry to bring you here so late on a Friday afternoon, but I wanted to talk with you in private."

Something is wrong. Why doesn't he look at me? Suddenly she was frightened. "What is it, Mr. Rollin? Did I do something wrong? Is it the paper I handed in today?" Her heart seemed to be doing flip-flops as she lowered herself slowly into the chair he indicated that faced his desk.

For a long moment he said nothing. She sat watching him, worry making her grip the arms of the chair. The soft music coming from the radio seemed to overwhelm the small office. *He thinks I've been cheating!*

"Mr. Rollin, please. What is it? Was it the last test?"

"No, no. It has nothing to do with your class work. You've done nothing wrong. It's, well, it's about your babysitting. I want you to know how much we have appreciated your help with Benji. You're very good with him. You're very . . . intuitive, and Benji loves having you to talk to." He hesitated. "Unfortunately we're going to have to make other arrangements from now on. Sydney, that is, we—my wife and I—have decided not to use college students with Benji any more. But, I want to make sure that you don't take this decision personally."

"I did something wrong, didn't I?" Unwelcome tears filled her eyes as she leaned closer to the edge of her chair, but still he didn't look at her.

"No, you didn't. Please don't think that. You were . . . you are, just great with Benji. Really. And he loves you. It's just that something has come up that makes it awkward for you to come over for awhile. I'm sorry, I'm saying this very badly."

An initial flash of anger was quickly followed by a deep hurt. She looked at him, but his eyes were still fixed on the pencil he held. "It's not all college students, is it? It's just me. Just tell me what I'm doing wrong and I'll try to change. Maybe I can talk to Mrs. Rollin about it."

Tears were falling from her chin making dark spots on her best skirt. Her fingers fumbled into the pocket of her jacket to find a tissue but the only thing there was his note. "No, no. Believe me, it would not be a good idea to talk to my wife," he said, his eyes finally meeting hers. "She is . . . not very understanding with students, but, I can tell you positively that this is not a reflection on you at all. I will write a glowing reference for your placement file. Oh, Karis, please don't cry. I'm so sorry."

"But, but, I don't understand." Her tears now combined with quiet sobs made her words hard to understand. "Please, tell me the truth. This is very important to me."

"Karis, I'm so sorry. It's better if I don't say any more," he said quietly handing her a tissue.

Turning her head away from him she started to get up to leave the office.

"Wait. Don't leave yet. All right, I'll try to explain. This isn't about you, it's about me. About my wife and me actually. Over the past couple of years there has been some gossip about me and some of my students. It wasn't true, but Sydney tends to be a bit jealous. And, well, I was seen taking you home from babysitting several times and that was apparently misunderstood by someone, and then someone saw us talking that day at the beach, and . . . well, I'm afraid there has been some talk."

"Talk? They think that you and I . . .?"

"My wife seems to think that I've been acting too 'familiar' with you and that people are getting the wrong idea."

A deep blush started at her collar bone and quickly flamed to her cheeks and ears as tears continued to course down her face. Clutching the tissue, now a soggy ball, she stood up again and turned to leave the office.

Before she could reach the door, she was stopped by Mike as he caught her in his arms. He held her, gently rocking back and forth, as she sobbed.

"Please don't cry, I'm so sorry," he said with a voice ragged with emotion. "But, it's probably better this way, because, well, to tell the truth I *am* very attracted to you. I think about you more than I should."

Her heart beat harder as a tide of conflicting emotions washed over her. Anger, shame, bewilderment, and to her amazement, exhilaration. His words echoed in her head making her light-headed. Then, with a shock, she realized that she was still in his arms. She moved to get free, but his arms tightened around her pulling her closer to him.

"But, how can that be?" she whispered. "You're married, and I, I . . ."

Mike lifted her chin with his hand to look into her face and with one finger he wiped the tears from her cheeks and kissed her lightly on the forehead. Then, as her body began to respond to him, he kissed her softly on the lips, first very gently, then more urgently, insistently.

The rush of her feelings drowned out caution. *This can't be happening. This is a dream. I'll wake up soon.* She tried to resist the unfamiliar pull of her body and the tingling sensations that were spreading through her senses.

Finally, overcome with the feel of her and her exciting response, he whispered against her mouth, "I think about you all the time. I want you so much." His kisses began again, ever more demanding as her arms moved up around his neck.

Finally she pulled away slightly and looked up at him. "I think about you all the time, too. I've been praying about it, but I just can't stop. I've never felt this way before. What's wrong with us?"

Holding her close he whispered, "nothing is wrong with us, Dear Heart. I think we might be falling in love." Then, without resistance, he began to kiss her again.

The chimes in the clock tower sounded distant and unreal as they rang the call to vespers. Engrossed with the wonder of their feelings they were unaware that the door to Mike's office had quietly opened.

Chapter 11

April 22, 1968, 2:15 A.M.

The Max and Susan Baker home

"Wake up! Susan, wake up! Max shook his sleeping wife, his voice shaking with fear, his legs trembling beneath the blankets. Did you hear that? Wake up!"

Susan struggled to open her eyes. "Yes, I heard it." She yawned and turned her back to him. "Honey, it's the village siren. It's for the volunteer firemen, Max, it's not for us. Go back to sleep, we both have to get up early tomorrow."

Max sank back on his pillow waiting for the trembling to subside. With a sigh Susan turned back to face him and began to gently rub his chest. She could feel his heart pounding and his perspiration wet on her hand. When he quieted down she turned over again and was soon asleep.

As soon as Max knew she was sleeping he carefully moved away from her and got up. Shivering from the perspiration drying on his skin he went down to the kitchen. Drinking a cup of hot herb tea warmed and calmed him as he stood looking out the window at the shadowy garden, its beauty far from his mind. The vivid memory of another siren and another fire filled him with a relentless fear. He would sleep no more this night.

The Terry and Jane Miller home

Dr. Terry Miller, full time Professor of Political Science, part time contract writer for the local newspaper and inveterate fire-chaser, heard the village fire siren at the same time that the pager on his bedside table began to crackle with static. **Code 3 wildland, Cresler Canyon, Code 3 wildland, Cresler Canyon**

"Jane, you awake, Honey? There's a code three fire. I'm leaving." Dr. Jane Miller, staff physician at the nearby St Helena hospital, whose sleep had already been interrupted twice that night, murmured acknowledgment and was immediately asleep again. Terry pulled on his clothes as he hurried through the darkened house, grabbed his camera case and tape recorder, which were always kept ready near the door to the garage, and was in his new Lincoln within minutes. The bright moonlight outlined his luxurious home as he sped down the dark winding road toward the orange glow he could see against the night sky.

The village volunteer fire station

At the fire station on College Avenue Bret Umek, the student watchman and fireman wanna-be, had all the lights burning and the engines started on the huge, red trucks even before the first car screeched to a stop in the parking lot.

"Boy, I'm glad you're here, Chief. Forestry says the fire's moving fast. It's already close to some homes and they're expecting it to jump the road any minute. They think the nursing home may be in danger. They said to send every available man we can round up."

Fire Chief Larry Morgan, an elementary teacher by profession, was short, slight, and bald; but when dressed in his "turnouts" and wearing his authoritative white hat, there was never any question that his crisp, skilled commands would be followed by his volunteer crew of professors, students, and community residents. He picked up the phone.

"T.W.? This is Chief Morgan at the fire station." The hand holding the telephone was sweating but only those who knew him most intimately would have guessed it. "There's a dangerous fire spreading quickly up from the Handley Ranch. It's threatening homes already and moving fast. We need help and lots of it. Can you get some additional teachers and students down to the gym right away? We'll have one of the firemen there to give them instructions and orders. We could use at least two to three hundred men—maybe more—all you can get. We may have to evacuate the college and the village, too, so we could use some of the older girls to help with that. Oh, and ask any of the men who have shovels to bring them along. Hurry, please."

The college president's home

T.W., now fully awake, reached for the phone beside his bed and dialed his secretary's memorized number.

"Peggy? This is T.W. Sorry to wake you, but there's a dangerous fire burning out of control and the fire chief asked me to enlist some teachers to help. Call the department chairmen and ask them to call the men in their departments. Everyone is to report to the gym immediately—with a shovel. Also, call Physical Plant and ask them to alert all their men. I'll call the administrators and, uh, maybe I'd better call Max Baker myself."

Peggy Kester immediately pulled her faculty list from the drawer by her bedside and began to dial the numbers.

The Max and Susan Baker home

Max was still standing by the window in the living room when the phone rang.

"Hello?

"Max, you awake?"

"Yes, we heard the siren."

"There's a big fire threatening some homes on the hill and possibly even the nursing home. The chief needs all the younger men teachers to go to the gym right away. Is this something you feel up to?"

"Yes, of course, why wouldn't I?"

"You're sure? Max, you don't have to go if you don't feel up to it. Everyone will understand."

"I'm sure. I want to help."

"Well, all right, if you're sure. Also call the other men in your department. Everyone should go to the gym right away. Oh, and each of you should bring a shovel."

Back upstairs in the bedroom Max touched Susan's shoulder, gently this time. "That was T.W., Honey. He wants all the men to help with this fire. I told him I'd go. Better get ready in case we have to evacuate. And call your mom. Maybe you should take some stuff and drive down there. Max continued to dress while he dialed Mike Rollin's number, his heart beating wildly. "And, Honey, keep the radio on. And don't worry about me. I can do this. I need to face this once and for all."

Through his brave words Susan could hear the panic rising in his voice. In the distance the siren again began to wail. She wanted to stop him, to hug him, to tell him he would be all right, or better yet, to tell him not to go. But she didn't. Her legs felt weak and she started to pray aloud as she went into the closet to pull out their boxes of family pictures. "Please God; don't let anything happen to him. I'm sorry I complained about him, Lord. Please, please, I can't face living without him. Please, please."

The men's dorm

Dean of Men, Jamen Hardy, felt his adrenaline rise as he put down the phone and switched on the microphone next to his bed. The old sound system, which often failed to work just when it was needed, hummed into life. He could hear his own voice, clear and vibrant, filling the halls and sleeping rooms of the old dormitory in which his small bachelor apartment was located. He was proud of that voice and hearing it with the slight vibrato caused by the out-of-date sound system always gave him satisfaction.

"Attention all men. Attention all men. This is Dean Hardy. We have just been informed by Dr. Patton that a dangerous fire is threatening the community and possibly even the old folks' home on the hill. Volunteers are needed right away to help the fire crew. All able men are to get dressed and report to the gym immediately."

He switched off the microphone and began to pull on his pants. *I'd better knock on each door just to make sure. Some of these guys sleep the sleep of the dead.*

The women's dorm

Dean of Women, May Wyant, listened to President Patton carefully . . . dangerous fire . . . He needed her . . . Don't frighten the girls . . . send most mature girls to help evacuation . . . hurry.

She was accustomed to dealing calmly in a crisis. Many years of widowhood and twenty-two years of coping with the lives and loves of more than five hundred girls each year had prepared her for anything—or so she reminded herself when each new challenge presented itself. She switched on the microphone next to her telephone.

"Attention girls. Attention all girls. This is Dean Wyant. Please come down to the parlor immediately for an important announcement. I repeat. All girls are to report to the parlor immediately for a very important announcement. All girls. To the parlor. *Immediately.*"

After the announcement she telephoned her two assistant deans, asking them to join her in the parlor—without giving them an explanation—then she dressed completely and combed her hair before leaving her apartment. Long experience had taught her that a dignified, unhurried demeanor was one of the most effective techniques for calming anxious young ladies, and assistant deans.

Chapter 12

3:30 A.M.

A hillside near the college

Above the fire line where Max and Paul Bradley had been assigned to dig fire breaks the outline of the Manzanita Manor Convalescent Hospital was starkly black against the flaming sky. Already Max's shirt was wet from perspiration and his growing fear combined with the heavy smoke was making it hard for him to breathe. His determination to continue, to be part of the community of volunteers, kept warring with his impulse to flee.

With each shovelful of dirt he dug he consciously tried to push away the memory of the searing, unbearable pain he had experienced in "that other" fire. His heart was beating erratically, but he continued to work, determined to win, determined to overcome.

He thought fleetingly of Susan; could she manage if he died? Maybe then someone else would give her the baby she yearned for, maybe she would be better off with someone else. His inability to grant her this great, overwhelming desire was a bitter taste in his mouth that never seemed to diminish.

Thirty feet away a yellow-hatted fireman was directing two students and in the distance others were clearing brush and digging trenches. They seemed to be talking to each other, even bantering. None of them looked frightened. *If they can do it, I can too, I can do this, I can. I must*

161

conquer this or "the beast" will win. That was how he always thought of fire; an insatiable beast devouring everything and everyone in its path. It had devoured his young manhood, destroyed his ability to have children, and made it impossible for him to ever make Susan truly happy.

The fire was an orange-hot raging fury still far beneath him in the canyon, but a strong wind was beginning to blow debris through the large Madrone and Pine trees. Max could hear the crackling of dozens of large Manzanita bushes burning in the distance. Above it all the eerie sound of the village fire siren still sounded its terrifying message sending waves of fear through his body.

Beside him, Paul Bradley continued to shovel while occasionally pausing to wipe the sweat and soot from his face. "I think they must be evacuating the old folks from the nursing home," Paul shouted above the noise of the wind and fire. "I can see a couple of ambulances and a line of cars. "Hey, Dr. Baker, look! There's someone coming down the hill! It looks like one of the old ladies from the home. "I'm going after her," Paul shouted over his shoulder as he started climbing up the hill. "I'll be right back."

Leaving his shovel in the trench he had been digging Max struggled to follow Paul up the hill, but he made little progress on the steep grade; his feet kept sliding back down in the loose soil he had piled up as he dug the trench. His breathing was becoming more difficult and his chest hurt from the exertion, and from the fear that continued to grip him.

Finally, clutching the branches of a small Manzanita bush, he was able to pull himself up to an outcropping rock that he could use as a toehold. He rested there for a moment to catch his breath. Then, as he stretched up to reach a higher ledge, the rock came loose and he fell, sliding farther and farther down the steep incline until he was able to grasp a small tree trunk to stop himself. As he tried to stand he groaned aloud as his knee buckled beneath him and a sharp pain shot up his leg. Lying there he realized that no one could hear him call for help. He couldn't move. He was helpless.

Flying dirt and debris blew in his face and eyes. The acrid smell brought back the terrible memory of his body burning. Panic gripped him in a paralysis of cold fear. His body began to shake uncontrollably. The siren continued to scream in his head.

Above him at the top of the hill he could see Paul Bradley grappling with the kicking, screaming woman her skirts up around her waist, her screams of fear drowned by the deafening roar of the fire.

Then he saw it. A solid wall of fire, rushing up the hillside. Furious, leaping, racing, bright red and yellow; the flames blocking all escape down the hill.

The tops of the trees above Max were exploding into fire with bright bursts of light. Tails of black smoke flailed the night sky. Beneath the trees the burning bushes hissed at his cowardice and formed a wall of thrusting, taunting tongues of flame . . . and eyes. There were eyes! He could see them clearly now, black-rimmed, hideous, laughing eyes, mocking him. *The beast. He's back, he's come for me.*

His head told him to get up, to run, but his body refused to move. It was happening again and this time—this time he would die. Smoke filled his every sense and the roaring sound of the wind was as a physical force surrounding him, hammering at him, stealing his will. Stealing his mind. An unbearable blast of heat forced him flat to the ground. His fingers scratched convulsively at the earth. As he pressed his face into the dirt, he could feel his mouth begin to scream.

Chapter 13

April 29, 1968

The college president's office

SAN FRANCISCO, CA (AP) Torrential rain during the last two days have doused the last smoldering embers of a forest fire which claimed the life of a young college professor and burned more than 1,850 acres near a small college town in Napa Valley. Destroyed in the fire were a small convalescent hospital and seven homes.

T.W. read the article again, sighed and laid down the newspaper. Leaning back and rocking slightly in his large executive-type chair, his mind returned to his phone call to Max Baker on the night of the fire and again the familiar wave of guilt washed over him. *I sent that fine young man to his death. I'll never forgive myself for asking him to help. I should have known better; I knew his history.*

He remembered Susan Baker's pretty face at the funeral; all swollen and red from crying. *Maybe it's a blessing they didn't have children. Of course, she's still young. She'll marry again.*

Shaking the thought away he reached for the phone and buzzed Peggy.

"Yes, T.W., what can I do for you?"

"Peggy, we need to find a secretary for Dr. Stevens. Any suggestions?"

"Do you want someone temporary or someone permanent?"

"Temporary, I think. I still expect Dr. Granados will be back next year and I suppose he'll want to choose his own secretary."

"Well, there is Rev. Anderson's wife, Laura. She used to be an executive secretary. She's retired now but she might consider it on a short-term basis."

"Good, good. She might be just the ticket; competent, no nonsense." *And no temptation to Jason Stevens,* he thought. "Call her, will you? Ask her if she would be interested."

As she turned to leave he called to her, "Oh, Peggy, one more thing."

"Yes?"

"Do you happen to know what Max Baker wanted to see me about when he asked for that appointment the day before the fire?"

"I had the impression it was something confidential to do with one of the men in his department."

"I see. Humm. Peggy, I hesitate to ask you this, but since Max is gone, uh, sit down, please. I've been hearing some comments about one of the Urban Studies faculty members that concern me. Have you heard anything that I should be aware of?"

"I've never heard anything about Dr. Lenz, but Mike Rollin seems to be a favorite topic of conversation."

The rocking mechanism on his chair creaked as he leaned forward in his chair. "And, the topic has to do with . . . ?" He raised his eyebrows and looked intently at her.

Peggy Kester was not a gossiper. She hesitated, "He seems to be quite the ladies' man."

10:10 A.M.

On the campus

Karis walked slowly from her class in Urban Hall down the still wet and slippery steps of the Religion building. After three days of no sunshine she was feeling as gloomy as the gray sky looked. Attending Mr. Rollin's Introduction to Urban Studies, once her favorite class, was now actually painful. In class they avoided eye contact with each other, but she was acutely aware of every movement he made.

166

After the shock of being seen embracing in his office, and the embarrassing "talking-to" and prayer by Dr. Baker, they had agreed not to ever see each other alone again—but that hadn't stopped her thoughts. No matter where she went or what she did the vivid memory of each kiss, every word spoken, each detail and nuance of his embrace replayed over and over in her mind. She was sure she was in love with him. She had never felt anything like this about Paul.

Dodging a puddle in the street she met Wally and Mark, coming out of the Physics building. They nodded to her but walked on without stopping to talk as they would have before she had broken up with Paul. It seemed strange not to be meeting Paul after her classes or in the library or the cafeteria. She saw him from a distance sometimes and she knew he was hurting. She missed talking with him, being with him, as a friend, but as each day went by she was more convinced that she had made the right decision not to marry him. *I think I won't date anyone at all until I'm finished with medicine. If I'm going to be a pediatrician someday I'd better begin to focus. No more men! Especially no more teachers!*

12:25 P.M.

The college cafeteria

As soon as Paul Bradley saw Karis come into the cafeteria he immediately stood up and began to gather his dishes onto a tray to leave. "I'll see you later," he said to Wally and Don who had been sitting with him.

Wally watched him leave through the opposite door to where Karis was standing in line and shook his head. "He can't bear even to be in the same room with Karis. And, did you notice that he ate almost nothing? He hasn't been sleeping either."

"Does he talk about her?"

"Naw. If I bring it up he just says it's The Lord's will."

"More likely it's Mr. Rollin's will."

"Yeah, I agree. After the stuff you told me about Rollin I've been thinking that someone should do something about him."

Don looked skeptical. "Like what?"

"Well, last night I was talking to some of the guys and . . . come on, let's get out of here. Here comes Karis. I'll tell you about it on the way to class."

167

5:35 P.M.

The Jason Stevens home

Eileen Stevens held the telephone in one hand while she stirred a pot on the stove with the other.

"Mr. Rollin? This is Eileen Stevens . . . Dean Stevens's wife. I just received a call from your sister, Grace. She's been trying to reach you. There was no answer at your home and my husband's office was closed so she called our home. I'm afraid she has some bad news. Your brother, Jim, has had a heart attack and has been taken to San Francisco General Hospital. Grace would like you to call her as soon as possible. You can reach her in the ICU waiting room at 415 721 0038." . . . "You're welcome. I'm so sorry; I hope he'll be all right. We'll be praying for you. I'm sure my husband will see that your classes are covered tomorrow, so don't worry about that. Let us know if we can do anything to help." . . . "Good bye."

5:40 P.M.

San Francisco General Hospital

Grace Rollin was pacing in the hall outside the I.C.U. waiting to be allowed back into the room to spend a few more minutes with her oldest brother, Jim, when a nurse motioned for her to come to a telephone.

"Oh, Mike. Oh, good! I tried and tried to reach you." . . . "Oh, Mike he's so bad. They have him heavily medicated so he isn't saying much but I can tell he's really scared. I've never seen him like this. He's been asking for you and for Mom and he wouldn't go to sleep until I promised I would call you." . . . "I know, but I need you here, Jim needs you. Can't you find someone else to stay with Benji while you and Mom come? He could die, Mike, he's very bad. Please come." . . . "Thank you, thank you. I'll tell Jim you're on your way."

Ten minutes later

"Karis? This is Mr. Rollin. I know we have an agreement, but I have a family emergency, a crisis, and I really need you. My brother has had a heart attack and my mother and I have to go to San Francisco to the hospital. My mom's been here taking care of Benji while my wife is out of town." . . . "Karis, please. I know I could get someone else, but both my mom and I think it's important for Benji to have someone he knows, in case, well, just in case. Will you come?" . . . "Thank you. I'll pick you up in 15 minutes. You may have to stay overnight so come prepared. I'll call Dean Wyant to explain."

7:30 P.M.

The Regency Hotel, Chicago

"Hi Benji. It's Mommy. How are you, Sweetie? Is Daddy there?" . . . "He's not? Well, let me talk to Gramma." . . . "Who's taking care of you?" . . . "Karis is there with you?" . . . "Daddy went away with Gramma and he asked *Karis* to take care of you?" . . . "Did Daddy tell you when they'd be back?" . . . " Are you sure Daddy said Karis is going to stay all night?" . . . "No Honey, I'll talk to Karis when I get home. Benji, will you tell Daddy that I know about Karis staying all night?" . . . "That's my good boy. Don't forget, OK? As soon as Daddy gets home tell him Mommy knows that Karis stayed all night." . . . "Don't forget. I'm counting on you. I have to go now, Honey. I miss you. Give yourself a big hug from me. Bye bye."

Very early the next morning

It was nearly two in the morning when Mike turned his Mustang into Terrace View Drive. His mind still numb from seeing his only brother die, he drove slowly down the dark road automatically swerving around the familiar potholes. All of the houses on the street were dark, the only illumination a dim light coming from inside his nearest neighbor's house. The surge of pride he usually felt when the garage door opened smoothly at his touch and the automatic light revealed his clean, orderly garage was absent as he brought the Mustang to a stop next to Syd's VW. *It's just as well that Mom didn't come back with me; Benji would just be upset seeing her so distraught. Thank God Sydney will be home tomorrow. I'll patch things up with her.* He realized, to his surprise, that he missed his wife and that he wanted her with him and their son. *Maybe Sydney and*

I can still make our marriage work, I'll talk with her tomorrow, he thought as he let himself into the kitchen, relieved to be home.

For a long moment he stood still in the dark room until the tension in his shoulders began to ease. The house was still. A night light shone faintly in the darkened hallway. He walked quietly through his silent, comforting home to the staircase. Draping his jacket over the newel post he slowly climbed the carpeted stairs.

Benji's small form was curled up under his favorite blanket; his teddy bear snuggled close beside him. The little wheelchair beside the bed reminded Mike, as it always did, that it was his driving that was the cause of Benji's weak legs. Standing in the doorway with the night light from the hall shining on the sweet little face, Mike was overcome with tenderness and sadness. *Syd's right, it is all my fault, the gossip, our fights, Benji's accident . . .* The familiar guilt that returned each time he remembered the accident overwhelmed him. Then, the unanswerable question; *why would God punish an innocent little boy for his father's sins? It's not fair that Benji should have to suffer for what I've done . . .* Wiping the tears from his eyes and sighing audibly he pulled Benji's door almost closed—the way Benji liked it—and walked toward his bedroom.

The guest room was across the hall from his and Sydney's bedroom and Mike hesitated before the slightly open door remembering; Karis was in there.

In bed.

Suddenly the intense feelings that she had aroused in his office came flooding over him and caution slipped away. *Just a look, then I'll leave. I won't wake her.* Slowly, quietly, he pushed open the door.

170

Karis lay quietly with her eyes closed knowing that Mike had come home, sensing that he was there, that he was looking at her. After a moment when he said nothing she turned, opened her eyes and smiled. Her hair was in disarray and in the faint light her face was luminous. Above the satin-trimmed blanket that she held up to cover herself the lacy straps of her nightie showed pink against her skin. *She is so beautiful,* he thought, *but, I can't . . . I must not . . . I won't.*

"How's your brother?" she whispered. "Is he going to be all right?"

Her questions brought back fresh anguish. *Jim, his brother, the dependable one, his best friend in the world had struggled for his last breath while he sat helpless beside him.* His chest hurt with the pain of his sorrow. He knelt beside her bed and whispered, his voice rough with feeling, "Oh, Karis, he's . . . he's dead."

He dropped his head to the blanket to hide the tears that had gathered and to try to control the sobs he had been suppressing ever since he left the hospital. Then he felt her hand stroking his hair, her voice murmuring, "shhh, I know, I know, I'm so sorry. Shhh, shhh."

After his sobs subsided he lifted his head and looked at her, sheepishly, his face still wet from his tears. He took her hands in his and kissed each of them in turn. "Thank you," he said, his voice strained with emotion.

Karis reclaimed one hand and reached up to trace the outline of his cheek as she wiped away an errant tear. "I love you," she whispered. "I love you so much!" Then, before she was aware of even moving, she was up kneeling on the bed, the blanket forgotten, her arms around him, pulling him up to her, an irresistible urge for him sweeping over her.

In the rush of sudden passion all resolve was forgotten as Mike's hands moved on her body. Karis held his face in her hands and their mouths remained pressed tightly together as he began to tug at her nightgown.

Unnoticed, Benji, on hands and knees, watched from the open door. His cries, at first only whimpering sounds, increased in intensity until Karis and Mike, dazed and speechless, finally looked up and stared at him.

"Daddy, Daddy, I . . . I . . . I for, forgot to tell you . . . Mommy made me promise and I forgot."

Mike jumped back from the bed and picked him up. As Mike carried him out of the room Benji, wide-eyed, looked back at Karis still kneeling, naked, on the bed.

Panicked at what had happened Karis jumped up and began to pull on her clothes, her hurried efforts making buttons and zippers nearly impossible to close. As she left the room she could hear Mike's voice quietly reassuring Benjil.

"It's OK, Sweetheart. Everyone forgets sometimes, even Mommy. But, now it's OK, because you remembered and now you can tell me. What did Mommy want you to tell me?"

She wanted me . . . she wanted . . . she wanted me to tell you that she knew Karis was taking care of me. Daddy, why were you kissing and kissing and kissing Karis, and she didn't have her clothes on?" The sobbing began again and he laid his head on Mike's chest. "Are you and Mommy getting revorced? Davie said you were getting revorced."

"Of course not, Sweetie. Davie doesn't know anything about our family. Mommy and I love each other and we both love you. I was just feeling bad because Uncle Jim got very sick. Karis was trying to make me feel better, that's all. Let's not tell Mommy about this, OK? We'll make a deal; I won't tell her that you forgot, if you don't tell her I was kissing Karis. OK? . . . that's my boy. Come on now, let me tuck you into bed."

Outside Benji's door Karis stood listening to Mike's explanation and thought her mixed emotions would suffocate her. She had been so sure that she loved him, but now his explanation to Benji, so calm, so . . . so false, added doubts to her feelings and she had to leave, to get away before he could stop her, before the unthinkable could happen. Before it was too late.

Unnoticed by Mike she tiptoed past Benji's room and crept down the stairs. In the dimly lighted living room she quietly opened the front door and ran out into the night.

Outside the door of Mike's house Karis hesitated. There were no street lights on the lonely road and the dark outlines of the neighboring homes looked menacing. The faint glow coming from a window in the house next door shed a tenuous light on the driveway as she tried to remember the length of the driveway and which direction she should walk to reach the highway. Glancing again at the neighbor's dimly lighted window, she thought she saw someone looking out, watching her, but then the light went out and the total blackness of the night closed in around her.

As soon as she felt the hard top of the driveway end and the gravel road begin she started to run, and to pray. *Oh, dear Lord, help me. Please, give me strength. I know I was wrong, please, forgive me. Help me. I'm sorry. I'm truly sorry.*

She had only run a short way when she stepped into a pothole, turning her ankle as she fell. Her hands and knees hit the sharp gravel as she fell and she cried aloud from the pain and from the realization of her vulnerability in the dark, dark night. Slowly she forced herself to stand up and, wincing from the pain in her ankle and knees and hands, she began to walk more slowly, more cautiously.

In the darkness her hearing became more acute and her muscles tensed as she became more aware of the night noises surrounding her. Suddenly she stopped to listen more carefully. *That rustling behind her.* It was getting louder. She walked faster. The rustling receded and finally stopped.

As her eyes adjusted to the darkness she could see more clearly the outlines of trees and rooftops against the night sky. Then she thought she saw a shadow, moving beside a darkened house. She remembered the faint outline in the neighbor's window and fear gripped her. She stopped, straining to see. *Suddenly she heard it again*, the ominous rustling. It was getting louder, And closer.

Terror clutched at her throat, "Who's there?" she cried aloud. "Is someone there?" Her voice sounded too loud in the darkness. The rustling seemed to stop. Did the shadow move again? She wasn't sure. She tried to scream but fear filled her throat and choked out the sound.

"Karis, it's me. Don't be afraid." His voice was quiet and pleading. "Please, please, come back. Let me drive you to the dorm. It's not safe for you out here." He continued to call, reassuring her, apologizing, pleading, but Karis, embarrassed and afraid of her lack of control, shrank back into the dark shadows and did not answer him.

She heard him finally retreating and shortly afterward saw a light go on in his house. She had to get away before he came again with a flashlight to find her. She tried to run, but the pain in her ankle was too great. She remembered that there was a path through the woods to the highway, a short cut, but could she find it in the dark? And there were rattlesnakes in these woods, sometimes even on the road. At that horrendous thought she began to walk faster ignoring the pain. Suddenly she tripped and fell heavily to the ground. Lying there, hurting and frightened, her body hugging the cold unyielding earth, despondency flooded her mind and she cried from fear and from pain and from the guilt that flooded her mind. *Oh Lord, save me, help me!*

After awhile she stopped crying and brought herself slowly to her bleeding knees. Feeling around on the ground with her hands she realized that she was no longer on the gravel road but on the edge of the asphalt highway. She knew the way now and that knowledge gave her strength as she stood up.

Clenching her teeth she shook herself, as though shaking the fear from her body. *I will not be afraid. I'm safe now, I'm almost there, I'm safe. I'm almost there. I'm safe, I'm almost there.* The mantra seemed to give her courage and she began to say the words out loud and to walk in their cadence. I'm safe, I'm safe, I'm almost there.

Twice the red Mustang drove slowly by her, Mike's head clearly visible in the light from the dashboard. Twice her mind compelled her to crouch behind low bushes beside the road while her body ached to leap out to call to him.

After awhile the clouds parted and the stars above shone clear and bright, but Karis limped on without noticing, her mind teeming with conflicting emotions, her determination to reach her goal the drumbeat that kept her going forward.

On she trudged, slowly, painfully, up the grade to the cusp of the small caldera that cradled the college. Her mind was in constant turmoil. *I love him, but . . . dear God, will I ever be the same again? I knew he could never be mine. Lord, help me to be strong, and forgive me for sinning with him, for wanting to sin with him,* she prayed as she struggled to keep going.

Her ankle was swollen and very painful, and she was exhausted from the confusing seesaw of her emotions, but there! She could see the lights of the campus before her. Her tears were dry now, replaced by a dogged resoluteness to make it to the dorm, to safety, to her bed.

3:20 A.M.

The Women's dorm

Usually the night receptionist in the dorm, Mandy Ferris, found her job boring, and she often found it hard to stay awake after midnight when the dorm quieted down. By three a.m. on this morning, as usual, the phone had stopped ringing, her homework was finished and she was dozing, her head cradled on her arms at the desk when the night bell rang. Opening the door she stared in astonishment at Karis. Karis' clothes, usually so immaculate, were dirty and disheveled, her face red and swollen from crying, and she looked as though she might faint. Mandy put her arm around her and helped her into the lobby.

"Karis! What happened? Are you all right? You're hurt, here sit down, I'll get Dean Wyant."

"No, no, please Mandy, don't . . . I'm all right. I walked home and . . . and . . . I sprained my ankle and fell. Please, promise me you won't tell the Dean, or anyone. Please, Mandy. Promise me. I'll be all right in the morning, I just need to sleep now."

"Well, all right, if you're sure you're all right. You should have let Mr. Rollin drive you home. He called a little while ago asking for you and he sounded really worried. Why don't I call him to let him know you're alright."

"No! No . . . please. If he calls again . . . tell him . . . oh, tell him I don't want to talk to him. I just don't want to talk to anyone." Karis turned her face away as she began to limp toward the hall, but Mandy could see her body shaking with sobs.

Chapter 16

3:25 A.M.

Room 103, West Hall men's dorm

Wally Darnell lifted a sleepy head from his pillow and looked up to see the night monitor shaking him.

"Darnell, wake up! There's a phone call for you. She says it's urgent."

"Who is it? Is it my mom?"

"No, it's Mandy and she says it can't wait 'til morning. You can take the call at my desk."

The distance to the front entrance where the monitor's desk held a telephone was reached in record time by Wally in pajamas and robe.

"Mandy? What's wrong? Are you OK?"

"Wally? I know it's late, but I don't know what to do. I'm working the desk at the dorm tonight and Karis just came in."

"It must be after three A.M. She just came in?"

"Yeah, just five minutes ago. You know what you were telling me about Karis and Mr.Rollin? Well, you might be right. She was baby-sitting at Mr. Rollin's house, but when she came in she was crying and her clothes were all messed up"

"Were her clothes torn?"

"No, not torn, but her blouse wasn't all buttoned and her skirt was on wrong and she was hurt and bleeding."

"What happened? Did she tell you what happened?

"She said she had walked back from his house and had fallen down. She made me promise not to say anything to anyone. Then she just limped crying to her room. Wally, I'm really worried about her. Do you think he could have raped her?"

"Oh, I doubt it, but—."

"—I can't believe it either, but something bad happened, that's for sure. I should tell Dean Wyant. I promised Karis I wouldn't, but I think I better. Do you think it would be OK to wait until I talk to Karis in the morning before I tell Dean Wyant?"

"Yeah. Wait 'til we know more then we can decide who to tell. Maybe we'll need to tell the president instead. Or the police."

"OK, I'll wait, but don't tell anyone else. OK?"

"OK, sure. Let me know as soon as you find out what's going on."

"Wait for me after Lit class and I'll tell you what she says. 'Night, Wally. Thanks."

"You're welcome. G'night."

The next day, 7:30 P.M.

Room 103, West Hall men's dorm

Wally paced while several of Paul Bradley's closest friends sat around his dorm room listening.

"I told you I was afraid of something like this. We still don't know exactly what happened to Karis, but it wasn't good. Whatever, he shouldn't be fooling around with her—or with any of the other girls either. Besides, he's a pinko and he has no business spouting his treason in class. OK, then, are we all agreed on the reasons to get Rollin fired? If any of you disagree you probably shouldn't be here. Well?"

"I'm in," said Don, "that guy's really bad news. I was in a class once where he—"

"—OK, Don, hold that thought. How about you Mark?"

"I think he should keep his hands off Karis, but calling his opinion of the war treason is pretty strong. I agree with some of what he says."

"We'll go over that later, Mark, but first I need to know if you're with us on this or not."

180

"I want to know what you have planned first."

"OK, that's simple; we plan to get him off the campus—get him fired if possible. We're not gonna hurt him or anything."

"Well, OK, I'm in, but this is for Paul and Karis, not for Rollin's politics, and only if we don't do anything illegal."

"Right. Good. The rest of you are in? OK then. Now, the first thing we need to do is . . ."

Chapter 17

8:55 A.M.

An Urban Studies Classroom

Dr. Bill Lenz, appointed Chairman of the Department of Urban Studies after Max Baker's death, had just finished writing an announcement on the blackboard of classroom B as the students of Mike Rollin's class began to straggle in. *Mr. Rollin's classes will not meet today. Try to be brave.*

As each student read the unexpected announcement their smiles gave evidence of their fortitude.

9:30 A.M.

Office of Jason Stevens

Mrs. Laura Anderson, wife of Emeritus Professor of Religion, Dr. Kevin P. Anderson, rubbed compulsively at the faint bristle of moustache on her upper lip. She wasn't used to these new electric typewriters. Trying to figure out all the gadgets wore her out. She had been at her desk for over an hour and she needed to stretch. The light rain falling outside had caused her arthritis to flare up and the knuckles on her right hand were swollen. Getting up from her desk she flexed her fingers and rolled her shoulders several times as she walked to the windows on the far side of the office. To make things worse, her feet hurt. Since she was alone in

183

the office she slipped out of her size ten and a half, AAA width pumps. *"Aaah, that's better"*, she said aloud to herself.

Strangers would often remark that everything about Laura Anderson was long and thin. Her five foot nine-inch slim frame, her thin face, the important-looking, slightly-humped nose, her fingers, her legs, even the severely-cut, mid-calf length clothes she wore all contributed to their impression. Her graying hair, worn in a long braid twisted into a bun just above her collar, combined with a face that had never known cosmetics made her look even older than her sixty five years.

Two floors below students talked and laughed as they hurried along the rain-slicked sidewalks to class. *How fast the years have gone by,* she thought. *Could it really be almost forty-five years since I was one of them? How different it is now; girls and boys holding hands—even kissing—right on campus, driving cars, going to movies. That certainly would never have happened when I was a student. It shouldn't be happening now! We've moved too far away from the Lord's blueprint.* Her sigh was long and heart-felt as she returned to her desk.

When Peggy Kester asked her to fill in as Dr. Stevens' secretary she had refused. It wasn't until T.W. himself called that she had, reluctantly, agreed. He had been persuasive. She was desperately needed. A critical Board meeting was coming up. He had reminded her how much college administrators relied on secretaries who didn't gossip about confidential matters. Still, she had resisted. It was his stern, "It's your duty, Sister Anderson, The Lord's Work is more important than your garden," that had finally made her agree.

Dr. Stevens, however, had made it clear from the beginning that she hadn't been his choice. *Not young and pretty enough,* she surmised. Not consulted in advance about her selection he had been barely civil to her from the beginning.

Rationalizing that she needed to "familiarize" herself with his files she had discovered some interesting things about this "Acting" dean. First, she found out that his real name wasn't Stevens at all; it was StevenSON. She knew then who his father was; every denominational worker knew him, or at least knew about him. He was one of the most influential men at the General Assembly with a reputation as a strong, rigidly righteous leader.

Her second surprise was learning that Dr. Stevens' mother, Ruth, had briefly been one of her own classmates right here at this college. *Jason Stevens must take after his father,* she decided, *Ruth was a timid, sweet, and polite girl.*

Laura hadn't seen Dr. Stevens yet that morning but she knew that the waiting memo from T.W. telling him to correct—yet again—his report for the board meeting would put him into a foul mood—yet again.

10:15 A.M.

Jason Stevens found the first note taped to the outside door to his office when he returned from a committee meeting. The envelope read PRIVATE—DEAN'S EYES AND HANDS ONLY. Puzzled, he tore it open and was reading it as he walked into Laura's office.

Mrs. Anderson, did you see who left this note?" he asked, without looking up or bothering to greet her.

Watching him warily she hesitated, "Good morning, Dr. Stevens. No, I saw no one. The note was there when I arrived. As it was clearly for you I left it there."

His forehead wrinkled in annoyance, "Get Mike Rollin on the phone for me. Tell him I need to see him right now." He stalked into his office and closed the door without waiting for her response.

Two minutes later Laura opened the door to his office. "Dr. Stevens, a student in the Urban Studies Office said that Mr. Rollin's classes have been cancelled for the day. I tried his home but there was no answer. I left a message in his office for him to call you as soon as he returns."

"Oh yes, there was a death in his family. Well when he calls get him in to see me as soon as possible. Make an appointment with Karis Radford for tomorrow morning, and hold my calls until I get this blasted report finished."

"Yes, Sir. Is there anything else?"

"No, just shut the door and give me some peace."

10:30 A.M.

"Mrs. Anderson?" His head appeared in the doorway to her office. "Why hasn't Physical Plant fixed this blasted pipe yet? How am I supposed to work with that infernal hissing sound? I'm never going to get this report done."

"I called them again yesterday, but they said that the part hasn't come in yet. If you had some duct tape I think you could keep it from hissing."

"Well, will you—" he watched her eyes narrow in annoyance. "—Oh, never mind. I'll bring some in." He closed the door and returned to his desk. *Old battle-ax . . . he might have let me pick my own secretary at least. T.W. treats me like a dumb kid. Maybe I'll ask Dad to suggest an early retirement for him. Hmmm. President Stevens. Nice ring.*

Fifteen minutes later he looked up to see Laura Anderson standing before his desk. "Dr. Stevens, there's a woman on the phone for you. I told her you couldn't be disturbed, but she says it's an urgent personal matter that can't wait. I'm not sure, but I think she said her name was . . . Desiree? Do you want to talk with her?"

He stared at her in disgust until she left the office and shut the door, then he picked up the phone. "I thought I told you NEVER to call me" . . . "what do you mean you don't want my business?" . . . "listen, you used up old bag, if you think" . . . "don't you hang up on me!"

Ten minutes later Laura opened his office door again and poked her head inside, waiting until he looked up. "Dr. Stevens, a Mr. Scott from Bank of America is on the phone for you. He says it's important. Do you want to talk to him?"

"No! Just tell him I'm not here."

"Dr. Stevens," she said, stepping inside the office to face him, her lips in a tight, thin line. "I think we should get something straight. I am not comfortable lying for you. I have never had to lie in any of my other positions and I don't intend to begin now." Her back stiffened as she stared at him.

"Well, Mrs. Anderson, we certainly wouldn't want you to be *uncomfortable*," he said, his voice dripping sarcasm. "Maybe you'd feel more *comfortable* working for someone else. Close the door when you leave, and next time use the buzzer to call me." He picked up the phone as she shut the door—firmly.

"Scott? Good morning. I was just picking up the phone to call you" . . . "yes, I am aware that it's overdue, but" . . . "no, sorry, can't make it today, but," . . . "look, I said I was sorry, you don't have to shout" . . . "Yes, Monday. Good by." *Self-important, pompous so'n so.*

11:15 A.M.

The inter-office buzzer rang. Jason ignored it. It rang again, longer and more insistently. He shook his head then picked it up, muttering under his breath. "I *told* you to hold all my calls."

"It's your father, Dr. Stevens. I told him you were very busy and didn't want to be disturbed, but he insisted that I interrupt you. What shall I tell him?"

His groan could be heard through the closed door as he pushed the button to talk.

"Look, Dad, I can't talk now, I've—"

"—Good news, Son. I just ran into General Williams. He tells me that he's retired and is moving to Napa Valley—St. Helena I think he said. He seemed really pleased when I told him where you lived. He'll be out looking for a house next weekend so I invited him to spend a couple of days with you and Eileen. I checked with Eileen first, of course, and she said it was fine."

"Absolutely not!" He could feel the anger tightening his throat making it hard to breathe. "You should have checked with me, not Eileen. I can't stand that man and I don't have time for this. I have commitments; a board meeting to prepare for, and I'm teaching the Sabbath school lesson this week, and—"

"—Nonsense, Jack, uh, Jason. He'll understand all that. He's very fond of you—told me so himself. He looks on you as the son he never had. He told me he was looking forward to spending some 'quality' time with you and your family—his very words. I told him about Davie and he said it would be almost like having a grandson of his own. In fact right away he mentioned outings that he could take with Davie if you were too busy."

"Dad, I—" the familiar feeling of impotence his father engendered in him made his head begin to pound.

"—Son, it's all arranged. Relax. It'll be good for you to be seen with a general; remind the good folks on the hill what kind of stock you come from."

"Dad, I'm not—" his hand gripping the receiver tightened until his knuckles were white.

"—Sorry, have to go. Eileen has all the details. Your mother sends her love. Bye now."

After he hung up Jason Stevens sat staring at the telephone. *Why doesn't he just leave me alone. I hate him. My own father. I hate the general and I hate T.W. I even hate my own father.*

11:35 A.M.

Laura turned off her typewriter on the third ring. "Dr. Stevens' office."

"Oh, yes, T.W." . . .

"He specifically asked me not to disturb him, but," . . .

"Yes, yes, of course. I'll put you through."

"Jason? How's that report coming? I'd like to see your changes by early this afternoon so we can go over it before Mrs. Anderson types the final copy. Remember, the board will look this one over carefully, so make it good." . . .

"Good, good. I'll expect you with your report in my office at 2:30."

11:37 A.M.

"Mrs. Anderson, get in here," he growled.

"Yes, what is it?"

"I said *no* calls. That means NO calls. Not the President of the college or the President of the United States. NO ONE. Is that perfectly clear?"

Laura stood before his desk unflinching, her back straight, her teeth clenched so tightly she could barely get the words out. "Yes, that's clear, *Sir.* Did it ever occur to you, *Sir,* that I just might be able to help you with that report? I am an experienced person you may remember."

"You want to help? Great. Pull the plug on the phone and get out of here so I can think."

A loud hiss from the old heater punctuated Laura's gasp of disapproval at his rudeness as she left his office.

12:20 P.M.

Laura was talking on the phone when Jason emerged from his office gripping a yellow legal pad. "Type this over lunch so I can work on it when I return."

Holding her hand over the telephone receiver, she paused, looked at her watch, then at him. She frowned, began to say something, then sighed, nodded, and removed her hand from the receiver. As Jason left the office she said into the telephone, "Looks like his majesty has outlawed lunch along with courtesy. I'll call you later."

12:25 P.M.

He saw the second note stuck under the windshield wiper on his car as soon as he approached his parking space. The envelope read, NEW INFORMATION—READ IMMEDIATELY. But, he didn't read it immediately because just at that moment he noticed an old beat-up VW van drive by. There were peace signs pasted on the windows and inside were two young men with the requisite long hair and scraggly beards of the San Francisco hippy community. He tried to flag them down, but they just smiled, raised two fingers in the peace sign, and drove on. Then he read the note.

12:37 P.M.

Jason's wife, Eileen, was reading a scribbled note when he opened the front door to his home. "Jason, look what I found in our mailbox mixed in with the regular mail." She showed him the envelope that read, ACTION DEMANDED—NOW.

"Just some crackpot kids. I got one at the office too. Is lunch ready?" he said starting toward the kitchen.

"Jason, I think you should read this. They're claiming that Mike Rollin is having an affair with a student. Is that true?"

"I don't know but I'm d— well going to find out."

"Jason! Please! Someday you're going to slip up and swear in front of—"

He whipped around, his face flushed, his lips tight in anger. "—OK, OK, and, don't give me that holier-than-thou look." *He looks just like his Dad when he's angry,* thought Eileen. "Now listen to me," he said, "I want you to call my Dad back and tell him to *un*-invite Williams. You had no business saying he could stay with us."

Eileen squared her shoulders and looked at him, "Call him yourself. He doesn't let me get a word in edgewise."

"Alright, alright, I'll take care of it. Now let's eat, I have to get back."

It was a very silent lunch.

1:20 P.M.

Rummaging around in the garage after lunch Jason found a roll of duct tape and some old garden gloves which he threw on the passenger seat of the car. *Physical Plant treats me like I'm one of the janitors.* He was still tense and grumbling to himself as he drove out of the driveway and turned toward the college.

I think Desiree may need a little persuasion tonight. Who does she think she is anyway, the washed-up old bag. After all the money I've pumped into her dump. That new girl she gave me last time? She needs to find out that the one who pays the piper picks the tune. Anyway, I didn't really hurt her. OK a few bruises maybe, but she should know by now that's a cost of doing business—her business anyway.

190

Chapter 18

The Mike Rollin home

Mike Rollin sat alone at the kitchen table, his head in his hands; Jim's death still unbelievable and nearly unendurable. His sister's tearful call asking for his help with arrangements for the funeral had brought back the terrible anguish of those last moments in the hospital. He could hear Benji talking softly to himself as he played with his legos on the coffee table in the family room. *Maybe he's already forgotten what he saw last night.* But as he remembered Benji's big eyes when he discovered him kissing a naked Karis he knew that wasn't likely. *And what about Karis?* What *was she feeling? I wish she'd talk to me. Will she tell anyone? Her roommate maybe?*

Karis still wouldn't talk to him when he called and, according to her roommate, she wasn't attending her classes. *Syd's bound to find out sooner or later. Then what? She'll probably take Benji and leave me. There'll be a huge scandal for sure. I could lose Benji, my career, everything. Would Karis be worth it?* As he remembered the feel of her hand on his face and the soft, sweet way she had told him that she loved him a strong stirring of desire rippled though him.

I have to pick Syd up at the airport at 3:15. He glanced at his watch. *An hour and a half, I'd better get going. What am I going to say to her? I*

191

doubt Benji will be able to resist telling her what he saw. I have to tell her something to neutralize what he saw.

2:35 P.M.

En flight, United Airlines Flight 714

Sydney Rollin was in torment about her decision, her mood vacillating between rage and despondency. *How could he! I'll never forgive him. Oh, Mike, I love you, how could you? You promised not to see her, then as soon as I'm out of sight you get her to stay all night; and with Benji in the next room! His promises are worth nothing. But how can I live without him?*

Her decision had been made immediately after her phone conversation with Benji the night before; she would divorce Mike and move close to her folks in Wisconsin. An unexpected wave of sympathy for Mike engulfed her as she remembered how much he loved Benji, but then Karis came to mind, and Synnove and the others, and all sympathy evaporated as her anger returned with a vengeance. *It's his turn to suffer.*

She dreaded the confrontation with Mike. *Maybe it'll be easy. Maybe he wants to be free.* The familiar throbbing over her left eye was already starting when she stepped off the plane in San Francisco. Outside the baggage claim area she could see Mike's Mustang waiting beside the curb and her budding migraine leaped into full bloom.

7:30 P.M.

The Jason and Eileen Steven's home

Jason slouched in his leather recliner, his feet on the uplifted footrest, his eyes hidden behind the day's copy of the Napa Register, his mind on the rape story on page one. *Women are so stupid! Why do they fight it? If they would just "lay back and enjoy it" as the saying goes, they wouldn't get hurt.*

Across the room Eileen watched him, covertly, over an open book, a worried look on her face. *This has been a bad day for him; T.W. chewing him out, the coming visit from the general. I wonder why he dislikes him so much.* She combed her fingers through her hair worrying about what he would be like in bed tonight; trouble brought out the worst in Jason.

10:45 P.M.

"Jason, I *said* not tonight. Now let go of me. I mean it . . . and don't you dare hit me or you'll be sorry. I've told you before; I will not sleep with you when you're upset. You're too rough. I still have the bruises you gave me last week."

Jason jumped from the bed, his face red with anger, "All right. I'll find someone who will." He yanked his jogging suit from the chair by the bed and without even putting it on he stalked out of the bedroom.

Eileen pulled down her nightgown from her chest where Jason had shoved it, drew the blanket up to her chin and snuggled down into the bed. *Let him take his frustrations out on someone who gets paid for it,* she thought as she turned on her side and tried to sleep.

1:35 A.M.

Napa, California

Jason drove slowly along Lincoln Avenue, turned north on Silverado Trail and headed toward home. He was still aroused and breathing hard after his last encounter. The woman he had picked up had fought like a banshee; screaming and kicking and finally managing to get away from him before he was half finished. It was exhilarating. He hadn't been aware of the scratches on his hands and arms from her fingernails until, looking down, he noticed small drops of blood on his pants. *So I had to hurt her a little. It was her own fault. If she had just shut up and let me do what I was paying her for . . . but no, she thought she could tell me what to do. Well, no one tells a Stevenson what to do!*

As he neared the campus his thoughts turned back to the day before. Especially embarrassing—and infuriating—was the dressing down from T.W. in front of the executive committee when he gave his report. *There was nothing wrong with that report! T.W.'s just out to get me and he has the others so buffaloed that they were afraid to admit how good it was. I'd better have a talk with Dad about this before he hears it from T.W. He'll prob'ly think it's my fault as usual.*

Suddenly he remembered the general's visit and his hands clenched. *If he so much as looks at Davie, so help me, I'll kill him. Dad had some nerve inviting him without asking me first. Eileen could have refused; she knows how much I hate him. She's becoming impossible lately . . . I should leave her, just take off for L.A. or New York.*

A satisfied smile erased the frown on his face at the thought that Eileen would have to deal with the overdue bank loan. *She'll be bent out of shape when she finds out about that. I don't care. Serves her right. She doesn't appreciate me. Maybe I will leave her and take Davie with me. Yeah, it would just serve her right.*

Chapter 19

6:30 A.M.

Jason woke up stiff from sleeping on the couch where he had crashed when he got home sometime after two a.m. He pulled on his jogging suit and left the house to run the daily three mile loop which had in recent years been substituted for his previous morning calisthenics. The air was crisp and cool with wisps of fog still lifting through the pines. On most days the run immediately cleared his head and gave him a feeling of empowerment, but not this time. His forehead was creased with a frown and his mind churned with the injustices he felt. *Everyone's against me,* he thought. *T.W. seems determined to see me fail, Eileen thinks she can refuse me anytime she wants to, even that disgusting prostitute; screaming like that before I was finished.* The bitterness of his thoughts added strength and power as he ran; it flowed like juice into his thighs and his stride lengthened. Rounding a corner he thought again of the coming general's visit and reminded himself that his strength was now greater than the general's. *Payback time,* he thought with elation spurring him on to run faster. *We're not in the Army now.*

7:15 A.M.

A tentative sun was just beginning to stream through the breakfast room window as Eileen poured milk on her cereal. Outside she could see an Anna's hummingbird hovering around the empty feeder. She made a

195

mental note to stop at the Mercantile to buy some red food coloring for the feeder after she dropped Davie at the day care center.

Hmmm, he came in even later than usual last night, she mused. *I wish I knew how to help him. It's frightening. I'm afraid he might really hurt some poor girl sometime . . . he hurts me.* She shivered, thankful that he hadn't forced her again. Her bruises from their last "lovemaking" session hadn't quite healed yet. She wondered sometimes if God didn't have a special blessing for prostitutes; they'd sure saved her a lot of pain through the years. She crumbled another half biscuit of shredded wheat into her bowl to finish the milk.

She chewed the crunchy cereal slowly thinking about her marriage. *It could be so good if it weren't for sex. I guess I was too young when we married—barely eighteen—but, I loved him so much and I never dreamed he'd hurt me.* She replayed in her mind the events of the night she and Jason had met.

I was so excited. I even remember what we ate, and the lace table cloth. That table looked sooo beautiful to me after six years at the mission. Mom Stevenson used her "good" dishes and her sterling silver spoons—she still doesn't have the knives and forks. Maybe we should give her at least a fork or two for Christmas. I should write that down so I don't forget. She told me on her last visit that someday her china and her spoons would be mine and Jason's.

I remember watching Jack across the table and thinking he must be in some kind of trouble; there was a lot of tension between him and his dad. Well, that hasn't changed.

Jack was quiet all through supper that night, but I could tell he was watching me. Afterwards we went into the living room and Dad told them a little bit about the mission. Then we knelt in a circle to pray—holding hands. Jack—I still think of him as Jack when I remember those days—made sure he was next to me. As the prayer went on and on and on, I felt Jack shaking and I could tell he was crying. I felt so sorry for him. When I squeezed his hand he looked up at me kinda surprised. The next month when he proposed he told me he had fallen in love with me when I squeezed his hand that night. Huh, maybe I should try squeezing his hand more often! I sometimes forget how really sensitive he is; I know he has a good heart; he's so good to people in need. I should have more patience with him. Not long ago he told me I reminded him of someone he had met in England during the war. I wonder if he was in love with her.

The telephone's ring shook her out of her reverie.

8:25 A.M.

The Jason Stevens office

Karis Radford was already waiting for Jason when he arrived at his office. Sitting primly in the outer office she looked up with questioning eyes when he came in. He nodded briefly to her, motioned for Laura Anderson to follow him, and entered his office closing the door behind him.

"Did you finish typing the revision of that report last night?" he asked without looking at her.

She stood, unflinching, before him. "Good morning, Dr. Stevens," she said.

"Good morning. Well?"

"I wasn't able to quite finish it. I stopped at 9:30 to go home."

"D—, you know I need that today."

"Dr. Stevens, I only took this job as a favor to T.W., I'm doing my best to put up with your rudeness, but I *will not* stand for profanity!"

"OK, OK, I'm sorry. That just slipped out."

"Sorry isn't good enough. I want your word that you will never curse in front of me again."

"All right, all right, I won't 'curse.' Now, when can you finish the report? I have to have it by ten this morning so it can be included in T.W.'s report for the board meeting. And, I don't want any typos, understand? It has to be perfect this time."

"My typing will be perfect; just as it was the *last* time. Anything else?"

"Just send in Karis Radford when I buzz you."

"Very well."

8:40 A.M.

Karis entered his office with apprehension replacing her usual confidence. "You wanted to see me, Dr. Stevens?"

"Yes, yes, I did," he said. He stood up, came around his desk and motioned toward the leather couch. "Come, sit here, it's more comfortable." *She reminds me of that picture of my mother when she was young.*

"What is it you wanted to see me about?" Karis asked, uneasy in his scrutiny.

"How are things going for you this year?"

"Well, uh, OK, fine. Why did you want to see me? Is there something wrong? Did my mother call you?"

Ignoring her questions he asked, "I hope you won't mind, but I have to ask you a personal question. Do you have a boyfriend?"

She looked at him in bewilderment. "Uh, no, not now. I did, but we broke up last week."

"I see," he said. "I understand that breakup was with Paul Bradley. Do you mind telling me why you broke up?"

Her face flushed and she looked at him in surprise. "I don't understand why you're asking this, Dr. Stevens."

"I'm asking because I've been receiving some disturbing notes during the last two days, and they were concerning you."

She looked at him more curious than alarmed. "Notes about me? What did they say?"

He watched her intently as he spoke. "They suggest that your breakup with Paul Bradley was because you have a secret lover. Could that be true?"

"No, no, of course not. That isn't true. I, well, I uh—"

He leaned his head so close to her that she could smell his cologne. "The notes claim that you are 'involved' with one of our male faculty members." Her face flushed crimson and she looked away from him. *She's guilty,* he thought. *Guilty as sin.* "It's true, isn't it?"

"No, I, I, what do you mean 'involved?' I haven't, that is we haven't" . . . her eyes welled with tears and her hands twisted in her lap.

"I think you know what that means. You're a very intelligent young woman. Surely I don't have to explain that tempting a faculty member to commit adultery is a very serious thing."

"But, Dr. Stevens, I haven't . . . all right, I admit, I was attracted to him, but I'm not 'involved' with him." She wiped the tears from her eyes and sat up straighter.

Jason studied her for a moment without comment. "Dr. Stevens, I give you my word that I will have nothing more to do with Mr. Rollin. I had already decided that."

"Karis, and I say this kindly, it's not fair, but the fact is that God places the responsibility in these affairs with the woman. Men are, that is, most men are—"

"—Please, Dr. Stevens. It's not necessary for you to go on. I have transferred out of his class and I will not be babysitting at his home again." She started to stand, but was restrained by his hand on her arm gently pushing her back down.

"Let me finish. As I started to say, men are not as strong as women are. Sometimes we're tempted more than we can control. A young teacher might become aroused just by noticing your figure in a sweater—like the one you have on now. Men can be ready for sexual intercourse at a moment's notice."

Frightened now, Karis tried to pull her arm away and, once more, tried to stand up. "Please, may I go now? I understand, really. It's not necessary for you to say anymore."

His hand moved upward to her shoulder and he tightened his grip as he pushed her back on the couch. "Look, I'm trying to be kind to you, but you're not making it easy. Don't you realize that I could—and maybe should—suspend you for what you're doing?"

"Yes, I know," she mumbled, fear in her voice. "Please, let me go, you're hurting me."

His grip on her shoulder tightened still more and she flinched with pain. "You'll go when I'm finished," he growled. He moved his face closer to hers as she cowered into the corner of the couch. "I know your type, you lead a man on, then refuse to satisfy him." And still his hand kept her from standing.

She tried to twist out of his grip. "Oh, no, please . . ."

The buzzer on his desk sounded, but he ignored it. It sounded again and again until, distracted, Jason took his hand from her shoulder, stood up and moved toward his desk. "You stay right there," he said with a scowl.

Karis immediately jumped up and rushed out of his office. Laura Anderson glanced up with surprise as Karis ran through her office and out the door.

In the hallway Karis stood for a moment rubbing her bruised shoulder. Finally, her eyes dry, her back straight, she strode back into the office, past a wondering Laura Anderson. Pulling open the door to Stevens' office she stood in the doorway, her eyes defiant, her lips in a determined line.

Jason Stevens stood up, his mouth open in surprise. "What do you want?" he asked

"How dare you talk to me like you did? Your behavior was uncalled for. You are despicable." Without waiting for a response she turned and walked with dignity out of the office.

Across the hall, through her open door, Peggy Kester watched the little drama unfold, but, as was her custom, she told no one.

Chapter 20

THE VALLEJO TIMES HERALD, May 1, 1968. RAPIST STRIKES AGAIN. A third city rape victim was found early this morning her eyes and mouth bound with duct tape. Police are reminding residents of North Napa to make sure doors and windows are securely locked at all times.

THE CAMPUS CRIER, May 1, 1968. The automatic sprinkling system on the football field which was recently re-timed to water the field during night hours is coming on unexpectedly at off times. Physical Plant is reminding students to make sure they are prepared to receive a surprise shower if they choose to walk on the football field.

Weekdays, from 11:30 A.M. until the one o'clock classes begin on the small secluded End-Time Christian College campus, there is a quiet interlude known as the "noontime lull." Faculty members retire to their nearby homes for lunch while in the college cafeteria students jockey for position in the gender-segregated food lines to make sure they emerge at the right moment to sit with the opposite-gendered student of their choice.

But, during the noontime lull on Wednesday, May the first, 1968, the people in this story did not follow that time-honored pattern.

Karis Radford, alone in her room, was strengthening her resolve to move on with her life after the difficult events of the past two weeks. Reflecting on her morning's meeting with the dean Karis wondered if she might have inherited some characteristics from Grandma Radford. It was evident that the kind of courage she had mustered that morning, as well as the temper she struggled to keep in check, could not have been inherited from her gentle, submissive mother.

In the college library Milly Munsell glanced at the empty chair which the late Dr. Max Baker had daily occupied before his death and she thought with real sadness that the subscription to the New York Times might as well be cancelled.

Mike Rollin, his eleven o'clock class in progress, was showing considerable less charm and enthusiasm in his lecture than usual; his thoughts were elsewhere. Sydney's firm decision to divorce him was more troubling than he had expected it to be. And then there was his pending appointment with Jason Stevens. That could mean trouble.

The "Acting" Academic Dean, Jason Stevens, was at home fuming about a "strictly personal" note he had received in the morning mail from the general. In the note he had made it clear he was expecting a close relationship with Jason *and his son.*

Eileen Stevens was at the Safeway supermarket in St. Helena shopping the weekend specials. She had purposely chosen the noontime lull to shop after a phone call from Laura Anderson had warned her that Jason was in a rage. Experience had taught her that the most effective response to her husband's temper was to be absent.

When the clock tower struck one bell, the noontime lull ended once more and, like an art tableaux come to life, the campus moved and mingled and laughed and worked and studied once again.

Chapter 21

3:30 P.M.

Office of the President

Peggy Kester was alone in the president's office. She had just finished the letter T.W. had dictated to her from his hotel room in Washington, D.C., where he was attending meetings.

Peggy didn't believe Christians should watch television, except for her church's programming, of course. Her evenings were spent quietly knitting or reading, but, she was quick to tell friends, her work was much more exciting than television and she got paid to live it. Anyone watching her typing on this day would not have suspected that she was all attention waiting for the second act of the drama that had started that morning in Jason Stevens' office.

Above her rapidly typing fingers Peggy discreetly observed Mike Rollin as he arrived for his appointment with Stevens. Laura Anderson, as usual, had left open the outer door to the hallway that separated their offices and Peggy had a direct view of Mike Rollin fidgeting in his chair as he waited for his appointment.

Peggy also knew what the meeting was about. She had read the memo Stevens had written to T.W. and she had typed T.W.'s reply. Mike Rollin was in BIG trouble.

When Stevens finally arrived he motioned for Mike to come into his office and the door was closed. Peggy Kester turned the page on her steno pad and began to type another letter.

Her concentration was broken abruptly fifteen minutes later. Stevens' office door flew open and slammed against a file cabinet in the corner. Windows rattled. She watched in amazement as Mike Rollin stalked out into the hall and then quickly ran out the front door and down the steps. Moments later she heard Laura Anderson gasp.

Jason Stevens was lying on the floor. He was not moving and blood was oozing from his nose and mouth.

3:45 P.M.

With trembling fingers Mike unlocked his parked Mustang while his mind reeled with what had just happened. *You stupid fool! You hit him, maybe you killed him! Alright, he had no business saying that, and maybe he wants Karis himself, but, Oh, God, why did I hit him! What am I going to do?*

His tires squealed in complaint as Mike drove, as though possessed, away from the back of his office building and around the dormitories to the end of the campus. Students who were used to seeing his sporty red car speeding by waved as he passed, but he saw no one. When he reached the edge of the campus he hesitated, his eyes shifting from side to side in indecision. Then, abruptly, he turned right toward Ink Grade Road. *I have to get away. I have to think. You stupid fool. You hit him! You knocked him down! What if he's hurt bad? What if he's dead?*

Ink Grade Road, a narrow twisting road on the east side of the mountain, is a favorite destination of hikers as well as a haunt of rattlesnakes and an occasional mountain lion. The few houses are hidden behind thick foliage and in winter the road is treacherous in the frequent fogs. Still, for those not prone to car-sickness, spectacular views of the valley below are the reward for driving the hazardous road. Mike was in no mood to appreciate the view. Speeding as he came into a sharp left curve he heard a loud "bang". He knew immediately that a tire had blown. As he struggled to keep control of the car his foot slipped and accidentally hit the gas pedal. The shiny red Mustang left the road and was quickly airborne. In the seconds before his car crashed into a hillside he thought of Benji and he screamed. Then there was only darkness.

3:46 P.M.

Jason Stevens' office

Peggy Kester and Laura Anderson were not excitable women, but a fist fight? In the Dean's office? Maybe even a murder? This was definitely a new experience. After an initial flurry of hand-wringing and shocked indecision Peggy Kester took charge. "Close the door, Laura, and lock it," she said, her voice returning to its normal pitch.

"Oh, Peggy, what should we do? Should I call an ambulance?"

"Not yet. Let's see how bad he is first." They knelt together beside the body, careful not to get blood on their good suits.

Peggy, feeling the pulse in his neck, looked at the pale-faced Laura and said, "He's still alive, just out cold. He'll probably be alright."

Laura wiped her forehead with the 'hanky' she kept stuffed in her sleeve. "Well, that's a relief. I thought sure he was dead."

Together they wiped the blood from Jason's face with a paper towel and tried to sponge the few drops of blood from the carpet. Peggy brought a cushion from her office and while Laura gingerly lifted his head Peggy slipped it beneath him. Covering him with a small blanket she found in the closet they left him lying on the office floor and closed the door.

Peggy, still in charge, said, "Now, Laura, keep the outer door locked and don't answer it if anyone knocks, then open the door to his office so you can keep your eye on him. If anything changes call me."

"Shouldn't we let someone know what happened? Maybe call a doctor or his wife?"

"Not until I've talked with T.W. I don't think he'll want this to be bandied about. Hmm, let's see, it's after six in Washington. I might be able to reach him in one of the Assembly guest rooms. I'll call right away and let you know what he wants us to do."

4:30 P.M.

Laura Anderson was talking on the telephone, having taken her eyes off "the body" in the inner office for only a moment, when Jason Stevens came to. He sat up, groggy, more embarrassed than hurt. Holding onto the edge of his desk he pulled himself up to a standing position and stood still for a minute to regain his equilibrium. Then he sat down at his desk, took a deep breath and opened the folder that held the day's mail.

"Oh, Dr. Stevens, thank goodness, you're awake," said Laura hurrying into his office. "We've all been so worried. Can I get you something? Some water?"

"No, no. I'm alright. I need to get some work done and then I'm going home." He opened his desk drawer and pulled out a tissue—kept for distraught students—and flinched as he dabbed at the blood dripping from his nose. *He broke my nose. I'll get him for this.*

He looked at Laura still standing in front of his desk with compassion on her face. "You can go now."

"Peggy has a call in to T.W. in Washington. I'm sure he'll want to talk to you."

"No, no, NO! I don't want T.W. to hear about this. You tell Mrs. Kester that she's not to blab this to T.W. or to anyone else. And, that goes for you, too. Understand?"

Laura's eyes took on a distinctly hurt look. "We were only trying to help, Dr. Stevens. We were very worried about you."

"All right, all right, I apologize, but I don't want this to get out. What if the newspapers get hold of this? Think what that would do to the reputation of the college."

"Well . . . all right, but you were unconscious for nearly an hour. You really should have a doctor examine you."

"I told you, I'm alright. So, I got a bloody nose and a loose tooth. I'll go to the dentist. It's no big deal. I can take care of myself, so just get out and leave me alone."

Laura shut his door with just enough force to let him know that she was angry; but not enough for it to be called slamming; executive secretaries do not slam doors. *That ungrateful wretch,* she thought, *we should have just left him there to bleed to death.*

206

Chapter 22

4:40 P.M.

The women's dorm

"Hi, Can I help you?" Crystal, the afternoon receptionist smiled encouragingly at Matt Whittaker who stood before her holding a plate wrapped in wax paper. He looked extremely uncomfortable. She had recognized her bathmate's brother immediately from seeing him several times with Joan. He looked nicer close up, cuter, but his long hair and beard still marked him as an outsider at best, maybe even as a hippy.

"Is Joan Whittaker or her roommate in?" He spoke in a subdued voice as though trying to match its sound to his surroundings.

"Let me buzz their room and find out." She spoke into the loudspeaker, JOAN WHITTAKER YOU HAVE A VISITOR IN THE LOBBY.

She looked at Matt and smiled again. "She'll be down in a minute. Why don't you have a seat."

He looked around and then sat carefully on the edge of a pink upholstered chair in the parlor, his eyes fixed on the carpet. *Poor guy, he looks like he's really embarrassed to be here. He's kinda cute. I wonder if he has a girlfriend.*

Crystal watched him, surreptitiously, until Joan came through the double doors from the hall, greeted him, and led him to a private corner of the parlor where they couldn't be seen from the lobby.

207

4:55 P.M.

Jason Stevens' office

When Jason walked through her office to leave for home Laura didn't bother to look up. She was still put out at his lack of gratitude—and even more by his rudeness. *Imagine! In an End-Time school! It's no wonder the Lord hasn't come yet. I must speak to T.W. about his behavior.* She glanced at the clock and decided to leave a little early. It had been a hard day.

4:55 P.M.

The women's dorm

As Karis Radford entered the lobby from her room she slipped a small volume of the psalms into her jacket pocket, smiled at Crystal, her bath mate and friend since childhood, and signed out for a walk. Leaving the rear door of the lobby she waved at Matt, who was just getting into his colorfully decorated, borrowed VW van, and began to walk toward the steps that led across the athletic field to the woods behind the elementary school.

4:55 P.M.

Still sitting in the VW behind the dorm Matt Whittaker hesitated before turning the ignition. Finally, taking a long look at the window of his sister's room, he started the van and drove slowly away.

4:58 P.M.

As Karis reached the steps that descended to the athletic field she glanced quickly at the first line of Psalm 130, then looked up and began to quietly say the ancient words she was memorizing; *Out of the depths have I cried unto Thee, O Lord. Lord, hear my voice . . .*

5:00 P.M.

Milly Munsell left the library precisely at five o'clock. She walked past the Prep school building and down the driveway to the path that led along the edge of the athletic field to the elementary school.

5:00 P.M.

Jason Stevens, driving along the campus peripheral road noticed the same hippy VW van he had seen on campus before and made a mental note to call security when he got home. Driving toward the athletic field he noticed Karis Radford walking on the path that led to the elementary school. Anger and curiosity mixed with a familiar excitement, arose within him.

5:03 P.M.

Karis walked onto the playground of the little elementary school and sat down on one of the swings. Swinging slowly, her eyes closed, she willed herself to forget Mike Rollin as David's cry to the Lord became hers, *I wait for the Lord, my soul doth wait, and in his word do I hope.* The words filled her mind with a peace she hadn't felt for days.

5:03 P.M.

When he heard the siren Matt Whittaker pulled the VW over to the side of the road beside the college welcome sign and watched as a police car and ambulance went speeding by toward Ink Grade Road. Instead of moving back onto the road immediately he sat there staring straight ahead and thinking again of the possible consequences of what he was planning to do.

5:03 P.M.

Turning away from the highway toward his home on Cold Springs Road, Jason Stevens tasted blood in his mouth as his tongue played with the loose tooth. *I'll get that jerk for this,* he thought again, *no one hits a Stevenson and gets away with it.* His head was throbbing and his mind was still churning with fury when he glanced toward the elementary playground and saw Karis swinging slowly back and forth. He slowed and then stopped the car and watched her until she got off the swing, walked behind the small elementary gym and disappeared into the woods.

5:08 P.M.

Milly Munsell had just reached the elementary school property when she saw Karis get up from the playground swing and walk behind the gym into the woods. As Milly cut through the school grounds she noticed Dean Stevens parked across the street in front of her house and her heart skipped a beat. *I wonder if he could be waiting for me!* At this exciting thought her steps quickened to an almost run—within proper limits of librarian decorum. Disappointed that he didn't even look up when she passed by his car she quickly slipped into the side door of her small home.

By July the mass of purple flowers on the clematis vine that covered the trellis on Milly's front porch would provide an impenetrable shady refuge from the heat, but this early in spring there were only leaves. Squinting a little, Milly watched the dean get out of his car and move toward the rear of the elementary gym. *Whatever can he be doing back there?* She moved closer and pushed aside some of the leaves, her earlier surge of hope in a possible visit fading as he disappeared from view.

Twenty minutes later, her light supper finished, she was sitting on the porch rocking, her cat on her lap, when she saw the dean emerge from the woods carrying someone. *My goodness, he's carrying that girl who was swinging a few minutes ago. I wonder what's wrong with her.* Dumping the cat off her lap, she jumped up and hurried down off the porch. Just as she reached the street Jason Stevens drove away with Karis in his car.

Chapter 23

5:50 P.M.

The Stevens home

Jason, a queasy feeling in his stomach, walked quickly away from the guest room where Eileen was consoling a hysterical Karis. Standing in the hallway outside the closed guest room door his five-year old son, Davie, was crying softly. Jason picked him up and carried him into his teddy-bear decorated bedroom. After Davie was comforted and assured that "the lady got hurt but she'll be alright pretty soon" and that "Mommy will tell you about it when the lady feels better," he left him, subdued, but playing quietly with his new kitten. Then, taking a deep breath and straightening his shoulders Jason went into his study, closed the door and dialed a number.

"T.W.? This is Jason. I hope the meetings have been going well. I wouldn't disturb you but we had an incident today that I knew you'd want to know about as soon as possible."

"What kind of incident?"

"Well, driving home from the office today I heard someone screaming behind the elementary school gym. I stopped to investigate and I found one of the dorm girls all bound up with duct tape on a jogging path. She'd been roughed up and is claiming that someone had tried to rape her."

"Was she really raped? Is she OK? Where is she now?"

211

"She's here. She's bruised but it doesn't look serious. I don't think she was actually raped. She passed out when I took the tape off and tried to get her to stand up so I carried her out and brought her home with me. Eileen is taking care of her now."

"That was good thinking. Thank Eileen for me. Have you called her parents or the police?"

"No, she doesn't want us to, and considering what would happen if the papers got hold of this, I decided that it was better to follow her wishes."

"Well, you're probably right, still, her parents will have to be told something. Who's the girl?"

"It's Karis Radford."

"What? Oh, too bad. She's one of our most promising seniors."

"Yes, she is, but remember, she's also the girl who's been chasing Mike Rollin."

"Do you think Rollin might have—?"

"—Oh, I doubt that. Why should he? He's already getting . . . uh, I mean, I'm sure it wasn't anyone on the faculty. I think it was probably one of those hippies that have been hanging around lately. I saw that VW van on campus again just as I left the office."

"Well call me tomorrow and let me know how she is and let me know if you find out anything else. I'll come back right away if necessary. Meantime tell Karis that I'm praying for her."

"Of course. I'll tell her. I'm sure it won't be necessary for you to come back early; I can handle it. I'll call you tomorrow."

6:00 P.M.

The Terry and Jane Miller home

Terry and Jane Miller were in the dining room eating dinner when the telephone in the kitchen rang. Terry took another quick bite before reluctantly getting up to answer.

"Miller house."

"May I speak to Dr. Miller?"

Terry Miller heard the anxiety in the speaker's voice and immediately signaled to this wife that it was for her.

212

"Dr. Miller? This is Eileen Stevens. I'm sorry to disturb you at home, but we have an emergency, and—" her voice broke into a choking sob and for a moment she couldn't continue.

"What is it, Mrs. Stevens?" asked Dr. Jane Miller, the college physician.

"I think one of our girls may have been, uh, ra, ra, raped," she stammered, tears in her voice. "She was beaten up too and she's—"

"—Someone was raped? On campus?"

"Yes, well, not actually on campus. It happened in the woods behind the elementary gym. Jason, uh, my husband, heard her screaming and found her all beaten up on a jogging path. Could you possibly come over? She's very frightened and in a lot of pain."

"Of course, I'll be right over. Or, better yet, why don't you take her down to the hospital and I'll meet you there."

"She won't go to the hospital. I wanted to take her there but she refused. She seems very frightened, I think she was threatened."

"I'll be right over." Jane Miller, M.D. quickly retrieved her medical bag from the hall closet and hurried out the kitchen door to her car. Hearing his wife's urgent responses Terry Miller knew this sounded like a potential story for the paper. He grabbed his camera, patted his pocket to make sure he had pad and pen, and ran out the door just in time to intercept his wife's car as she backed out of the garage. They were at the Stevens' home in less than three minutes.

Eileen Stevens, an anxious look on her face, was waiting at the door. "Oh, Dr. Miller. Thank you for coming. This is so awful." Seeing Terry behind his wife she hesitated, "Oh, Dr., uh, Mr. Miller, would you mind waiting in the living room? My husband's in there. He found her and he's very concerned."

"Sure, Mrs. Stevens."

In the Stevens' living room Jason sat tilted back in his recliner reading the Napa Register, a can of 7up on the table beside him.

"Terry, good of you to come along. Sit down, sit down. How are things going in your department? Would you like a soda?"

Terry, struck by the nonchalance of the greeting and the casual body language, refused the drink, took the proffered chair, and pulled out his reporter's pad and pen. "Why don't you give me the details of what happened."

Jason lowered the recliner, put down the paper and picked up his can of 7up before he answered. "Terry—I hope you don't mind if I call you Terry—I know you work for the Register and probably would like to get a 'scoop', but" . . . he took a long swallow of his 7up and burped discreetly before answering, "I hope you'll consider the girl's wishes before you decide to give out this incident for public consumption."

"The Register doesn't print the names of rape victims; her identity will be protected."

"Well, but even a mention of the, uh, incident would raise questions in people's minds. You may not be aware of this, but the college policy is to handle these incidents internally to save embarrassment to the victim and, of course, to the college. Also, I'm sure your wife would agree, it would just frighten the other girls unnecessarily."

"With all due respect, Dr. Stevens, that's a very poor policy. This is bound to get out and it's always best to get the facts out 'up front' rather than to try to gloss them over afterward"

"Well, I'm afraid I must insist that you keep this confidential—at least until T.W. has had an opportunity to decide how we will handle it. After he clears it I'll see that you personally get all the relevant details. Fair enough?"

"But, I understand that T.W. will be gone for the rest of the week. I couldn't keep this quiet that long even if I wanted to; it's bound to come out."

"Come on Terry," he leaned forward, "I wouldn't say this in front of the women, but, after all he didn't really hurt her. He just tried to have sex with her. Who knows, she may even have asked for it. I know this girl."

Terry looked at Jason with amazement. "That sounds a bit heartless; your wife said she was beaten up."

"My wife tends to exaggerate sometimes. She has a few bruises, nothing serious; some women like it rough, they tell me, and this could just be that."

"I can't believe you said that! You know the girl? Who is it?"

"Remember—this is strictly confidential. Her name is Karis Radford."

"Karis Radford? Isn't she Paul Bradley's girlfriend?"

"*Was* his girlfriend. I understand he broke it off. She was also, and again this is absolutely not for publication, having an affair with a faculty member. And, she's been seen around campus several times with a couple of hippies. Frankly, I think that's who was probably responsible for what happened to her."

Jason took another swallow of his 7up, put the can down on the table and leaned forward again toward Terry. "Just between you and me, I suspect the reason she's so adamant that this doesn't get out is that she's afraid Bradley will find out about her 'extra-curricular' activities. She probably wants to get back with him and knows that he'd never marry her if he found out what's been going on. And, of course, she's right about that. No Assembly committee would call a ministerial intern with a promiscuous wife. Now, do you understand why this has to be kept out of the paper?"

"Still, if there was an attempted rape near the college we should be warning the other girls and we need to—"

"—Terry, Terry, this could easily have been a consensual thing that got out of hand. Just this morning I counseled Karis about her affair with the faculty member and I've asked the girl's dean to talk to her about her provocative clothes." He tilted the recliner back again and rested his feet on the foot rest before he continued.

"We had a similar case back East once, but we were able to keep it under wraps and it turned out better for all concerned."

Terry's skepticism was obvious. "Oh? What happened to the girl?"

"She was counseled to leave school for awhile and then to transfer to another college. We were able to keep the whole thing quiet, which was what they both wanted. I understand she's happily married now."

"And the boy? What happened to him?"

"Well, the administration gave him a good talking-to and he was suspended for a couple of weeks. He was basically a good kid, later became an administrative trainee at the G.A. and he's in The Lord's Work today. That would never have happened if there had been a lot of publicity."

Terry just sat shaking his head in disbelief.

"I spoke to T.W. on the phone just a little while ago and he assured me that he wanted this handled confidentially. But, don't take my word for it; talk to him about it when he gets back."

"I'm sorry, I just don't agree with you. Keeping a serious crime quiet is not good for the college, or for The Lord's Work, and I'm *very sure* it's not good for the victim."

Stevens, his face flushing with annoyance took his feet off the foot rest and pulled himself upright again. "Well then, you should at least consider the girl's feelings. She's the one who should make the decision and she's insisting that we tell no one—not even her mother."

Neither man had paid any heed to the little curly-headed boy who had entered the room and stood quietly tugging on his father's sleeve.

"Davie? Honey, Daddy is busy now. Shouldn't you be in bed?" Jason's face visibly softened when he looked down at the beautiful child.

"Daddy", he whispered, "Is the lady really going to be all right?"

"Yes, Honey. Mommy and Dr. Miller are taking good care of her. She'll feel better tomorrow."

"I'll let her play with my kitty if she wants to, and maybe we could give her some ice cream."

"I think she'd like that. Why don't you ask her tomorrow? I think it's your bedtime now. Come, say good night to Mr. Miller and then give me a hug."

"G'night, Mr. Miller."

As Davie was hugging his father his mother entered the room followed by Jane Miller. "Come on Honey, it's your bedtime," Eileen said as she disengaged Davie from his father's embrace.

Jason and Terry rose at the same time and asked Jane in unison, "How is she?"

"Her injuries are painful, but not too serious. Emotionally however she's in very bad shape. She was still close to hysteria when I arrived, but I gave her a shot and she's quieted down. I've alerted the Emergency Room at the hospital that I'm bringing her in, and—"

"—Dr. Miller, you said she wasn't seriously hurt; is it really necessary to take her to the hospital?"

216

"Yes, it is necessary. I need to have some tests done and I need to gather the forensic evidence for the police investigation."

Clearly annoyed Stevens stood up and moved closer to her; a ploy he had found useful in intimidating female teachers. "You should have cleared this with me first. College policy is that we look into student accidents ourselves before outsiders are involved. I must insist that you cooperate by not involving the police."

Dr. Jane Miller was not easily intimidated. She stood up straighter and looked steadily at him. "I can't do that Dr. Stevens. As a physician I am legally obligated to report this to the police, but even if that were not the law I'd do it anyway. I want this animal caught before he tries to hurt her again—as she says he threatened repeatedly to do."

Stevens' face turned red and his eyes narrowed. "Very well, if you refuse to cooperate I must insist that I be the one who reports the incident to the police."

She shrugged, "As you wish. In any case the police will be given the evidence and my report, but since you're the one who found her I'm sure they'll want to talk to you first."

Turning to Terry she said, "The police will want the clothes she's wearing for evidence so will you go over to the dorm, pick up some things for her to put on and take them to the hospital? I've called her roommate and she'll have a package waiting for you at the reception desk. Mrs. Stevens will go with me in her car to take Karis to the hospital."

"Dr. Stevens, . . ." Jane paused and looked at him more closely. "Dr. Stevens, are you alright? You look a little faint and your nose is bleeding. Have you been hurt?"

Terry quickly pulled a handkerchief from his jacket pocket and handed it to Jason who held it to his nose. A red stain immediately appeared. Still holding the handkerchief to his nose Jason put his other hand on the arm of the chair to steady himself from the disorientation he suddenly felt. After a short time the bleeding stopped and Jason seemed to have recovered. Terry extended his hand for the handkerchief and Jason, with a nod of thanks, gave it to him.

"I'm fine," he said to Jane, "I bumped into a cabinet door in my office. It's nothing."

Jane Miller's trained eye noted the momentary glazing of Stevens' eyes, the scratches on his hands and another small gash on the side of his face. *There's something fishy here,* she thought.

Jason, his composure restored, turned annoyed eyes on Jane. "I suppose you told the roommate just what happened."

She looked at him in disgust. "Don't worry, I was discreet. I told her that Karis wasn't feeling well and that she'd be all right after a few days' rest."

She turned to Terry. "Let me use your camera. I should take some pictures of her injuries here before we go. She'd be more comfortable—"

She was interrupted immediately by Stevens. "—No! Absolutely not. There will be no pictures taken in my home. You're going too far, Dr. Miller."

Terry looked at him in disbelief, "What are you afraid of, Stevens? Afraid they might implicate you?"

While Jason glowered at Terry, Jane put her hand on her husband's arm. "It's all right, Honey, just give me your camera. I'll take the pictures at the hospital."

Shaking his head in disgust Terry handed her the camera and walked out the door.

"Dr. Miller," said Eileen quietly, "Karis is ready to go. We can take her out through the kitchen door." Turning to Jason she said, "Davie is in bed and he's waiting for you to tuck him in."

Jason watched them go before he walked into the hall toward Davie's room. *How dare she lecture me? Just who does she think she is coming in here and acting like she's the one in charge. And, her husband—he'd just better watch his step. I'm still the dean.* Without warning the same disorientation he had felt before came again and he eased himself down into his chair and sat with his head in his hands until it passed.

11:30 that night

The women's dorm

Joan Whittaker picked up the telephone and was surprised to hear her mother crying. "Mom? Mom, what's wrong?"

. . . "Yes, I did see Matt. Just this afternoon. He brought Karis and me a piece of his birthday cake."

. . . "Mom, please, don't cry. I'm sure he's OK. He's probably off celebrating his birthday with some of his friends. I guess I don't understand why you're so upset; he's often out this late."

. . . "Oh Mom, I'm sure he wouldn't leave for Canada without telling us."

. . . "Yes, he told me the other day that a couple of his friends were leaving, but I'm quite sure they left sometime ago."

. . . "Yes, of course. I'll call you right away if I hear from him. Do you want me to come home?"

. . . "OK, if you're sure. Please don't worry. He'll probably show up home any minute."

. . . "I know Mom, I love you too."

Joan hung up the phone and stood in place for a moment trying to replay in her mind her brother's visit. *Come to think of it he did seem different today, quieter, more thoughtful. I wonder . . .*

Chapter 24

1:30 A.M.

The next morning

It was after midnight before Eileen Stevens brought Karis back from the hospital emergency room. The medication given her had taken its intended effect and she was unresponsive to Eileen's murmured comments. As Eileen slipped over her head the nightgown that her roommate had sent from the dorm she was shocked at the large dark bruises on her breasts and at the raw, nasty-looking scrapes on her arms and legs. It looked to Eileen as if she had been beaten first and then dragged in gravel.

Karis slept intermittently. No matter which way she turned in bed the pain from the bruises and cuts kept partially waking her, but each time as the medication gave her relief she slept again.

7:45 A.M.

For a moment Karis couldn't imagine where she was or why she hurt so much. Then the memory of horror flooded her senses with a sickening immediacy. At first it was the smell, a mixture of dirt and perspiration and a somehow-familiar cologne, but that was soon overwhelmed by the voice; guttural, menacing, shouting obscenities, threatening to hurt her, to kill her. She could feel his hands on her breasts and the searing pain from his pinches; she could feel his—suddenly she couldn't breath, she turned her face to the wall and began to cry with great gulping sobs.

After awhile her sobbing dwindled to whimpers and she felt a small hand touch her arm. Half turning she saw a little boy in pajamas standing by the bed with a kitten in his arms.

"You can play with my kitty if you want to." The little boy looked as if he might cry along with her. "That's what I do when I'm sad," he said softly.

Karis' answer, through lips swollen and cut, was muffled and low. "Thank you. Who are you?"

"I'm Davie Stevens and I'm five years old now because I just had a birthday. What's wrong with your face? Does it hurt? Is that why you're crying?"

"I was, uh, I got hurt last night and it does hurt a little." She tried to smile but her face felt stiff and sore and her eyes hurt too much to keep them open.

"Davie, come out and don't bother Karis. You can talk with her later when she feels better. Bring the kitty with you. It's time for you to get ready for pre-school."

Eileen shooed Davie out of the room and handed Karis a glass of water and a pink pill. "The doctor left this pill for you to take. She said it would help you sleep a little longer." She helped support Karis as she tried to sit up and then waited while she swallowed the pill. "I'll be right here if you need me. I'll check on you after I get Davie ready for pre-school. My husband is taking him this morning so I can stay here with you."

When she was alone again Karis closed her eyes and tried to sleep but the growing realization of what had happened to her inundated her thoughts and she began to sob again. After a long while, her tears exhausted, she slept.

8:15 A.M.

The college library

A dour Dr. Moore entered the library expecting his usual flirty smile from Milly Munsell. His trips to the library were always brightened by what he perceived as her infatuation with him. It had been a long, long time since anyone had shown him that kind of attention. *Very gratifying*, he told himself, *very gratifying, indeed*. But, for the first time ever, he was disappointed; she didn't seem to even notice him as he stood there waiting expectantly.

Milly Munsell wasn't noticing anyone this morning. She sat unmoving behind the counter of the reference desk distracted and flustered by indecision. *Should I tell someone? But, what if I get that nice man in trouble over something entirely innocent? But, my goodness it certainly didn't look innocent.*

"Of course, Dear, you'll find it on the third shelf, near the end," she told the student asking her a question for the second time. *Who should I tell? Maybe T.W.? No, he's out of town. Maybe I should just ask Dr. Stevens himself about it? No, that might not be wise. I just know he was carrying the same girl that I saw on the playground. But, surely that good man wouldn't hurt her. Oh, I just don't know what to do.*

"No, no, of course you can't take it out! It's a reference book," she said with uncharacteristic sharpness to the surprised student standing before her desk. She sighed then and smiled in apology at the student, "I'm sorry. Can I help you find what you need?"

I know, I'll ask May Wyant what to do. She's the girl's dean, she should be told about this. Relieved that the decision was made Milly looked up just as Dr. Moore walked by the counter. She gave him her usual sweet smile and his step quickened as he left the library.

8:50 A.M.

The Stevens home

By the time Dr. Jane Miller arrived to check on Karis the pill Eileen had given her had taken effect and Karis slept though the thorough examination.

"How is she?" Eileen asked when Dr. Miller came out of the bedroom..

"Not good. It looks like the rape itself was not successful—she is still a virgin—but what went on during the attempt was almost as bad. Those deep bruises where that monster pinched her will take a long time to heal . . . and the emotional toll will be high. The Sheriff will be here to talk to her in about an hour. She should be awake by then. Talking to the police will be very difficult for her so after he leaves give her these two pills. She will probably be very distraught so stay near her as much as you can. She shouldn't be left alone for very long right now."

"Couldn't we ask the Sheriff to wait a few days until she feels better? Poor little lamb, she's in such misery."

"He won't want to wait. It'll be hard for her, I know, but it's critical to the investigation. She may be able to identify who did this to her. I have to go now, but call me at the hospital if you need me. If I don't hear from you I'll stop back this evening."

9:30 A.M.

Office of the college president

Still keeping her eye on the happenings in Jason's office, Peggy Kester picked up the ringing telephone. "Good morning. Dr. Patton's office."

"Peggy?"

"Oh, good morning, T.W., I'm glad you called." She glanced down at her 'REPORT TO T.W.' list. The list was longer than usual—and much more interesting. She took a deep breath and began to read.

REPORT TO T.W.

1. Dean's altercation with Mike Rollin (actions taken)
2. Mike Rollin's subsequent disappearance Front page news story about accident in newspaper (read)
3. Police in Dean's office (questions asked)
4. Call from Clayton Wolfe (daughter reported "strange goings-on" late night in dorm. Stopped payment on last check)
5. Furious call from Dean May Wyant. (Claims she was not informed about a rape on campus. Getting calls from parents.)
6. Letter received signed by 5 students about Mike Rollin (flirtations and anti-war comments in class. Want him fired)

7. Letters from several constituents with usual complaints and suggestions for changes
8. Suggest you return (ASAP)

When the phone conversation with her boss was finished Peggy Kester leaned back in her secretarial chair and folded her hands behind her head. *Yes, indeed, her job was definitely better than television.* She turned, contented, back to her typewriter and opened her shorthand pad.

10:00 A.M.

En route to the Stevens home

Sheriff Tom Whittaker was troubled. The disappearance of his son, Matt, at about the same time this attempted rape of his daughter's roommate was committed, was a disturbing coincidence—if it *was* a coincidence. Matt's recent run-in with the Calistoga police and his wife's comment that Matt was acting like he might be using drugs came to mind. Then there was Joan's report that Matt had a crush on Karis and had been on campus just before 5 p.m. *No! Not Matt! He may have some problems, but rape? Never.*

After his second interview with Jason Stevens his immediate, visceral, reaction was that Stevens himself was probably the "perp." Stevens had tried to convince him that some "hippie" he'd seen around campus did it. *Was Matt who he'd seen?* Stevens, however, looked like he'd been in some kind of struggle and his story sounded like fiction. Tom was quite sure that when they had the lab results from the crime scene and from the girl's clothing it would show Stevens' involvement. Nevertheless, he was uneasy. *I just wish I knew where Matt was.*

He wasn't looking forward to interviewing Karis either. It was always hard for a rape victim to talk about her ordeal and these End-Time girls were especially sheltered from such things.

Driving into the Stevens' driveway he wondered just how safe Karis was to be staying in the home of the man who might be the one who tried to rape her.

225

10:30 A.M.

The Stevens home

After the Sheriff left Eileen returned to the bedroom and found Karis sitting up in bed sobbing. After giving her the pills Dr. Miller had left she sat down beside her, put her arms carefully around her and held her while softly singing one of the lullabies she sang to quiet Davie.

As the medication began to take effect and Karis' sobbing quieted Eileen carefully eased her down on the bed, covered her and stood looking down at her. *Poor child. So young and vulnerable. She must be very pretty when her face isn't swollen. She has the same black curls and blue eyes that Davie has; if I had a daughter she might have looked a lot like her.*

She wondered how Karis' mother would act when she arrived later in the day. She hoped, for Karis' sake, that her mother was the comforting type.

Suddenly she remembered Jane Miller's words . . . "her breasts had been savagely pinched" . . . and a cold chill went through her. Her own breasts had been pinched and bruised more than once . . . by her own husband. She was still shaking from the ugly thought when the phone rang.

"Mrs. Stevens?" asked the distinctive voice of her husband's secretary. "Dr. Stevens asked me to let you know that he will not be coming home for lunch today and possibly not for dinner either. He'll call you later."

"Thank you," she answered, relieved. She didn't want to face him while she harbored such terrible thoughts.

226

Chapter 25

11:10 A.M.

Like her mother before her Eileen Stevens made soup when there was trouble at home. She was cutting up vegetables when the doorbell rang. She wiped her hands on her apron and went to the door. A clearly distraught woman stood there.

"Mrs. Stevens? I'm Karis' mother. Can I see her please? How is she?" Katherine was trembling and close to tears.

"She's sleeping right now. Won't you come in and sit down?"

"No, please, just let me see her. No one will tell me what happened to her. Is she alright?"

"She's alright. Come. Have a cup of tea first and I'll tell you everything I know. It's best if you know before you see her. But, she's going to be fine." Eileen took Katherine's arm and drew her into the kitchen. "After we talk I'll take you in to see her."

Please God, give me the right words, let me help her to cope, Eileen prayed, as she prepared and poured the tea.

"What happened? Please. Tell me," Katherine said, her voice anxious and quivering with unspent tears.

"I'll tell you as much as I know. Last evening my husband was driving home from the office when he heard someone screaming in the woods behind the elementary school gym. He stopped the car, ran toward the screams and found Karis there.

"What? What do you mean 'found her there'?" Katherine's voice rose in near hysteria. "Is she . . . is she . . . no! No! She's dead?" Katherine stood up trembling so hard that Eileen thought she might collapse.

Eileen went quickly around the table and put her arm around her shoulder. "No, no, no, she's not dead. She's going to be OK. I don't think her life was ever in danger. She has some bad bruises and scrapes, but she'll be alright."

"What happened? Tell me. Did someone try to kill her?"

"Someone tried to rape her—but they didn't succeed, thank God. However, it was a very frightening time for her and she was hurt, but it was not life-threatening."

"Where is she? Can I see her now? Please, take me to her."

"Of course, come this way. Be prepared though; her face is badly swollen and she hasn't seen herself in a mirror yet."

Karis was sitting on the edge of the bed when Katherine came in. One side of her face had already turned an ugly blue and her eyes and mouth were swollen nearly shut. She ran into her mother's arms with a cry.

"Mama, I . . ."

"Shh, shh, It's alright, Honey. Don't try to talk. I'm here now and I'm going to take you home where you'll be safe."

"Oh, Mama, it was so terrible. I tried to fight, but he was so strong—"

"—I know, Honey. I know you did. I'm so sorry this happened to you. We'll talk about it later when you're better. I'm here now and I won't let anyone hurt you ever again."

Eileen Stevens backed out of the room and closed the door as mother and daughter cried together.

After a while Katherine opened the door and Eileen heard her say, "All right, Honey, lie back down. We'll talk later. Try to sleep if you can. I'm going to go get your things from the dorm and as soon as you feel up to it we'll go home. Daddy is so worried about you."

After packing up Karis' things from her dorm room, and reassuring her roommate, Katherine drove slowly away from the campus. Suddenly her mind filled with the horrific detailed memories of her own humiliation; memories she had pushed to the back of conscious thought for many years. Mindlessly she drove on past the small hospital where Karis had been treated and on down the mountain. Somehow she found herself stopped on a narrow dirt service road within a vineyard, and there, in the beautiful valley, she cried. Amidst the few remaining mustard plants, and the new bright green leaves, her weeping grew into loud, wrenching cries that could no longer be contained in the car. She got out, for only the earth and sky had room for her despair. It was as though the hard ball of sorrow that had so long been resident in her had suddenly grown to an unmanageable size and was now pushing up through her body, rising up her throat to escape. The beauty around her seemed to mock her. Her darling little girl, her only joy, her very life blood; was nothing sacred? She shook her fist toward the sky and screamed, "How could you? *How could you?*"

4:30 P.M.

The Mike and Sydney Rollin home

Sydney wasn't sure whether she should be angry or worried. Mike hadn't come home the night before. That wasn't like him. All night she had waited, her bed cold and empty without him. *He was so angry at me when he left and so upset about Jim's death . . . I should have believed him. I should have been more understanding. I shouldn't have told him about the divorce . . . but still, he could at least call. Maybe he was telling the truth about him and Karis. Maybe he really does love me like he said. Oh God, let him be OK and bring him back to us.*

Sydney was still praying when the message came.

11:30 P.M.

The Stevens home

Katherine lay quietly in the twin bed across the room from Karis wishing they were home. Each time she heard Karis moan or cry out in her sleep she knew the doctor had been right to insist she stay one more night, but she had a strange feeling that she couldn't quite shake. Eileen Stevens had been very helpful and kind, and their little boy had helped to distract Karis from her torment, but . . . there was definitely something unnerving about this home that made her uneasy. She turned toward the wall, closed her eyes and willed herself to go to sleep. She needed to be strong for Karis and for the long drive home tomorrow.

Still half awake three hours later she suddenly had the sensation that someone was in the room. Slowly, slowly she turned her head toward the door, straining to see in the darkness. Did she see someone or was it her imagination? Did something move? Was that a quiet step? It was closer now, she could smell a faint fragrance that was eerily familiar. Someone was here . . . they were leaning over Karis. "Who's there?" she whispered as she sat up, her muscles tensed in fear. Silence. "Get away from her or I'll scream," her voice, louder now, was hoarse with fear. There was a swift movement toward the door, a faint click, and then nothing. Karis stirred and moaned softly.

Katherine quickly got out of bed, pulled a chair in front of the door and sat down to guard her sleeping daughter through the long night.

Chapter 26

6:30 A.M. Friday morning

When Jason rolled out of bed Eileen was still asleep facing away from his side of the bed. He tugged his sweatshirt over his head and pulled on his running shorts in preparation for his daily run. Tying his sneakers he remembered that it was his turn to teach the Sabbath School lesson the next day and he wondered when he would ever find the time to prepare. He hadn't even looked at the Teacher's edition of the Lesson Quarterly yet. He would have to 'wing it' again. He decided to "prepare" while he ran.

Forgiveness was the subject.

I wonder if God could ever forgive me . . . probably not. He glanced at the mound that was the sleeping Eileen and a momentary flicker of remorse for how he had treated her came to his mind. *She's so good. She deserved someone better. I should try to be nicer to her.*

In the hallway outside his room he could hear someone stirring in the guest room. *I hope they go home today. It was her own fault for fighting me . . . and now Eileen is acting like she suspects me.* As he unlocked the kitchen door to leave he heard the guest room door open and footsteps coming toward the kitchen. He left quickly hoping to avoid facing Karis' mother whom he had yet to meet.

6:40 A.M.

Katherine was standing in the kitchen staring out the window when Eileen Stevens entered. "Thank you," she said simply, without turning around. "I haven't thanked you for all you've done for Karis. I'll always be grateful to you."

"You are very welcome. Katherine, you look so tired. I don't suppose either of you got much sleep last night. Please feel free to stay with us another day or two if you feel it would help."

"Thank you, but I must get Karis home. Her father is anxious to see her. We'll be leaving this morning as soon as I can get her ready."

As Katherine was speaking a tousle-headed, sleepy-looking Davie came into the kitchen and was pulled into his mother's arms for a wake-up hug. When he pulled away he looked at Katherine and smiled shyly. Katherine's hand flew to her mouth and she caught her breath. She had been aware of the little boy talking to Karis but in her anxiety she had not actually looked closely at him. The resemblance to Karis at five years old was uncanny; his big blue eyes, his black curly hair, his smile. *Why, he looks enough like Karis to be her twin.* She blanched as a terrible thought went through her mind. Randy Brekke had told her that Jack Stevenson had a little son . . . *Oh, no!* . . . that frightening sensation in the night . . . that strange familiar scent . . . *could it be? Could Dr. Jason Stevens actually be JACK StevenSON?*

"Are you alright Mrs. Radford?" asked Eileen. "You look like you're going to faint. Here, sit down, let me get you something to eat. I don't think you ate anything at all yesterday."

Obediently Katherine sat down at the table. "I'm alright now. It's just that your little boy looks so much like Karis did at that age that it gave me a start."

Opening the refrigerator Eileen looked down at the still sleepy Davie and smiled. "You know, I noticed the same thing. Actually, Davie looks a lot like his father's side of the family. My husband has the same hair and eyes—black Irish, the family calls it. He'll be back from his morning run soon and you'll see how much Davie looks like him.

The phone rang just then and Eileen picked up the receiver still speaking to Katherine. "Maybe you know my husband's father, he's— hello, yes, this is Mrs. Stevens," . . .

"Mr. Scott, I think you must have the wrong Stevens, we don't have a loan with Bank of America."

. . . "But, there must be some mistake."

Sensing Eileen needed privacy Katherine quickly left the kitchen as Eileen's puzzled responses grew more alarmed. "*How* much?" . . . "Are you sure?" . . . "No, he's out on his morning run, but—"

. . . "Yes, I will certainly have him call you. Good by."

7:15 A.M.

The Tom Whittaker home

Sheriff Tom Whittaker was just finishing his breakfast when the telephone rang. "Get that Grace, will you?"

His wife's eyes were red from another night of sleeplessness and her hands trembled as she picked up the phone.

"Hello."

"Mom? It's me."

"Matt? Oh, thank God. Are you all right? Where are you?"

"I'm staying with some friends. I'm OK."

"When are you coming home, Son? We've been so worried."

"Mom, I'm fine, really. I only called so you wouldn't worry."

"Matt, Honey, talk to your father—" There was no answer. She held the phone until the line went dead.

7:30 A.M.

The Stevens home

Back in the guest room with the still sleeping Karis, Katherine heard Jason return from his run. She heard the shower running and later his heavy footsteps in the hall and the murmur of voices. She waited long moments dreading to go out to face him, but knowing that she must. *I have to know if he's Jack . . . if he was in our room . . . if he was the one who hurt Karis.* She squared her shoulders, took a deep breath, and opened the door.

Standing in the hallway outside the guest room Katherine could hear loud voices coming from the kitchen and she realized that Eileen and her husband were arguing about money. This isn't the time to confront him she thought as she went back into the room. A few minutes later

233

she heard the kitchen door close and a car drive out of the garage. She sighed with relief at the momentary reprieve and began to wake Karis in preparation for the trip home.

7:45 A.M.

The college cafeteria

Wally hurried into the cafeteria breathless with the news. He threaded his way through the maze of tables until he found Paul Bradley sitting at a table with Mark and Don. Leaning over so that only those sitting at the table could hear, Wally whispered, "Mike Rollin was found yesterday afternoon at the bottom of a ravine off Ink Grade Road."

"What? Is he dead?" said Paul half rising from his seat.

"No, he's alive, but he's seriously hurt and his Mustang was totaled."

"What happened? Do they know what happened?"

"They think he blew a tire and went over a cliff."

The group of friends were silent for a few minutes each engrossed in his own thoughts. Paul finally broke the silence.

"I hope he'll be OK."

"Personally," said Wally, "I think God was punishing him."

"Oh, come off it Wally. You know better than that. God doesn't use accidents to punish people."

"OK, but maybe He'll use this one to get him off campus at least."

The rest of the meal was more somber than usual as each kept his thoughts to himself. Their breakfast finished, the friends left the building together. It was time for class.

7:50 A.M.

The Stevens home

Katherine waited until she thought that everyone had left before she ventured out of the guest room. She walked swiftly down the hall, her footsteps quieted by the hall runner, and into the living room. A group of pictures stood on the mantle and she moved quickly toward them. Holding her breath she picked up a family picture. There, with his arms around a toddler Davie, was the smiling face of Jack Stevenson.

"Hello, Katherine," said a low menacing voice behind her. "It's been a long time."

9:00 A.M. the same day

The college library office

"Hello, is this the sheriff?" . . .

"Well, may I speak to him, please?" . . .

"Hello, Sheriff? My name is Mildred Munsell and I'm a librarian at the End-Time College. I think I have some information that you may need." . . .

"Well, last Wednesday as I was on my way home from work . . ."

11:30 A.M.

The Jason Stevens office

Laura Anderson rolled her shoulders up and back and flexed her long fingers in a vain effort to ease their stiffness; she had been typing nearly non-stop since she arrived at eight that morning. Across the hall outside her open door she watched Peggy Kester greet T.W. as he arrived back from Washington with his loaded briefcase weighing down one shoulder. She picked up her phone and buzzed Jason Stevens.

"Yes?"

"T.W. just walked in, shall I tell him you need to see him?" When he didn't respond she shrugged and hung up the phone. Two minutes later Jason came out of his office. "I'm leaving," he said, as he laid a file on her desk and walked out.

Laura shrugged again and looked at her watch. *11:40. Good. Almost time. It's a blessing we have Friday afternoons off or I'd never be able to get ready for the Sabbath.* She began to make a mental list of all the things she wanted to get done before sundown.

Twenty minutes later Laura had just covered her Selectric and was tidying her desk to go home when two policemen entered the office.

"Hello, Ma'am," said Tom Whittaker. "Is Mr. Stevens in?"

"*Doctor* Stevens? No, I believe he has gone for the day."

"We'd like to look around his office, Ma'am," he said as he handed her an official-looking piece of paper.

"What—"

"—it's a search warrant, Ma'am. Now if you will just step out into the hall and wait there, please."

7:30 P.M.

The Stevens home

They had just finished dinner when Eileen answered the doorbell. A tall, very erect, heavy-set man stood at the door. "You must be General Williams," she said with a smile. "Come in." She opened the door and stepped aside. "I'm Jason's wife, Eileen."

"Jason?" he looked confused. "Isn't this Jack Stevenson's home?"

For a moment Eileen mirrored his confusion, then she smiled, "Oh yes, perhaps you didn't know. Jack changed his name a few years ago to Jason Stevens. Won't you come—"

"—just a minute, Eileen," said a grim-faced Jason who appeared at the doorway and elbowed Eileen to one side, "I'll handle this."

"General. You can't stay here. I've made arrangements for you at a motel for one night in St. Helena, and then I want you to move on. Wait there, I'll get the directions to the motel for you," he said as he closed the door in the general's face.

When Jason returned he stepped outside and faced a furious General Williams. Handing him a piece of paper Jason turned without a word and started to go back inside the house.

"Just a minute. Stop right there. Just who do you think you are, Soldier? How dare you—?"

"—I am not a soldier, *Sir*," said Jason advancing toward him. "And, we need to get one thing straight right now. My family is out of bounds to you. I want nothing to do with you. Nothing. Understand?"

Williams pulled himself up into a military stance and said with a smirk, "I see. Yes. You're right. We do need an understanding." He glanced toward the window where Eileen and Davie could be seen watching them. "Now, listen up. *This* is our understanding: you *and your pretty little son* will have a close and personal 'friendship' with me just as you and I had in England, or—"

"—Or what?" growled Jason moving still closer to him with fists clenched at his side.

"Or, that pretty little wife of yours, your sanctimonious father, and all your so-holy friends at that so-holy college will hear all about your war-time fun and games. *That's* our understanding. Understand?" He threw the piece of paper on the ground and walked toward his car. Then he turned and said with a leer, "I'll expect a visit from you *and your son* very soon. I'll call with the time and place. It'll be just like old times, Jack."

Jason could hear him laughing as he drove away.

6:00 A.M. Saturday

The Stevens home

The persistent ringing of the telephone woke him. He sat up in bed and picked it up, still groggy from the wretched night just past.

"Good morning, Son." Jason heard his father's cheerful voice with dread. "I know it's early, but I wanted to catch you before your day got started."

"What is it, Dad?" he said, wariness in his voice.

"I'm getting hints that there might be trouble on the hill. That so, Son?"

Such strong hostility toward his father rose in his throat that Jason could scarcely answer. "Nothing I can't handle."

"Well, whatever it is we—your Mother and I—we want you to know that we're praying for you." The line went silent for a long moment, "and, uh, Son, I've been wanting to talk to you. I, uh, uh, I think I may have been too hard on you while you were growing—"

"—Dad, it's early and I have a busy day. Can this wait?"

"Sure, Son. Well, just remember we're counting on you to do the right thing. I'll make a few phone calls. We want you to succeed this time." His booming voice seemed to continue vibrating over the telephone line after each sentence was finished.

"No phone calls! I TOLD YOU I CAN HANDLE IT. I don't need your help."

"I don't know what's going on, Son, but your mother and I are getting worried."

Jason gritted his teeth to hold back an oath, "I'm telling you it's nothing, just drop it or—"

"—well, whatever it is, I'm sure you'll do the right thing. Just remember, you're a Stevenson; make us proud, Son. Your Mother sends her love."

Still sitting on the bed, wide awake now, the night's worries returned; *the sheriff's incessant questions . . . my daughter! Could I actually have attacked my own daughter? The general's threats . . . if he ever so much as looks at Davie, I'll—now Dad wants to throw his weight around and make me out a failure again.*

He got out of bed and began to pace. *OK, first, I have to take care of the general. I may have to fight him, maybe even . . . I have to keep him quiet somehow; get him away from here for good.*

Then he stopped and took a deep breath as it came to him again; Karis was his daughter! Why hadn't he seen it before? His stomach reeled with nausea when he remembered what he had done to her. Now he could see how much she looked like Davie. He had tried to get a good look at her in the night while she slept, but Katherine had heard him so he hadn't been able to. Later that night, half asleep, he had actually confused her with Davie for awhile.

All at once he was confused again. *Maybe it was Davie I attacked. No, of course it wasn't. Not Davie, it was Karis! But why would she fight me? I didn't mean to hurt her. My own daughter; God will never forgive me now.* The strange disorientation that he had been feeling lately came over him again and he sat down on the edge of the bed until it cleared.

When the room stopped spinning he stood up and again began to pace. *Good thing Katherine took Karis and left so quickly. I think I scared her enough so she won't go to the police. She turned white . . . almost fainted when I threatened to tell Karis who I am and how she was conceived. She'll probably keep quiet. Since Eileen and Davie had already gone she couldn't have told Eileen about us. That's one good thing.*

Eileen, awakened by his pacing and mumbling, got up and began to dress. Avoiding his glance, her back stiff with disapproval, she said, "I want you to tell me the truth. What did you do with all that money you borrowed from the bank?"

"I needed it, OK? I'm sorry. We can talk about it after Sabbath."

"All right but you better have a *very* good explanation," she said as she started toward the bathroom.

"I'm going to the office to study. I have the lesson today," he said to Eileen's retreating back. There was no answer from the retreating back. Shouting through the closed bathroom door he said, "I *said* I was sorry, whadaya *want* from me?"

A sleepy little Davie came into the hall just as Jason left his bedroom. In a rush of tenderness he picked him up and hugged him close.

"Don't ever forget, I love you, Davie," he said, his voice husky with emotion.

"Daddy, put me down," he said as he squirmed to get loose. "You're squeezing me too tight. I hafta go to the bathroom."

Chapter 29

Jason stood momentarily outside his office looking at the shiny brass letters on the door, JASON P. STEVENS, Ed.D. ACADEMIC DEAN He reached up and traced the letters with his finger. Then, with a sigh, he opened the door and went in.

He glanced at Laura Anderson's empty desk as he walked by to open the door to his own office. *When they make this job permanent she's out, first thing.*

Now where 'd I put that Lesson Guide and that Bible? Oh, yeah, in the credenza. He looked at the clock and frowned. *20 minutes? I can do this. I have to just forget what's happening and concentrate.* He glanced at the clock again. *I'll just read the texts and wing it.*

Squinting in concentration he fanned through the pages of the seldom-used Bible until he found the memory verse for the lesson.

ISAIAH 1:16 & 17, PUT AWAY THE EVIL OF YOUR DOINGS FROM BEFORE MINE EYES; CEASE TO DO EVIL; LEARN TO DO WELL.

No problem God, my 'evil doings' have been out of Your sight for years. It's a little late. You gave up on me years ago. Remember?

He turned easily to the next text, his childhood memorization of the books of the Bible still resident in his mind.

PSALM 51:10, CREATE IN ME A CLEAN HEART, OH GOD, AND RENEW A RIGHT SPIRIT WITHIN ME.

His mother's voice came to mind then and he pictured her reading this verse as part of their morning worship. *This was one of Mom's favorite verses. Aw, God, You know it's too late for me. My sins—that abomination with the general? Attacking my own daughter? All the other stuff? . . . No, there's no way, . . . but, what if it weren't too late? . . . What if I could start over?*

ISAIAH 1:18, COME NOW, AND LET US REASON TOGETHER, SAITH THE LORD. THOUGH YOUR SINS BE AS SCARLET THEY SHALL BE AS WHITE AS SNOW.

Mine are scarlet all right; more like black and blue. White as snow? With my long list? No way. I've sinned, really bad sins, for too many years, hurt too many people. No, God, you know I'm a hopeless case.

I JOHN 1:9, IF WE CONFESS OUR SINS HE IS FAITHFUL AND JUST TO FORGIVE US OUR SINS AND TO CLEANSE US FROM ALL UNRIGHTEOUSNESS.

It's too hard, Lord. Even if I wanted to I'm not strong enough. The temptations are stronger than I am. You know that, Lord. It's too late for me. Isn't it? Could You really forgive someone like me? No, it's too late. I'm too weak; I'd just fail.

ISAIAH 26:4, TRUST YE IN THE LORD . . . FOR IN THE LORD IS EVERLASTING STRENGTH.

EPHESIANS 2:8, BY GRACE ARE YE SAVED THROUGH FAITH; AND THAT NOT OF YOURSELVES: IT IS THE GIFT OF GOD.

His years of pretense at living the Christian life flashed before him and for a long moment Jason sat still struggling with the knowledge of his unworthiness and with a strong yearning to confess, to be accepted once more by God. Finally, in bitter tears of emotional turmoil Jason fell to his knees beside his desk and fixed his eyes on the picture of Jesus on the wall. His tears splashing on the carpet he cried aloud, "I confess,

Lord, I confess. Cleanse me like You promised. Forgive me. Give me strength to be Yours again."

MATTHEW 9:2, JESUS SAID . . . SON, BE OF GOOD CHEER; THY SINS BE FORGIVEN THEE.

9:30 A.M.

Paulin Hall Sabbath School

The program was already in progress when Jason slipped into a back row seat in the auditorium. He waited through the "special feature" given by a former student missionary and while a student quartet sang. Then it was his turn. He walked to the front while the Sabbath School Superintendent was introducing him as the guest teacher for the lesson.

With a prayer in his heart, he began. "The title of our lesson today is 'Forgiveness.' The gist of the entire lesson is God's willingness, in fact His eagerness, to forgive our sins. God's Word tells us that we all have access to that forgiveness no matter what—even if our sins are horrendous, even if we have blood on our hands. God says 'tho your sins be as scarlet He will make them white as snow." *Even mine Lord, even mine. Thank you Lord.*

Sheriff Tom Whittaker's two deputies sat waiting at the table while he pondered the list of evidence on a chalk board.

"We can add blood to the list now," he said. "The sample on that handkerchief matches what we found under the victim's fingernails. That professor, or reporter, or whatever he is, gave us some good stuff."

He added the words 'blood match' to the list, relieved that his son was no longer a viable suspect.

". . . in James 1:14 we learn that every man is tempted when he is drawn away of his own lust, and enticed. We know that Satan is well acquainted with our weaknesses, and that he suits his enticements to our frailties. Therefore, we each of us have to be on guard at all times lest we fall." But, my friends, God is faithful to forgive us if we are willing to forsake our sins, even those most grievous to Him—even, my dear young people, even sexual sins." *I'm ready to change, Lord, help me.*

"OK, that's what we have so far. I think it's enough," said Tom.

"I still think it was just opportunity," one of his deputies said. "Remember, that librarian saw him slow down and watch before he stopped. Pretty girl, alone near the woods . . ."

"Then what about the duct tape we found in his car? Also, his secretary's testimony that he'd had a confrontation with the same girl that morning. I say it's premeditation, maybe even lying in wait," added a burly deputy with his feet resting on the table.

"While we know that God forgives, we shouldn't think that gives us license to do anything we want. In Messages to Young People, p. 82, we read: Keep yourselves away from the corrupting influences of the world . . ." *I need your help on this Lord.*

"Think we can tie him to those prostitutes who were beat up in Vallejo, Sheriff?

"I think we might," said Tom. "We have his blood now, and they each described the guy as very strong."

"Yeah, and they each remembered that distinctive cologne smell. Our victim mentioned that, too. Two bits we find that cologne in his bathroom when we search his house today."

"And don't forget those deep bruises on the victim's breasts—same as the others."

"Yeah, we're gonna nail this creep," said Tom.

". . . in verse 15, we read: Then when lust hath conceived it bringeth forth sin; and sin, when it is finished, bringeth forth death."

"I think we've got our man alright," said Tom as he picked up his file and walked toward his office.

"Aren't we gonna go pick him up?"

"Not just yet. Don't want to disturb the good folks on the 'holy hill' while they're in church. We'll pick him up at his home right after the service."

". . . and in conclusion; early this morning my father called. Thinking of his counsel to me reminds me that in the same way parents are ready to forgive their children so is Our Lord ready to forgive us. And, my young friends, remember that just as my father wants to be proud of me, so God wants to be proud of each of you.

"Let us pray. Our Father in heaven. Forgive us our many sins and help us to live our lives in such a way that You will be proud to call us Your sons and daughters. Amen."

The twenty minute interlude between the Sabbath School classes and the worship service is a favorite time for End-Time Christians. Old friends stop by to chat, the children in their Sabbath finery pour out of their classrooms, and the latest campus gossip is exchanged.

On this day, Saturday, May 3, 1968, as Dr. Jason Stevens walked from Paulin Hall to the sanctuary for the worship service he noticed that friends seemed to be avoiding him, no one mentioned his lesson study and—could he be imagining it?—did conversations stop when he walked by? Suddenly his mind flashed back to his last day in high school, but he quickly dismissed the thought, shook his head, and continued down the walkway.

As he entered the foyer to wait for Eileen and Davie, T.W. caught his eye and beckoned him into a corner. As he listened to T.W.'s whispered comments Jason Stevens, a.k.a. Jack Stevenson, knew that his career in The Lord's Work was over.

Ignoring the stares of worshippers he hurried out of the church, up the mall steps two at a time, across the interior campus street and up the stairs to his office. The office door opened to his key. Fumbling in the credenza drawer for an envelope of petty cash he kept for emergencies his eyes were drawn to the picture of a smiling Eileen and Davie. His tears came then and his body rocked with grief as he dropped to his knees once more crying out to The Lord for forgiveness.

As he drove out of the campus he saw two police cars turn into Cold Springs Road. Suddenly panic gripped him. Keeping his head low he slowed until they were out of sight then increasing his speed he fled down the winding mountain road to the valley floor. *They're after me. I knew it was too late for me. Oh, God, why didn't You listen? You could have stopped them. They know what I did to Karis. I'll go to jail, I'll lose everything.*

He drove on without awareness of traffic or direction, his mind agitated and blurred. *They know it was me. They know she's my daughter. I tried to rape my own daughter, my beautiful Davie—no, no, it wasn't Davie—it was Karis, my daughter. I didn't know she was my daughter, please God, I didn't know. Is there forgiveness for even that? Oh Lord, forgive me! You promised!* The strange loss of his bearings came over him again and he drove faster and more recklessly without conscious plan along the country road. *A Stevenson would never rape anyone. Not his own daughter. Someone else did it. It wasn't me. I love Davie. I didn't mean to hurt her but she kept fighting me.*

After a time Jason found himself in Sonoma County traveling without awareness of the panoramic views of groomed vineyards. Soon he was driving into the affluence of Marin County still unaware of his surroundings. His mind was muddled and he fought an unsettling disorientation as he drove erratically on. In the distance he saw the Golden Gate Bridge and his mind suggested a final solution. He cried aloud as he drove, *"They all hate me. The general will tell everyone what I did. I can't ever go home again. Not ever see Eileen or Davie. I'll go to jail. Never again in The Lord's Work, no heaven, disgraced. They'll be better off without me. They'll be sorry when I'm gone, no, maybe they'll be glad. Eileen will lose our house. Eileen, I'm sorry, I'm so sorry. I love you, Eileen. And Davie, Oh, Davie, I'm so sorry, I wanted to be a good father."*

The traffic began to pile up as he approached the bridge toll gate. A sign above the highway flashed on and off, "Slow; Accident on bridge." His car crawled slowly onto the bridge behind a battered VW van driven by two long-haired kids with colorful scarves tied around their foreheads. "Hippies," he said out loud in disgust. For a moment he found himself planning to report them to college security; then he remembered: he was lost to the college. He was lost to everyone he cared about; everyone who cared about him. Tears filled his eyes again. *Oh God, I know You forgave me. Please give me another chance and I will sin no more.*

The slowly moving line of traffic was nearly to the center of the bridge when the VW van in front of him backfired twice, hesitated, coughed, and stopped. Immediately the two kids got out and while one of them came around to the rear of the van to look at the engine the other circled looking at the tires. As one of the boys made eye contact with Jason he smiled and held up two fingers in the victory sign.

In the lanes to Jason's left all the cars were now stopped, bumper to bumper. To his right the orange pillars of the bridge shone in the sunshine under a bright blue sky. In the distance he could see the flashing lights of police cars and not far ahead two uniformed policemen were waving their arms as they began to walk in his direction.

Then he heard the sirens. The sound grew louder and louder in a frightening crescendo as it moved closer to him. Abruptly he was gripped again with panic. *They're coming for me! I have to get away! They know who I am.* He began to honk his horn and race the motor, but the young hippie standing in front of his car just smiled and again raised his fingers in the peace salute.

Disoriented and dizzy he opened the car door and stumbled out. *It's the police. I have to get away. They're coming for me.* He ran to the back of the car and looked frantically around trying to decide which way to run. Then his father's voice came to him like a vibrating echo. "You're a Stevenson, Son. A Stevenson, a Stevenson, make us proud, Son, do the right thing, the right thing."

He sprinted toward the sidewalk and climbed up on the railing. "You win, Dad," he shouted to the sky. "I'm doing the right thing." At that moment he felt a tug on the back of his jacket. Looking back he saw that one of the young hippies from the VW was holding tight to the end of his jacket.

"Don't do it, Man, please, don't do it," he kept saying over and over.

Jason hesitated, looked back at him, then climbed down from the railing and straightened his clothes. "I'll be all right now. You can let go. Thank you."

"You sure you're OK?" he said, releasing his hold.

"Hey, Matt," Called the second kid from inside the van. "Come on, let's go. The traffic's beginning to move."

Matt hesitated and looked at Jason again. "You sure you're OK?" he asked again. "You won't try to jump again?" Cars were beginning to honk now, impatient to move forward.

"I'm OK now. I just lost it for a minute. Go ahead. I'll be all right. Really, I'm OK. We need to move our cars." He began to walk slowly toward his own car.

Matt started toward the VW still watching Jason over his shoulder as he walked. Then he got in and the van started to move.

Ignoring the honking of the cars behind him Jason stood hesitantly at the open door to his car, his father's voice once more invading his mind. "Do what's right, Son. Make us proud, Son. Do the right thing."

The orange railing was easily vaulted. His piercing scream rent the air until the cold, angry waters closed over him.

Chapter 30

SAN FRANCISCO CHRONICLE May 6, 1968. This year's 16th jumper from the Golden Gate Bridge survived today with serious injuries. Forty-four year old Jason Stevens, Academic Dean of a small North Bay college, was immediately pulled from the bay by a Coast Guard cutter and taken to the Ft. Baker pier where he was then transported to Marin General Hospital in critical condition. His jump once again generated a rally supporting the building of a safety barrier on the bridge. "This bridge is about beauty; if they don't jump here they'll just find another bridge somewhere. We can't stop them," said a Golden Gate Bridge official who declined to be identified.

ST. HELENA, CA. (AP) May 7, 1968. Anthony J. Williams, General U.S. Army, retired, was arrested today charged with kidnapping and molesting a ten-year-old Napa County boy. Williams, a top aide to General Dwight D. Eisenhower during World War II, was picked up inside a motel room with the child. A motel housekeeper who claimed to have seen Williams carry a struggling child inside the room called police. Williams' attorney, Earl Smale said today that the housekeeper was mistaken, that his client maintains his innocence and looks forward to being acquitted at trial.

ST. HELENA STAR May 9, 1968. The coed victim of attempted rape at the End-Time College has asked prosecutors to drop all charges against her alleged assailant according to Napa County Sheriff Tom Whittaker.

THE CAMPUS CRIER May 15, 1868. President T.W. Patton announced today that Dr. Herman Granados is returning to the college next school year to resume his position as Academic Dean. Dr. Granados, who has been on a year's sabbatical in Washington, D.C., told this reporter in a telephone interview today that he is eager to rejoin the college community.

NAPA REGISTER May 20, 1968. Real Estate News: Beautiful valley view home for sale near End-Time College campus. Spacious 4 bedroom, 2 bath home with plenty of extra custom touches. Must see to appreciate. Owner is motivated. Call Heli at 707 252 0348 for details.

June 3, 1968

The college campus

Joan Whittaker crossed the street by the library and began to walk slowly down the broad steps of the mall toward the church. She was thinking about last night's phone call from Karis. She missed her, but she wasn't worried about her any more. Karis had sounded upbeat; she would finish her last quarter in summer school and she had been accepted in medical school for the fall. Even more surprising she said her mother had decided to move to Loma Linda with her to work toward a college degree. *They're going to be just fine,* Joan thought.

Below her several girls in their bright spring dresses were talking and laughing near the fountain that splashed at the bottom of the mall steps. *I know those girls.* She smiled at the satisfaction she felt in knowing them. *I'm part of God's family now and part of this special place. Maybe someday my children will come here and they'll know the children of my classmates. Thank you, Lord, for bringing me here. Soon I'll make my public stand for You, but You know I'm Yours already.*

252

As she reached each descending terraced level of the mall she stopped to admire the ornamental cherry trees in bloom and to watch the bees buzzing among the blossoms. Above her the sky was blue and cloudless. As the bell tower came into her view between the flowering trees the carillon began to play. *When peace like a river . . .*

The beauty of the day, the flowering trees, the lovely hymn, all combined to fill her with a sweet, quiet feeling. *This is what it feels like to be happy,* she mused.

"Hey, Joanie, wait up." Running down the steps of the mall Paul Bradley caught up with her just as she reached the fountain.

Paul watched as her welcoming smile made her eyes shine and her curls bounce and gleam red-brown in the bright sunshine. *Why, she's really pretty. Funny, I never noticed before how pretty she is.*

"Uh, Joanie, I was wondering. Would you like to come to Cloverdale with me this afternoon? A bunch of us have been helping out with a branch Sabbath School there and it would be nice, that is, well, actually I would really like it if you would come with me."

Joan's smile widened as she looked up at him and nodded her answer.

NEWSLETTER OF THE GENERAL ASSEMBLY August 14, 1968. Letters to the Editor. Dear brothers and sisters in Christ. Thank you for your many cards and letters and, most especially, for your prayers. So many have asked about Jack's injuries and prognosis that this seemed a way to answer your questions. Jack's fall from the bridge caused many serious injuries including a broken pelvis, clavicle, sternum, several ribs, and both ankles. He had extensive internal bleeding and both lungs were punctured. Although his recovery is still uncertain we thank God daily that he is alive.

He is, finally, fully conscious and during my many hours at his bedside we have had a precious time together. Last week Jack told me of the childhood abuse he suffered from a trusted neighbor and its terrible results. My heart aches to know that I was unaware of it and indeed unwittingly helped it to happen. Dear brothers and

sisters stay close to your children; our enemy, the Devil, is ever ready to devour them!

In agony of soul Jack has confessed many dreadful sins. Together we cried and in prayer beseeched our gracious God to forgive us both. I am fully persuaded of Jack's sincerity and of his remorse and I ask your continued prayers for him as he faces the consequences of his sins. He is hoping to make restitution to those he has grievously harmed, but as it is probable he will face prison if he recovers sufficiently, that will not be easy.

Jack's wife, Eileen, has sold their home in Napa Valley to pay debts that he had incurred and she and their son are temporarily living with us. Please continue to pray for us. David Stevenson.

THE END

To order additional copies of

TEN MILES
FROM THE NEAREST SIN

Have your credit card ready and call

Toll free: (877) 421-READ (7323)

or order online at: www.winepressbooks.com